DATE DUE

6415413		

The Library Store #47-0152

PRESSURE

ALSO BY BRIAN KEENE

PRESSURE

BRIAN KEENE

Thomas Dunne Books
St. Martin's Press
New York

This is a work of fiction. All of the characters, organizations, and events portrayed in this novel are either products of the author's imagination or are used fictitiously.

THOMAS DUNNE BOOKS.

An imprint of St. Martin's Press.

www.thomasdunnebooks.com

www.stmartins.com

Designed by Omar Chapa

Library of Congress Cataloging-in-Publication Data

Names: Keene, Brian, author.
Title: Pressure / Brian Keene.
Description: First edition. | New York : Thomas Dunne Books/ St. Martin's Press, 2016.
Identifiers: LCCN 2015051265| ISBN 9781250071347 (hardcover) | ISBN 9781466882492 (e-book)
Subjects: LCSH: Marine biologists—Fiction. | Scientific expeditions—Fiction. | BISAC: FICTION / Action & Adventure. | FICTION / Sea Stories. | GSAFD: Adventure fiction. | Sea stories. | Suspense fiction.
Classification: LCC PS3611.E3397 P74 2016 | DDC 813'.6—dc23
LC record available at http://lccn.loc.gov/2015051265

Our books may be purchased in bulk for promotional, educational, or business use. Please contact your local bookseller or the Macmillan Corporate and Premium Sales Department at 1-800-221-7945, extension 5442, or by e-mail at MacmillanSpecial Markets@macmillan.com.

First Edition: June 2016

10 9 8 7 6 5 4 3 2 1

For Brindi, from one black sheep to another . . .

ACKNOWLEDGMENTS

Thanks to Nicole Sohl; Brendan Deneen; Kelli "Gypsy Smurf" Owen, Mark "Dezm" Sylva, Tod "I Can Drink It" Clark, and Stephen "Macker" McDornell; Cathy and Hannah Gonzalez; Christopher Golden; William Bevill; Paul Legerski; Paul Goblirsch; Weston Ochse and Yvonne Navarro; Linda Addison; Jonathan Maberry; Jeff Mariotte; Mandy Walters (for distracting me with Words); Mary SanGiovanni; Nathan Carson, Mike Scheidt, and Kasey Lansdale; Keith Giffen and J.M. DeMatteis; Comix Connection, The York Emporium, IKO's Music Trade, and Tom's Music Trade (all four of which provide me with weekly fuel); Cassandra Burnham; and my sons.

PROLOGUE

Off the coast of Mauritius, shrimp and crabs scurried about like soldiers on important missions. Armies of ethereal jellyfish floated on the currents, aimless and drifting. A school of tuna dodged out of their way. Below them, sea anemones perched precariously on the seafloor with their adhesive feet, and waved vibrant, multi-colored tentacles with which to lure and capture their prey. A female octopus rested after the laborious, exhausting task of laying a string of eggs above her lair. A lonely green sea turtle searched for a mate—a sad task that grew increasingly difficult with each passing year. Two dugong gorged themselves on plants, feeling the turtle's plight. They had not seen another of their kind in recent memory. Orange-and-white striped clownfish darted between colorful coral, and massive schools of sapphire devils darted into holes and crevices, changing their color from blue to black, in order to hide from a group of bottlenose dolphins. The dolphins played as they hunted and fed, but their frivolity ceased, and their movements became cautionary as a great white shark slowly cruised by, cleaving the water like a slow moving missile.

Less common, but still present, a blue whale sang out from somewhere in the dark depths—a haunting, phantom melody that echoed of the past—but its mournful, yearning song went unanswered.

There was life here, off the coast of Mauritius. It was a quieter, slower existence, but life still lived. Life still moved amongst the warm, silt-laden waters.

Then, something new arrived in the ecosystem, something dark and predatory, and all other life ceased moving beneath its ominous shadow.

Slowly, the warm waters began to grow colder.

The darkness deepened, spreading in concentric waves.

And life began to fail.

PRESSURE

PART ONE

AS BELOW

ONE

". . . while we wait for Carrie Anderson and Peter Scofield to resurface from this unprecedented expedition. But even as the Mouth of Hell continues to open, and preparations for the possible evacuation of Mauritius proceed, there is now concern that the islands of Rodrigues and Réunion may need to be evacuated, as well. One researcher, who spoke to me on the condition of anonymity, said—"

"Hang on, Jessamine. We lost the connection."

Jessamine Wheatley sighed in frustration. "Damn it, Hank."

"It's not my fault. Stand by."

Frowning, Hank turned his attention to the equipment. He cursed beneath his breath. Jessamine crossed her arms in frustration. Their cameraman, Khem, tried defusing the tension by smiling at each of them in turn.

"Oh, knock it off," Jessamine told him. "Just because your name means 'one with peace and joy' in Hindi doesn't mean you have to live it every day."

Khem's smile slowly faltered. "I'm sorry."

Jessamine handed him her microphone. He accepted it without comment.

"Somebody's in a mood." Julio, the fourth member of their team, stepped forward with his makeup kit. "Let's do something with your hair while we wait. This tropical climate has made those red bangs go limp as spaghetti."

He reached for her hair, but Jessamine pushed his hand away.

"My hair is fine. Do something useful for a change. Help Hank get our connection back."

Julio clucked his tongue against the roof of his mouth and gave Khem a knowing glance. The two of them turned their backs to her, whispering amongst themselves. Jessamine immediately felt guilty, and then felt guilty about feeling guilty.

My therapist could have a field day with this, she thought. *She'd probably call it displaced aggression against the patriarchal news industry—because she says everything I do is that.*

Jessamine decided she should try to make peace with them both, but before she could apologize to either man, another swell rocked the ship, lifting it up rapidly and then dropping it back down. Jessamine's stomach roiled. Although she had reported from all around the world during the last five years, this was her first time doing so from a ship. They had been afloat off the southwestern coast of Mauritius for two weeks now, and her seasickness still hadn't abated. She'd tried an assortment of supposedly surefire cures and aids—scopolamine patches, Dramamine, Bonine, ginger, crackers and bread, chewing gum, and even a wristband—but she still suffered from intermittent nausea, headaches, dry mouth, and balance issues.

Her mood was worsened by the fact that this news story was quickly shaping up to be horribly anticlimactic. It shouldn't have been. After all, as a peer from the BBC had put it, the "bottom was falling out of the Indian Ocean." That should have been newsworthy. It should have been one of the biggest stories ever.

Mauritius was renowned for its stunning beaches, as well as being home to some of the world's rarest animal and plant species, but one of the island nation's main draws had always been its underwater waterfall—an optical illusion created as ocean currents sent sand and silt plunging off the island's coastal shelf to a much deeper second shelf off Mauritius's southern tip. The shelf, as well as the phenomenon, were fairly recent in geological terms, having been created a few million years ago by a slow and gradual spreading of the sea floor. As the silt and other debris drifted downward into the dark depths, it looked remarkably like a waterfall beneath the ocean. The illusion was especially prominent from the air. Long a curiosity for scuba divers, tourists flocked to see it, and the phenomenon had been featured endlessly on various travel and science programs. Private guides did big business in helicopter tours of the area.

Now, for unknown reasons, the seafloor's collapse had gone from gradual to rapid, and the once jewel-colored waters were murky due to the cascade of sand and debris created as the crevice expanded. Mauritius appeared to be the apex of the collapse, though how long the island would remain above the growing abyss—and not sink into it—was a matter of concern. As the trench, dubbed the "Mouth of Hell" by Jessamine's colleagues in the press, expanded toward the neighboring islands of Réunion and Rodrigues, emergency plans were being drawn up to evacuate the entire population of Mauritius island if need be.

Like other recent natural disasters such as the 2004 Christmas tsunami, Hurricane Katrina, the Tohoku earthquake, and its subsequent tsunami which had triggered the Fukushima nuclear meltdown, the collapse of the sea floor should have been a riveting news story. And at first, it had been. A plethora of ships congregated off the coast of Mauritius. The largest vessel was the *R/V Aloysious Novak,* named after a Virginian Senator who had been assassinated while on a humanitarian mission to Sumatra. The Novak was a well-equipped, Global Class research ship owned by Alpinus Biofutures, a biotech company that had financed the expedition team and was contracted by the United Nations to investigate the oceanographic and seismological crisis. Manned with scientists, researchers, and crew, it was accompanied by three support vessels (also owned by Alpinus Biofutures), another research ship from the National Oceanographic and Atmospheric Administration (acting strictly as observers), and two United Nations peacekeeping ships, as well as several Mauritius naval vessels. The rest of the flotilla was composed of various international news teams, all of whom had descended upon the Mouth of Hell in competition for a scoop. One night, while Jessamine, Hank, Julio, and Khem had stayed awake drinking tequila on board their CBS-chartered yacht, Hank had equated their presence to a school of piranha. She had begrudgingly admitted the producer's description was apt.

But as the days dragged on, the story drifted away, just like the sand swirling in the water beneath them. Despite the possible outcome, and the toll it might have on the populace and the environment, this was still primarily a science story— and science moved slowly. Much too slowly for the twenty-four-hour cable news cycle. The research was slow, the results slower, and the majority of their reports lacked any sound bites that would appeal to the laymen back home. Viewers wanted excitement and drama. They wanted riveting footage and breathless reporting. Instead, all they'd gotten were statistics and data and scientific reports.

There had been a host of other problems, as well. For some unknown reason, both the research expedition and the assembled press corps' electronic equipment and gear were experiencing intermittent but pervasive glitches and malfunctions. Diving robots had shorted out or been lost in the crevasse. Communications coverage was spotty and problematic. Video cameras turned themselves off. Ship engines had stalled, and several vessels—while not colliding—had bumped into each other to the point that they had to motor to shore for hull repairs. Jessamine thought she'd find more drama if she covered college kids drunk boating at Cairns. Minor electrical snafus did not make for exciting news coverage, and as a result, viewers at home were tuning out, looking instead for the next celebrity meltdown or manufactured political crisis.

Sighing, Jessamine stared out at the water, waiting for her nausea to subside. She'd noticed that the seasickness was even worse back on the smaller, CBS-chartered yacht. But currently, like the rest of the press corps, they were assembled here on the Novak, covering Anderson and Scofield's dive.

The sun had just sunk beneath the horizon, and the stars were beginning to come out overhead. She had to admit, no matter how despondent she was over their current assignment, there was something calming and peaceful about seeing stars and constellations that weren't visible back home. Jessamine breathed deeply and tried her best to relax. A light breeze caressed her face.

Maybe things would pick up again once the evacuation began. Surely, an operation of that magnitude should provide some human drama. But then again, maybe not. As the only African country other than Ghana with full democracy, Mauritius's National Assembly was generally well-loved by its people, with the government earning high marks of satisfaction from its populace time and time again.

The ship rose high, and the ocean disappeared momentarily. It seemed as if the deck was pointed at the sky. Then the vessel slammed back down again. Jessamine's stomach mimicked the sudden movements. Fighting back her gorge, she turned away from the churning water and surveyed her peers. Reporters from three-dozen different international networks were lined up on the deck of the Novak, all jostling for position in the small press area that had been set aside for them. She noticed, with some satisfaction, that several of the others were also experiencing technical difficulties with their live broadcasts.

"Okay," Hank said. "I think we've got . . . shit, nope. Lost it again. Hang on . . ."

"Maybe we'd have better luck back on our yacht," Khem suggested.

"The story is here on the Novak," Jessamine said. "I mean, let's be honest. Right now, until the evacuation begins, Anderson and Scofield are the *only* story."

Khem shrugged. "Yeah, but we've got booze on the yacht. Unless Hank drank it all again."

Jessamine and Khem shared a smile at this, but Hank ignored them. His attention was focused on their equipment.

"What's the problem, anyway?" Julio asked.

"We're a major network," Hank muttered. "And yet we're working with gear that was new during the first Clinton administration. And move, Julio. You're blocking my light."

"GNN doesn't seem to be having any trouble," Jessamine said.

"That's because GNN is owned by the Globe Corporation. They've got more money and better gear than we do."

"Alpinus Biofutures isn't exactly a small company either, Hank. Their electronic equipment seems to be just as glitch-prone as ours."

"Well, maybe it's all just a conspiracy against me, then. Now, let me focus, please. And Julio, I thought I asked you to quit blocking my light?"

Laughing, Jessamine and Khem moved a few feet away, while Julio stayed to tease Hank some more.

"You admire her, don't you?" Khem asked. "Carrie Anderson?"

Jessamine paused, and then nodded. "Sure. I mean, how could I not? She's certainly become a favorite figurehead for this expedition. People remember her from when she was a world-class free diver. Now she's an oceanographer. She's glamorous. Takes no shit. Able to deliver a sound bite. She's got . . . *story*. People like story."

"Well, let's hope she brings back a story when she surfaces. Because right now, we don't have much."

"No," Jessamine agreed, "we don't. But once the evacuation begins, we'll have plenty to cover."

Khem arched an eyebrow. "You almost sound like you actually *want* it to begin."

"No, it's not that. But you have to admit, if it happens, it would be an unprecedented event. To evacuate an entire population? That's huge, Khem. I just hope . . ."

She trailed off, distracted by a sudden commotion amongst the scientists. They were rushing over to a bank of computer monitors and huddling around them in what she first took for excitement. After a few more seconds of observation, she realized that what she'd mistaken for excitement was instead panic—and fear.

"Get that," she told Khem, nodding at the researchers. While he shouldered his camera and focused, Jessamine hurried over to Hank. "We've got something."

"Yeah," he replied, not glancing up from his equipment. "We've all got something. Julio's got a hard-on. He's over there talking to that sound tech from NBC. I've got a migraine. And you've got a big case of boredom."

"Over there, numb-nuts." She pointed at the commotion. Crew members hustled about, their expressions grim and determined. More researchers had gathered around the monitors, and were shouting at each other in agitation. "Something's happening. They're all stirred up."

"Shit." Hank's eyes went wide. "Khem, get—"

"He's already on it," Jessamine interrupted. "Let's go."

They hurried toward the excitement, as did the other news crews, each jostling for position and angle, trying to get as close as possible. Jessamine spotted Jennifer Wasco from competing network GNN, and her mood immediately soured. The two were not friends. They'd known each other since they'd both worked for WKNY, a local New York affiliate. Jessamine had gone from there to CBS, but since then her career had faltered. Jennifer, meanwhile, had risen from WKNY to a channel in Austin, and then to GNN. GNN had come onto the scene just a few short years ago, ostensibly presenting itself as a source for unbiased, non-partisan reporting—a counter to the punditry and commentary so prevalent on FOX, MSNBC, CNN, and others. What they didn't admit publicly was that the news they reported and the stories they covered were all dictated by their shareholders. Despite that, they had dominated in the ratings for the last six quarters, something Jennifer loved to prod Jessamine with every chance she got.

"Jessamine!" Jennifer's smile was as fake as her breast implants and nose job. "It's nice to see you. I didn't realize CBS had the money to keep you guys here this long. I assumed you'd already headed home."

Jessamine struggled to keep her composure. "We do just fine, Jennifer."

"Oh, Jess." Her tone was patronizing. "I'm sure you do."

Jessamine hated being called Jess. Worse, she knew that Jennifer knew this. She forced a smile of her own.

"It's nice," she said, "not taking editorial notes from a military-industrial shell company."

Jennifer laughed. "You sound like those alternative news nuts on the Internet, Jess. Next you'll be telling me about how 9/11 was an inside job, or how Black Lodge secretly controls the world."

Jessamine was about to respond when Hank interrupted them both.

"CBS. GNN. We're all on the corporate tip. So how about the two of you leave the alpha-kitty bullshit to someone else? There's news happening. Let's be professionals for a change."

Jennifer gasped, clearly offended. Smiling, Jessamine took advantage of her distraction to push past her and get to the front of the throng. Khem and Hank hurried along behind her.

"Good job," she muttered. "I hate that bitch."

"Yeah, well, she's beating us in the ratings, so go kick some ass."

Nodding, Jessamine grabbed the microphone from Khem and turned her attention to the scientists. One of the expedition's spokespeople, a scientist named Keith DeMatteis, approached the reporters. He was short and thin, in his late sixties, and constantly peering over the top of his thick-lensed glasses. He often seemed befuddled, but when responding to questions or giving a briefing, he was reliably and consistently acerbic and witty, which had made him a favorite amongst the press corps. Now, however, he seemed neither befuddled nor good-humored. His face had a pinched, nervous look.

He's scared, Jessamine realized.

DeMatteis swayed on the balls of his feet as the ship rolled again. When the reporters began to all shout questions at him simultaneously, he held up his hands for quiet. When he spoke, it was without his usual charm or sarcasm.

"I'm going to give a short statement, and that's all. I'm not—I repeat—not taking questions. When I'm done, I'm going to ask all of you to clear this area. We have an emergency situation. Approximately two minutes ago, Carrie Anderson and Peter Scofield reported some problems with their equipment."

"Just like everything else on this tug," Jessamine whispered.

"They're currently about one hundred eighty meters below the surface. Their communications array has now shorted and the oxygen monitor is on the fritz. The . . . the seals on both of their oxygen tanks appear to be compromised. I would remind everyone that Carrie Anderson is one of the most experienced free divers in the world—"

"What about Peter Scofield?" Jennifer elbowed her way past Jessamine and Khem. "Can they make it to the surface from that depth without their equipment?"

Scowling, DeMatteis shot Jennifer a withering glance, and then pretended he hadn't heard the question. Jessamine felt a sudden and overwhelming urge to go hug the old man.

"I would caution all of you that . . ."

DeMatteis broke off as the commotion increased behind him. Researchers began to shout, as their monitors went crazy. An alarm blared overhead, echoing throughout the ship. Then a second alarm began to wail in unison. Crew members rushed to the port side. Some members of the press began to follow them, but DeMatteis yelled at them to get back. Then, distracted by a colleague, he turned his attention away from the reporters. Jennifer and her crew charged ahead.

Jessamine glanced at Khem.

"I'm following you," he said.

"Is your camera still working?"

He nodded. "For now, at least. Let's make the most of that while we can."

Jessamine pushed forward, weaving her way between other members of the press. Khem stayed right behind her, filming everything with his camera, which almost seemed to be an extension of him.

The alarms stopped blaring. For one brief moment, everything fell silent.

Jessamine and Khem made it once more to the front of the crowd just as the commotion began anew. There, lying on the deck in a pool of water, was Carrie Anderson. She was curled into the fetal position and appeared to be unconscious and unresponsive. Freed of her suit and gear, her exposed skin was covered with an ugly red rash, and judging by the discoloration on her thighs, she'd lost control of her bowels during her rapid ascent.

Several crew members crouched next to her in concern. Jessamine heard one of them mutter about "the bends." Then a scientist shouted at the team to call for a helicopter and to get the hyperbaric chamber ready.

"Hopefully the hyperbaric chamber's not malfunctioning like everything else," Khem murmured.

Jessamine turned to him, realized that he had zoomed in on Carrie, and put her hand in front of the lens.

"No," she said. "Give her some dignity. Let's go over to the rail. We've got a story to report."

"Is she okay?" Hank asked as the three of them retreated starboard. "What's going on?"

"News," Jessamine replied. "News is what's going on. Do we have a connection yet?"

"Not yet. The damn uplink is still on the fritz."

"Shit . . . okay. Let's go ahead and tape anyway. We'll send it later. And somebody track Julio down."

"Speak of the devil and I shall appear," Julio said, maneuvering between reporters and crew. "You look fine, by the way. I think we can get by with just a quick touch up."

Jessamine waited patiently while Julio expertly attended to her hair and makeup. When he was finished, she nodded at Khem and Hank, indicating she was ready. The two of them both signaled their confirmation.

"Get the moon in the background," Hank told Khem. "That will make for a nice shot."

"I've got it. Kind of cloudy, though. I need better lighting."

"You want to light the moon?"

As Jessamine approached the railing, Hank and Khem's bickering faded into background noise. As a journalist, she'd trained herself to sort through information she was hearing, focusing on what was useful and disregarding the unimportant. She did that now, and heard several reporters inquiring about Peter Scofield's status. None of the research team responded to their shouted demands.

Jessamine realized that her seasickness had finally subsided. The research vessel was no longer swaying.

"There we go," Hank said. "Look at that, Khem. Perfect lighting. Somebody up there must like us."

The clouds cooperated with the shot, sliding across the night sky, and the almost-full moon shone down upon a dark ocean that had suddenly gone completely still.

Peter Scofield never resurfaced.

TWO

If you didn't look too closely, Carrie Anderson decided, then it was easy to pretend that the end of the world wasn't possibly due at any time now.

Cured of the bends, she had just been freshly released from a small hospital in Chemin Grenier, a village of about twelve thousand souls located in Mauritius's Savanne District. Well, perhaps released wasn't the most correct terminology. Left early, against doctor's orders was probably more apt. She hadn't even waited to inform her superiors at Alpinus Biofutures, whom she was currently under contract with as a freelancer. Although, that really didn't matter, since she was sure the hospital staff would notify them for her in short order.

The day was warm, the sky clear and crystalline blue, and the town bustled with people. A public transportation bus chortled down the street, belching exhaust. Impatient drivers honked their horns behind it. A group of older men sat outside a tiny sidewalk café, eating cheap seafood and listening to a football game—or soccer, as she thought of it—on an even cheaper transistor radio that looked like it had probably been new during the Nixon administration. The match was FC Dodo versus Garrison, judging by the snatch of the broadcast Carrie overheard. It had taken Carrie many years to think of soccer and football as the same game, rather than the Americanized version of football that she'd grown up watching with her father. One of the men wore an immaculately cleaned and pressed Toshan Gunness jersey. For a moment, she thought of her father and the various New England Patriots apparel he'd worn over the years.

The men good-naturedly ribbed each other in Creole, but stopped to stare at Carrie as she passed them by. Carrie didn't notice, still lost in thoughts of her own. Memories of her father always made her smile.

Reggae music rumbled from a nearby coffee shop. A few doors down, competing Sega music blasted from a corner bar, along with the sounds of dancing, clapping, and raucous laughter. Carrie paused in front of the doorway, considering for a moment, but then moved on, seeking some place quieter. The last thing she wanted right now was to be surrounded by a crowd.

She passed a bicycle shop and saw customers inside. Likewise a bakery, bookstore, and pharmacy. None of the businesses were closed or shuttered. Within a block, she walked by a mandir, a mosque, and a church. None of their doors were boarded over. A signboard outside the Village Council chambers was plastered with flyers advertising upcoming events. For a country that was facing the mounting possibility of a forced, mandatory evacuation, the people of Mauritius didn't seem to care. Or perhaps this was just their way of dealing with it. Maybe they chose to face it by pretending that life was still going on, as normal.

Carrie thought that she could almost like it here. Smiling, she inhaled deeply through her nose, trying to get rid of the smell of the hospital, which still seemed to linger about her. She smelled flowers and food. Her stomach grumbled.

Then she thought of Peter, and her mood soured again. She shivered, despite the tropical heat.

The events of the last three days were still a jumbled blur, but she decided to focus on them, so as not to think about Peter. Not yet. She would have to, at some point, because there were things she needed to do, but first, she needed time to consider her next moves carefully. She had experienced something during this last dive—she wasn't sure what. A hallucination, perhaps? She was no stranger to the sense of euphoria that came with free diving. Being that far down, with no scuba gear, was very much like what being in outer space must feel like. But this had been different. She hadn't been free diving, for one thing. She'd had the protection of state-of-the-art diving gear. And when the sensation had overcome her, it wasn't euphoria she had felt. It was . . .

No. She wasn't ready to go there yet. She needed to plan first.

And she also needed a drink. Or more likely, several of them.

She remembered the equipment malfunctioning. Of course it had. That had been the one constant on this expedition—everything that could go wrong, had gone wrong, especially when it came to electronic gear. Such mechanical failures had been the reason she and Peter had attempted such a dangerous dive in the first place. Her memories were more confused in the moments after that—just snatches, really. A jumbled mess of images and impressions and sounds. She remembered freeing herself from her tank and gear, and making for the surface, managing to save her own life with her ascension-breathing techniques, but because she experienced compression so suddenly, she'd gotten quite a case of the bends. She didn't remember blacking out, but it must have happened after she'd surfaced. She had snatches of memories in the moments after that—the severe itching she'd felt all over her skin, being brought out of the water and placed in the hyperbaric chamber, (which, thankfully, was one piece of equipment that had not malfunctioned), the dim awareness that she'd soiled herself, concerned faces of colleagues whose names she couldn't remember as she drifted in and out of consciousness, the numbness in her arms, legs, and tongue, and a brutal pain in her lower back—all symptoms of decompression sickness.

The next thing she remembered was waking up in the hospital, alive, thanks to her skills as a free diver, and her ability to hold her breath until resurfacing. And, she supposed, the doctors and the EMTs.

Peter wasn't a free diver and the monitors had lost track of him as he descended deeper into the trench.

She'd learned yesterday that he was missing and presumed dead.

Carrie thought that was a safe assumption.

After walking a few more blocks, she found a quiet bar nestled between two apartment buildings. It was dimly lit, even in the daylight, and didn't echo of music or laughter or fighting. Deciding to try her luck, Carrie stepped inside and paused for a moment, letting her eyes adjust. When they did, she saw that the establishment was nearly empty, save for a drowsy-looking bartender with a thick, graying mustache, and an even sleepier-looking patron nursing a drink at the end of the bar.

The customer seemed lost in his own morose thoughts, and didn't look up as she wove her way around a series of rickety, beer-stained tables and chairs, and approached the bar. The bartender smiled and nodded. Carrie was about to try her Creole, a language she spoke minimally at best, but felt relieved when he greeted her in English.

"What can I get you?"

"What do you have on tap?" she asked.

He shrugged. "Ti La Biere, Flying Dodo, Stella Pils, Black Eagle . . . oh, and Phoenix Fresh Lemon, which is fruity."

Carrie made a face. "Got anything that I don't need a little umbrella with? Maybe a nice Weizen Bock?"

The bartender grinned. "Flying Dodo Mean Wheat Bock."

Carrie hesitated, not sure if what he had just said was a mistranslation or just an oddly named beer.

"I'm sorry. Are you saying that Flying Dodo means Wheat Bock?"

The bartender's smile grew broader. "No, that's the name of the beer. Flying Dodo Mean Wheat Bock. It's delicious, and has a mean kick."

"Sounds perfect. One of those, and a shot of whiskey, please. Can I run a tab?"

Nodding, the bartender drew her beer, topping the glass off nicely. He placed the beer in front of her, returned with a shot glass of whiskey, and expertly picked up that she wasn't in the mood for conversation. He checked on his other customer and then returned to his stool behind the bar. Carrie downed the shot and then chased it with a sip of the beer. It was cold and delicious and tasted like happiness. Carrie made a mental note to tip him well.

She pulled out her phone and was pleased to see she had service. Whatever the reason for the electronic malfunctions onboard the Novak and its surrounding flotilla, her cell seemed to be working fine here on land. She tapped the app for her e-mail and frowned in frustration when she saw that she had over two hundred new messages. She scanned the senders and subject lines, weeding out the obvious interview requests and best wishes from well-meaning strangers, and focused instead on friends and family. All of them were concerned about

her. The incident had been all over the news. Rather than
e-mailing each of them separately, she decided to post a message
on Facebook.

As a public figure, Carrie had two Facebook accounts. One
was a Carrie Anderson page that the public could "Like" and
comment on. The other was a private profile she'd created under
the pseudonym Jojo Anderson, which was in no way connected
to her public page. She kept the friends list on her private profile confined strictly to family members, current friends, and
trusted peers. She logged into the private account and checked
the news feed. Her sister, Rachel, had posted pictures from her
home in Boston—Rachel, her husband Chris, and their two
sons, playing in what looked like about two feet of snow. They
were bundled up—hats, coats, scarves, and gloves. One of the
pictures showed them building a snowman. Another showed
their dog, Timber, pulling the kids on a sled. It seemed strange
to Carrie that while she was here, sweating and sunburned,
her sister was back home dealing with temperatures in the
twenties and a mound of snow. But then again, it also seemed
strange to her that Rachel was married, and a mom. Carrie
still thought of Rachel as her little sister. It seemed inconceiv-
able they were now both in their thirties, with lives of their
own. And Rachel with a family . . .

She spotted a slightly older post on Rachel's timeline—a
picture of their father, posted a week ago on his birthday. The
caption read: "We miss you, Pops. Happy 60th!" Carrie had
spent that day out at sea, trying not to think about it. Their
father had been killed in an automobile accident on rain-slicked
roads when Carrie was a sophomore in college and Rachel
was finishing high school. And their mother, gone two years
next May to cancer. Things had not ended well for Carrie and
her mother. It had begun when Carrie was a teenager, and
her father's death had only increased the gulf between them.

Her mother had always thought Carrie was headstrong, stubborn, and unnecessarily reckless by pursuing such a dangerous career, if she could call it that. Even early on, when Carrie's aptitude for diving had first manifested, her mother had been less than supportive. That had remained so as years went by and Carrie began to train. She'd always viewed Carrie's free diving as nothing more than a phase, like dying her hair pink or listening to Morrissey—something that Carrie would eventually grow out of, before settling down with a husband like Rachel had done. Carrie was pretty sure her diving would have been received differently if she were a son instead. Though her mother insisted that she truly wanted the best for Carrie, seeing her so restless and (in her mother's mind) unhappy as a young woman, troubled her. Her mother thought that, because Rachel had found happiness by settling down with a nice young man, Carrie would do the same. All she had to do was find the right guy . . .

Her mother had wanted more grandchildren, while Carrie had just wanted her mother to be proud of her. Just once.

Then, her mother had died, leaving both of them wanting and unfulfilled.

She sat the phone down on the bar beside her, finished her beer in one long gulp, and caught the bartender's attention.

"Two more of those, please?"

"Of course. Coming right up."

She posted a quick update, letting everyone know she was out of the hospital and assuring them she was okay. She waited a few minutes, responded to a few comments, and then closed the app. Sighing, Carrie picked up her glass and took another deep draught.

Damn it, Mom . . .

There was a bustle of noise from the doorway. The bartender looked up, and Carrie judged by his expression that this was far more traffic than he was normally accustomed to at this time of day. She half-turned on her stool, and saw four people entering the bar. One was a paunchy, middle-aged, balding white man dressed in a rumpled pair of shorts and a shirt that had never been introduced to an iron. A taller, thinner white man in his late twenties followed. Unlike his companion, he was immaculately dressed, with crisp, creased khakis and an eye-catching Hawaiian shirt. The third customer was a young Indian man with beautiful eyes that immediately caught Carrie's attention. But then her gaze was drawn to the video camera the man was holding. This was no mere tourist, taping his vacation for posterity. The camera was a professional-grade rig, just like the one the reporters had carried onboard the Novak. Lastly, a woman entered the bar. Carrie recognized her luxuriant red hair and creamy complexion right away— Jessamine Wheatley of CBS News.

The four of them paused, letting their eyes adjust to the dim light. Spying her, they conferred amongst themselves for a brief moment. Then, the two white guys pulled out chairs and sat down at a table while Jessamine and the cameraman approached her cautiously, as if Carrie were a tiger and they were two timid mice.

Carrie drained her second shot of whiskey and slammed the glass down on the bar, not hard enough to shatter it, but loud enough to make her displeasure known. The bartender, picking up on the tension, eyed the two women as if they were gunfighters. Carrie had a sudden, bizarre image of him ducking beneath the bar as gunshots rang out, like in an old western movie. The only thing missing was a piano player and a set of swinging doors. Despite her annoyance, she grinned at the thought.

The reporter must have mistaken her grin for friendliness, because her timidity vanished and she strode boldly toward the bar, hand outstretched. The cameraman hurried along in her wake, obviously uncomfortable and nervous.

"Carrie Anderson! I'm—"

"Is this on the record?" Carrie interrupted.

"Um . . . no?"

"Then go fuck yourself." Carrie turned back around to face the bar, and coolly considered her half-empty glass. The reporter gave an audible huff, and paused, speechless. Carrie stifled a grin. She knew reporters, knew how they worked, and she wasn't about to let one get over on her just because she was a little buzzed.

The bartender eyed them both, and slowly began to approach.

Jessamine stammered. "I . . . I'm sorry?"

"No, you're not," Carrie replied.

"We got off on the wrong foot. Maybe you don't remember me? I'm—"

"Jessamine Wheatley, currently of CBS News. Yes, I remember you. It was nice not having you people looking over my shoulder for three days."

"I . . . I just . . ."

"You just want to finish your story. Is that it?"

Before Jessamine could respond, the bartender interrupted them.

"Get you folks anything?"

"Um . . ." Jessamine frowned, clearly off balance by the turn of conversation. "A pitcher of Corona?"

"We only have beers brewed here in Mauritius. If you want an import, the closest thing I have is Guinness Foreign Extra Stout, and that's not on tap."

"They have a nice, fruity Phoenix Fresh Lemon," Carrie suggested.

The bartender smiled slyly at her and she winked.

"Yes, four of those, please," Jessamine said. "No, wait. Hank won't drink that. One Guinness and three of those . . . what did you call them?"

"Phoenix Fresh Lemon," Carrie and the bartender said in unison.

As he left to fill their order, Carrie and Jessamine appraised each other. The cameraman let his eyes dart all over the restaurant, looking at everything but Carrie. He shifted from foot to foot, clearly uncomfortable.

Carrie sipped her beer and said, "Don't bullshit a bullshitter. That's what my father always used to say."

Jessamine held her posture. "Meaning?"

"Meaning no offense, but get to the point. I've had a hell of a week and I'm not in the mood. What do you want?"

Jessamine took a deep breath, and exhaled. Her shoulders sagged.

"You're right," she admitted, with a conciliatory tone. "I want to finish my story. Right now, you're the only story here."

"How did you find me?"

"A spokesman for Alpinus Biofutures told everyone you were at the hospital in Port Louis. That made sense, since that's where most of the flotilla has been docking. But we checked into it, and found out you were here in Chemin Grenier instead. After that, it was just a matter of waiting for you to be released. I take it your employers don't know you left early?"

"Not yet," Carrie admitted. "But they'll figure it out soon enough."

"And you're fully recovered?"

The Indian man began to raise his camera. Carrie noted that the power light was on.

"Is this an interview?" she asked.

Jessamine shrugged. "We'd like it to be, if you're willing."

"Then be honest about it and quit dicking around."

"I thought I just was honest?"

"I'm talking about the fact that your camera is recording this when I thought it was off." Carrie turned to the cameraman. "What's your name?"

"K-khem . . . I'm Khem, ma'am."

"Okay, Khem. Do your job. Obviously, your partner here isn't going to leave me alone until I give her a sound bite. Let's get it over with."

"Wonderful! Thank you so much, Carrie." Jessamine smiled. "Would you care to join us at our table?"

"No, thanks. Right here is fine."

"Actually," Khem said, "the lighting in here isn't all that great."

"I'm sure professionals such as yourselves will be able to make do," Carrie said.

"Maybe if you could stand over there?"

Smiling, Carrie shook her head. "I have drinks on the way."

As if on cue, the bartender returned with their drinks. The balding man slipped out of his chair and walked over to retrieve them. He nodded at Carrie.

"Hi, I'm Hank. I'm their producer. And I'd just like to say that we're all glad you're okay. That's what's important. And I'm sorry about what happened to your colleague."

"Thank you, Hank."

"Yes, Hank." Jessamine scowled. "Thank you. Why don't you take Julio his drink? We'll be over in a bit."

"Don't get mad at me, Jessamine," he muttered under his breath.

Jessamine waited until he had departed, and then she tried smiling again. Carrie could see that beyond the surface bravado, the reporter was flustered.

Good, she thought. *Let's see if I can tweak her some more.*

"Could you tell us what happened to you down there?" Jessamine asked.

"No."

"Do you have any idea what might have caused the critical breakdown your equipment suffered?"

"No," Carrie lied.

"And you don't remember what happened to cause the accident?"

"I think what I said was that I wasn't going to tell you what happened down there, not that I don't remember. I don't want to talk about it. A man died, after all."

"Yes. Noted researcher Peter Scofield, who is presumed dead."

"He's not presumed dead." Carrie took another sip of beer. "He is dead."

"So, you're then confirming that—"

"I'm not confirming or denying anything."

"You just said he was dead," Jessamine protested. "I have a responsibility to—"

"Your responsibility begins and ends with your bosses, and their responsibility is to their shareholders and advertisers. I don't care which network you're with. They're all the same. The only thing that matters to them are their earnings. They pretend to appeal to one particular group or another, but in the end, it's all bullshit. The only thing they care about are dollar signs—big corporate interests that stand in the way of good science being done."

"Your research is funded by Alpinus Biofutures," Jessamine shot back. "They hardly qualify as a small company."

"But Alpinus wants results," Carrie argued. "Your bosses just want ratings."

"What, then, are your thoughts now that the United Nations has officially removed Alpinus Biofutures from the site and turned over further exploration in the area to the NOAA instead?"

"What?"

Carrie regretted the question the second she voiced it. She knew how to play politics. This wasn't her first time jousting with the press. She was something of a public relations expert when it came to her scientific interests. She knew how to handle investors, government officials, and members of the press. But so far, she had anticipated where Jessamine wanted to lead her, and had instead successfully steered the conversation in the direction she wanted to go—namely, away from Peter and what had really happened during their dive. Although now, it occurred to Carrie that it had been she who had brought Peter up. Why was she being so hot-headed all of a sudden, rather than her politically savvy self? Was she just tired? Off her game? This new, unexpected revelation regarding the United Nations and Alpinus surprised her, giving Jessamine the advantage.

"That's correct," Jessamine replied. "The U.N. removed Alpinus yesterday. In their report, they cited the constant equipment malfunctions, the lack of progress, and the fact that, so far, the scientific results are inconclusive, amongst other things."

"You can't rush science," Carrie said.

"No," Jessamine agreed, "you can't. Do you think the United Nations is making a mistake with this move?"

Carrie paused, choosing her words carefully. "I don't believe that the NOAA will have any better luck than we did."

"Would you care to comment on why?"

"No. And I have no further comment regarding any of this. Now, if you don't mind, I've just spent three days in the hospital. My skin still itches and I've got a rash, and what I really want to do right now is get drunk."

"A rash?"

"From the bends. It's a side effect. And it's terrible. Feels like tiny insects are crawling all over me. Itches like crazy."

"I'm sorry."

"Thanks." Carrie shrugged. "I got off lucky."

Jessamine started to respond, but Khem lowered the camera and turned it off.

"Come on," he said to her. Then he turned to Carrie. "I'm sorry for your loss, Ms. Anderson."

"Thank you," Carrie answered.

Nodding, Khem walked away to join his companions at their table. The man in the Hawaiian shirt, Julio, called out to him, but Carrie couldn't hear what was said. Jessamine began to walk away, staring at the floor.

"I'm sorry if I came off as snippy," Carrie apologized. "You just surprised me, is all. I really wasn't prepared for this—for giving any sort of interview. Usually I'm a bit more camera-savvy."

"No," Jessamine replied. "You have every reason to be snippy. You're right. You're absolutely right. We caught you unawares. I don't like staking out your hospital and following you into a bar when you obviously just want to be left alone. If it were any other profession, they'd call that stalking. But right now, this is what the public wants to hear about, and it's my job to ask. Even if I don't, somebody else will."

"I get it. Hey, can I buy you and your crew another round?"

Jessamine smiled. "I'd like that. But what I'd like more is to really interview you sometime."

"Isn't that what you just did?"

"Not about this. I mean a real interview. I just . . . I find you fascinating. So do a lot of other people. I'd love to hear about what it's been like for you in your field. And as a free diver, too. You still hold more CMAS- and AIDA-recognized world records than anyone else, man or woman."

Carrie shook her head. "I'm afraid you'll have to settle for a drink instead."

Jessamine shrugged. Carrie signaled the bartender and ordered another round. They were quiet for a moment, while they waited for the drink order to arrive, and then Jessamine cleared her throat.

"Look, I'm really sorry about what happened to your colleague. And I'm glad you're okay. Like a lot of other people, I genuinely admire you. If you change your mind, or if you want to stay in touch, here's my card."

She handed Carrie a business card. Carrie accepted it, and stuck it in her pocket without a glance.

"Thanks. I'll do that."

"I hope so."

"I guess I'll see you guys around?"

Jessamine shook her head. "Not us. The network wants to move on to other stories, at least until an evacuation order is given, and that doesn't appear to be happening anytime in the immediate future. The international community is dragging its feet."

"It would definitely be a massive undertaking," Carrie agreed. "But that explains everyone's behavior. When I first got out of the hospital, I thought it was weird that people weren't acting more concerned."

"Oh, they're concerned. There's just not a lot they can do until something is officially decided."

Carrie nodded. "It has to be frustrating and scary."

The bartender sat Carrie and Jessamine's drinks in front of them, and then carried a tray over to the news crew's table.

"So where are you off to next, then?" Carrie asked.

"Australia. They're dealing with an influx of jihadists. We're going to cover that."

"Australia's beautiful."

"It is," Jessamine agreed. "I'm from there, originally."

"You don't have an accent."

"Dual citizenship," Jessamine explained. "My parents moved to the States when I was young, but we also maintained a residence in Australia. I grew up in America, but I'm Australian at heart."

Carrie stuck out her hand again. "Well, good luck to you."

"Thanks." Jessamine shook her hand. "You, too. I hope you find what you're looking for. What will you do, now that your expedition has been sidelined?"

"Oh," Carrie said, her tone vague, "I'll just have to wait and see."

Carrie waited until the news crew had left the bar, which gave her time for three more rounds. Then she paid the bartender, tipping him generously and thanking him for his time. He told her to come back again, and she assured him that she'd try. When she stepped back outside into the sunlight and the heat, her vision momentarily blurred and she felt dizzy.

I should have eaten something, she thought. *Jesus Christ, all I've had was hospital food for the last three days.*

When the dizziness had passed, she glanced around to make sure no more reporters were following her. Then she pulled out her cell phone and called Abhi.

Serving as the research team's jack of all trades—pilot, instrument manager, repair man, boatswain's mate, laborer, and sometimes authority figure to the younger crew members—Abhi was one of Carrie's favorite people onboard the Novak. In the short time they'd known each other, the two had become fast friends. While he certainly wasn't a father figure, Carrie supposed her fondness for the older man was akin to that of a favorite uncle. She couldn't explain it, but the two of them had immediately clicked upon their first meeting, and had since become thick as thieves.

He also, unbeknownst to their superiors at Alpinus Bio-futures, ran an impressive makeshift still in the ship's boiler room, and freely shared the fruits of that still with discerning crew members who promised not to hold him responsible for any ill effects they might suffer from drinking what he termed his "special bulkhead cleaner."

Abhi answered on the second ring, sounding breathless and out of sorts.

"Hey, Jailbreak, I figured you'd be calling at some point. Need a ride back to Port Louis?"

"No, that's okay. I can grab a cab."

"Are you sure? I can get a car, no problem. A cab is going to be expensive."

"I might as well spend it while I've got it."

"Oh, so I take it you've heard?"

"That we're shut down? Yes, I just found out. From a re-porter, which was lovely. It's such bullshit."

"Aye," Abhi agreed, "it is. But what can we do? We aren't the ones making the decisions, Carrie. It's above our pay grade."

"Except we're no longer getting paid."

"Well, there is that, but as I said, what can we do? Not much, other than look for another job."

"I'll tell you exactly what we're going to do," Carrie replied. "We're going to do our own survey. And I don't want the press finding out about it, either. I'm betting most of them will be clearing out soon."

Abhi protested, but Carrie pushed ahead, insisting on his help. She then asked him to get a pen and paper, and gave him a list of equipment that they'd need—all analog gear, nothing electronic. When she was finished, there was a long pause. At first, she thought the call had dropped, but then Abhi spoke again.

"Carrie, why are we doing this?"

"Because," she said, "I saw something down there."

"What do you mean? What did you see?"

"I'm not sure. At least, not yet. But I think I saw something, and I can't explain what it was without seeing it again. No one's going to take what I say seriously until I have some actual evidence. We have to go back."

She thought Abhi would make another effort to talk her out of it, but instead, he simply asked one question.

"When do we leave?"

THREE

With only moderate traffic on the M2, the drive from Chemin Grenier to Port Louis took a little over an hour, which gave time for the effects of the alcohol to work its way out of Carrie's system. They rode in silence, for the most part. Carrie, lost in her own thoughts, watched the southwest coast roll by, and the cab driver seemed content to listen to the radio, which was tuned to a Creole talk show. From what she could tell, the conversation between the host and his guest was dominated by the trench, and the possible evacuation. Diego Garcia and Madagascar were mentioned as two locations where temporary shelters were being constructed. The host was apparently incensed by this, as Diego Garcia was part of the Chagos Archipelago. Although Carrie didn't understand all of the internal and regional politics involved, she knew that the archipelago was at the forefront of a long-running territorial dispute between Mauritius and the United Kingdom, who had leased Diego Garcia to the United States for a military base. Mauritius had unsuccessfully lobbied the United Nations several times for sovereignty over the Chagos region.

"We should take it by force," the cabbie muttered. "What use is having a military if we do not use it?"

As the landscape flashed by, Carrie thought about how different the little island nation was from most other nations associated with the African continent. While poverty still existed in Mauritius, the current government played an active role in trying to help their people overcome it. A visitor might assume all of the money was located along the beaches, resorts, and tourist areas, but when driving through the rural areas, as they were now, one encountered textile mills, farms, sugar plantations, and fisheries. She knew the latter was struggling recently, as a result of the spreading collapse. Fishermen had been banned from the waters around the southern coast, as the sea floor's spreading grew worse. This meant that the fisheries had to rely on the waters on the other side of the island, or amongst the lagoons. As a result, both their economy and their environment had taken a hit. But even before that, the fishing industry had struggled, confined to mostly trawling for shrimp and tuna, as bigger commercial fleets from Russia, Japan, Taiwan, and South Korea emptied the seas farther out.

The taxi slowed as they encountered a backup, caused by a minor traffic accident up ahead. Grumbling to no one in particular, the driver turned off the radio and rolled his window down. A wave of sticky, wet heat wafted into the cab. The driver leaned out of the vehicle, craning his neck for a better view. Carrie looked, too, and spotted a wooded park off to the side of the road. In the park's center was a huge bronze statue of a dodo bird.

"I am sorry for this, Miss." The driver ducked back into the car and turned to face her. "It looks like they are moving it to the side."

"That's okay," Carrie assured him. "You can't control what happens."

"You are looking at the statue?"

Carrie nodded. "That's your country's mascot, right?"

"Yes." He smiled, apparently pleased that she knew this. Then, the smile faded and his expression became worried. "I fear that will be us soon."

"What do you mean?"

"Before there were people, Mauritius belonged to the dodo. Before the Arabs came here, there was the dodo. When the Portuguese arrived, there was still the dodo. Then the French and the British. Soon, no more dodo. Now, we have independence. We are our own people. But we are not the original. We are not the dodo. And soon, I am afraid the dodo will have their revenge."

"You mean the trench?" Carrie leaned forward. "I'm actually one of the researchers working on that."

"Then you know," he said. "You can tell me how bad it is. I think the government are not telling us the whole truth. I think we are facing extinction, just like the dodo."

"I don't think it will come to that. Yes, the collapse is growing larger, but the absolute worst-case scenario would just be evacuation."

"Is that not the same as extinction?"

"Of course not," Carrie said.

The driver smiled sadly. "You would think they are the same thing if, like me, you had lived here all your life. This is where my home is. It was my parent's home. I was raised here. Now I raise my family here. Mauritius is all I have ever known. Every memory from my life is on this island. It is the same for my wife, and for our children. It is all we have, and soon, it may be gone. Is that not extinction?"

"I don't think it will come to that."

Carrie tried to sound convincing, but she could tell by his expression that she had failed.

"You're the first person I've met who has seemed concerned about this," she said.

"Oh, they're all concerned." The driver waved his hand, motioning at the people in the other cars. "But I am in this taxi all day, with only the radio for company, and this is all they talk about. I guess I think about it more."

Eventually, the vehicles involved in the accident were cleared to the side of the road and traffic began to move again. Carrie watched the statue of the dodo until it disappeared from sight.

The cab driver grew quiet again, returning to his own thoughts. Although he rolled the window up and turned the air conditioning back on, the radio remained off. They rode in silence once more. This time, the stillness seemed oppressive.

Carrie had the taxi drop her off at a resort far away from the harbor where their research vessel was docked. The last thing she wanted right now was to be recognized, or to run into anybody else from the expedition. After tipping the driver and wishing him luck, she entered the resort's restaurant. Light jazz played softly from hidden speakers somewhere overhead. The air conditioning was on just enough to make the establishment cool, but not uncomfortable.

A waiter guided her to a table overlooking a wooded grove. Placing her order, Carrie stared out at the trees and then around the restaurant. It was a faux-posh affair, catering to the tourists with a plastic type of elegance, but she didn't care. They offered the two things she needed the most right now— something to eat, and anonymity. She regretted that the former would have to be a small portion for now. After three days of hospital food, Carrie was ready for a five-course meal. But since she planned on meeting up with Abhi and possibly returning to the rift as early as tonight, a pre-dive meal would have to suffice. And as for the latter, it would be nice to relax for a while, safe from the press, or her fellow scientists, or anybody else who knew her.

Which was why, halfway through her meal, Carrie was surprised to look up from her table and see Paolo, the oceanographer and diver who she had supplanted on the Novak's research team, approaching from across the room. Carrie smiled at him, too stunned to speak. Paolo was slow to return the gesture.

"Paolo! I didn't expect to see you here. I figured you'd be back at the ship."

"I'm surprised to see you here, as well. You were released early?"

"Something like that."

Carrie played with her napkin, folding it and then unfolding it again. She felt flustered and unsure, and hated the uncertainty and effect that Paolo's sudden appearance had on her. Things had been tense between them over the last few weeks, although they'd interacted professionally, if somewhat coolly toward one another, in public—especially in front of the press. But Carrie knew that Paolo privately resented her for getting the lead diver role on this expedition, rather than him.

In truth, their rivalry went back further than just this recent research mission. A few years earlier, after her transition from world-class free diver to oceanographer, Carrie had gone to work for the Scripps Institute. That was where she and Paolo had first met. They started out as acquaintances, but had eventually gone out on a few dates, and then started a serious relationship that had lasted six months. Carrie had just started to let her guard down around him when Paolo unexpectedly broke it off one night. He said that he disapproved of Carrie's using a program leader's crush on her to get positions on prestigious teams. They had argued about it for hours. Carrie was convinced Paolo was just jealous of the fact that another man had a crush on her, and jealous that she got the position. After all, it wasn't like she had slept her way to the top. But Paolo had insisted on his moral stance. She'd argued that a woman who uses men's attraction to get what she wants was akin to men bonding over cognac and cigars—it was that same edge of nepotism. Paolo had stubbornly stuck to his guns, insisting that there was no difference between what she was doing, and using sex to get what she wanted. Angered by his belligerence, Carrie had decided that it was good he was breaking things off with her, because the decision was now mutual.

And that was the end of that.

Two months later, the Scripps Institute picked Carrie over Paolo for a position on a team that was embarking on a major survey mission in the Gulf of Mexico and she hadn't heard from him since.

Secretly, Carrie had always suspected that there was more to their breakup than just that argument. She had always battled insomnia, and usually had a bottle of Ambien on her nightstand. One night, early in their relationship, Paolo had asked if he could have one. Carrie had said fine. But then Paolo began floating the idea of selling the pills to raise extra cash for them both. Carrie had declined, gently at first, when she thought he was just kidding around, but more vehemently when he continued to suggest the idea. Paolo stopped bringing it up after that, but then she began to notice that her pills were going missing. When she eventually confronted him about it, he'd blown up, angrily denying any knowledge, and implying that perhaps she was taking more Ambien than she realized. It wasn't until a year after their breakup that Carrie had learned through a mutual colleague that Paolo had in fact been selling the pills regularly.

"May I join you?" Paolo motioned to the empty chair across

from her. He seemed almost timid, a behavior which was quite unlike him.

Intrigued by his demeanor, Carrie shrugged. "Sure. Have a seat."

Paolo wore a cream-colored shirt, pressed khakis, and brown leather shoes with no socks. She had to admit, he looked good—not at all like a man who had spent most of the last two weeks at sea. She suddenly—and uncharacteristically—wondered how she herself must look, having spent the last three days in the hospital.

As he pulled out the chair and sat down, Carrie smiled again. This time, Paolo returned the gesture much more quickly.

"It's a shame about Alpinus getting sidelined," she said. "What's next for you?"

"Oh, I'm staying onboard. Just because the NOAA is taking over doesn't mean we'll be leaving completely. Alpinus Biofutures still has a vested interest in what's occurring here. I'm sure you'll still be a part of the team, as well?"

"I guess," Carrie replied. "Honestly, I don't know yet. I haven't talked to anyone from Alpinus since I got out of the hospital. I don't know if I still have a job or not."

This time, Paolo's smile was wistful. He stared out the window, seemingly lost in thought.

"Same old Carrie," he said. "Always up to something."

"Excuse me?"

He turned back to her. "You're staying on. Maybe not for our current employer, but you're definitely staying here."

"Honestly, Paolo, I haven't decided anything yet. Have you forgotten that Peter died? Or that I almost did?"

"I've forgotten nothing. Especially how you operate. And I know exactly what you're up to."

He waited for her reaction. Carrie started to protest her ignorance, but something in his expression told her that it was pointless to do so.

"Goddamn it, Abhi," she cursed. "Let me guess. He told you because he was worried about me?"

"I haven't talked to Abhi since yesterday." He pointed at the table. "But I know a pre-dive meal when I see one. You just got released from the hospital. You are probably famished. And the food here is fine. Yet all you've ordered is a small bowl of fish soup, and a large pitcher of water. You've drank seven glasses."

"How long were you watching me, Paolo?"

He ignored the question. "You're hydrating, and you're not gorging yourself, which tells me that you're diving soon. Possibly tonight?"

Carrie remained silent, waiting for Paolo to make his next move. He was right. They both knew that. A diver lost lots of water while swimming, and it took a human body several hours to store water, so hydrating before a dive was essential. So was a diver's food intake. Diving on a full stomach meant that their body would use energy and oxygen to digest the food—oxygen that was needed elsewhere during a dive. And diving on an empty stomach increased a swimmer's chances of freezing more easily, because if they ran out of carbohydrates, their body would begin metabolizing their fat stores, which once again used up crucial oxygen. She felt a pang of guilt for having assumed that Abhi had broken her confidence. The question now was, what did Paolo want?

"I thought so," he said, finally, breaking the silence first.

"So, what are you going to do, Paolo? Tell Alpinus I'm diving without their permission? Get me fired? Is this about revenge?"

Frowning, he placed a hand over his heart in a broad,

sweeping gesture. "You wound me, Carrie. There has been plenty to occupy us both these last few weeks, and despite all of the setbacks the mission suffered, we have each made valuable contributions, regardless of our positions—a position, that I must admit, I'm curious how you obtained."

"Fuck you."

"I see that is something else that hasn't changed, Carrie."

"What's that?"

"You still curse like an American gangster rapper."

"I've got ninety-nine problems and you're not one."

He wagged his finger. "That is a Jay Z song, yes?"

"It is, but Ice-T did it first. People forget that. And don't try to change the subject."

"Well, Jay Z or Iced Tea, you curse enough for both."

Before she could respond, the waiter sidled up to their table. He cleared his throat nervously, as if the tension between them was a palpable thing, and asked if there would be anything else. Carrie shook her head slightly, barely acknowledging him. Her gaze remained leveled at Paolo. She did not blink. The waiter shuffled off.

"I'm sorry," Paolo apologized. "Perhaps I could have said that more tactfully."

Carrie didn't reply. She simply continued to stare at him, refusing to speak, to blink, to move. Her body felt like a tuning fork, vibrating with anger and frustration. What did he want? What was his angle?

The answer, when it came, surprised her.

"I'm not here to jeopardize you, Carrie. This isn't about revenge or blackmail. Despite what you might think, I still care about you. I know we're not exactly friends anymore, but I wish we could be. Time has a way of changing a person—of making a person see things in ways they didn't before. There are things from the past I regret, very deeply. I'm sorry for what I did."

Carrie finished her seventh glass of water to keep herself from responding.

"Obviously," Paolo continued, "you have your reasons for wanting to go back down there. Judging by the fact that you haven't informed our employers and have apparently enlisted Abhi and sworn him to secrecy, I have to assume it's important. If you want to guarantee my silence, all you have to do is let me come along with you."

Carrie nearly spit her water out. "W-what?"

Paolo grinned. "Exactly what I said. I want to accompany you."

"Well, that's an interesting offer, but as it happens, I've already got a sidekick."

"Abhi?" Paolo laughed. "Oh, Carrie. I like him, too. But you know as well as I do that you'll need a diving partner. That's one of the first rules of free diving. Always have a partner—a partner who understands the intricacies and special challenges that can occur. Peter was a good diver, but he was not a free diver, and he wasn't nearly as experienced as you. You barely survived, and Peter is . . . gone. And while Abhi might be clever and capable, and can work miracles with a wrench and a roll of duct tape, he can't help you if you run into trouble down there again."

"And you can?"

"Of course, I can. I am better than Peter is . . . was. You and I both know that. But you made this personal. You played politics, to get back at me. Had it not been for that, I would have been your dive partner, rather than him, and things might be very different now."

Carrie gripped the edge of the table. She wanted to shout at him for implying that she was somehow responsible for Peter's death, but worse, she wanted to shout at herself out of fear that Paolo might be right.

"So," Paolo continued after a moment, "with that in mind, I'm going along this time. I'll spot you, and ensure no other accidents occur."

Carrie considered his offer. "Why do you care, Paolo?"

"It's not just your reputation that's on the line here, Carrie. You may have been picked as the lead on this expedition, but my name was attached to this, too. Maybe you can fall back on your celebrity, but my name in this field is all I have. This research mission already has too many black marks against it in the public eye. If another mishap occurs, it might render all of our reputations unsalvageable."

"So, your interest in this is purely self-preservation?"

"No. It's also scientific, the same as you. And, to be perfectly honest, I'd rather not hear tomorrow that you've died, too."

The waiter returned with the check. Carrie paid cash, leaving it on the table, and rose up from her chair. Paolo followed, walking her to the door. She caught a whiff of his cologne. Apparently, he'd changed scents since they'd dated. She preferred this new smell. It didn't come with memories or wistful nostalgia.

They stepped out onto the street. After having been inside the resort's air-conditioned comfort, the heat struck Carrie like a wave. She had a brief moment of dizziness, but quickly concealed it from Paolo. A car horn honked from the curb, loud enough to startle her.

"Are you okay?" Paolo asked.

Carrie nodded as they walked out onto the sidewalk. "I'm fine, thanks. Just a little tired, still."

"You should get some rest."

"And miss all this?" She gestured at the sweltering, bustling street. "Besides, you know me. I'll sleep when I'm dead."

"That's what I'm worried about," Paolo smiled. "So, when are we diving?"

"I haven't agreed to your terms."

His smile vanished. "Then, I'm very sorry. You leave me with no choice but to inform our superiors at Alpinus, for both our sakes. I do not imagine they will react favorably, nor will the broader scientific community. Our peers . . ."

He trailed off, shrugged, and made a sad, pitying expression.

Carrie clenched her fists at her side. "Goddamn it . . . okay. I'd planned on going tonight, if the press has cleared off by then."

"They won't be. Tomorrow would be better."

"Why?"

"Because you're exhausted. You just said so yourself. You know how dangerous it is to dive when tired. Plus, if you wait until tomorrow, then you can have more to eat today."

Although she was frustrated, Carrie couldn't help but laugh at this.

"Tomorrow," Paolo repeated. "Then you'll have more light."

"I can work without light. I can't work with reporters following our every move and getting in the way."

"It's not just them you have to worry about."

"What do you mean?" Carrie asked.

"You'll need a different, lower profile craft. And tell Abhi he can't leave straight from the Novak. He'll need to go elsewhere first."

"Why?"

"Because the Novak is under surveillance."

"What? By who? Reporters?"

"No, it's not the press. This is something . . . different. I'm not sure who they are, to be honest. Spies from an intelligence service, or perhaps a rival corporation. Those seem to be the most likely suspects."

"How do you know this? How do you know it's under sur-veillance?"

"Because when my father ran afoul of Pinochet, he taught my entire family anti-surveillance techniques that I never for-got. Sometimes they come in quite handy."

"Maybe so. But they also make you sound paranoid."

"Perhaps. But that doesn't mean I'm wrong. And I'm not."

He said it in his brief, off-handed way that, at different times in her life, Carrie had seen as alternatingly smug, sexy, infuriating, or endearing. Now, she saw it as simply annoying. But despite her annoyance, Carrie was secretly relieved at Paolo's relative cooperation, and the prospect of having him along below the surface.

She still wasn't sure what she had seen on her last dive, but she knew that whatever it was, she didn't want to be down there alone.

FOUR

Carrie arrived at the wharf the next morning. It was located in a less-trafficked, disused section of the harbor, surrounded by leaning tin shacks, vacant storage buildings whose outer walls were covered with graffiti and gray-black mildew, and decrepit marinas that looked ready to fall into the sea. It was a depressing, unwholesome sight, but it was also far away from the research flotilla, for which she was grateful. There was no chance of a reporter finding them here. Most of the press corps had indeed moved on to other parts of the world and other stories, leaving behind only a few stringers, all of whom were spending their time on the island, rather than at sea. Mindful of Paolo's paranoid warning, she'd paid attention to her surroundings, making sure she wasn't followed. Doing so had been disconcerting—but also exciting, like being in a spy movie.

A warm wind blew in from the water, bringing with it the smell of rotten fish and salt. Sunlight reflected off the sea in brilliant red, orange, and yellow hues. Carrie sighed, trying to ignore the stench and enjoy the simple breeze on her skin. She watched the colors stretch across the water, marveling at them. Even here, in this desolate armpit of a wharf, there was beauty. Carrie could almost pretend she was staring at a New England woodland in autumn rather than the Indian Ocean.

Then she thought about how dark the waters were below the surface, and how the colors wouldn't reach there, and her momentary joy vanished.

Paolo and Abhi were already waiting for her when she arrived at the dock. The two men stood on the docks next to a few storage containers and a small boat. Abhi waved enthusiastically, and Paolo nodded a greeting. Waving back, Carrie paused to study the boat Abhi had obtained for them. It was a fourteen-foot zinc affair that looked weather-beaten and barely seaworthy. Abhi looked right at home next to the aged vessel, dressed in threadbare, faded cutoff shorts with a missing back pocket, and a blue and white Hawaiian shirt that barely covered his belly. Salt and pepper curls of chest hair stuck out from between the shirt's buttons. Atop his head was a dirty ball cap emblazoned with a logo for Mercury Optimax motors. Paolo towered over the shorter man, and was dressed much like the day before, but this time his leather shoes had been replaced with open-toed sandals. Both men smiled as she approached. Abhi's expression was broad and delighted, while Paolo's was subdued and reserved.

"There she is," Abhi exclaimed. "You are looking well, Carrie. That hospital stay must have agreed with you."

"Thanks." Carrie smiled. "Although that was not exactly the vacation I had in mind."

Abhi shrugged. "Any time off is still time off. Some of us had to work while you were laying around in the hospital."

"You work?" Carrie gave him a quick hug. "That's new. I didn't think you knew how to work."

"Nonsense. The whole thing would fall apart without me."

"Were you followed?" Paolo asked, interrupting their banter.

"No," Carrie said. "I don't think so. I took all the necessary precautions, just like you said. I still don't understand why we'd be under surveillance though, or by who."

"I would like to know that, as well," Abhi agreed. "And I would also like to know why we're meeting in secret, and just what you intend to do, Carrie. What have you gotten me into?"

"Nothing illegal, Abhi."

"Then I am disappointed. Illegal is always more fun."

"Is that why you make that illegal rotgut hooch?"

"I don't know what you're talking about," Abhi said, feigning mock protest. "I make deck cleaner and paint thinner. I am not responsible for what happens if someone drinks it."

"Did you have any trouble getting all the equipment I asked for?"

Abhi shrugged. "Not much. We've got nothing electronic, just like you asked, except for some underwater communicators, and of course, the boat's emergency radio and the engine components. Other than those, it's all analog. Some of it wasn't easy to get with such short notice. I had to call in a few favors. Make a few deals. Oh, and I may have borrowed a few items from the Novak, but I don't think anyone will miss them. I'm hoping one of you will reimburse me for the boat, though?"

"I'll make sure you get reimbursed." Carrie eyed it skeptically. "Although, I hope you didn't pay too much for it. This thing looks like it's ready to sink."

"I have to agree," Paolo said. "Are you sure it's safe?"

"Looks can be deceiving." Abhi grinned, flashing tobacco and coffee-stained teeth. "It may be old, but it is sturdy. Like me. More importantly, it won't attract attention."

"Also like you," Carrie quipped.

"The bends look good on you," he teased, not missing a

beat. "That rash is a particularly lovely color. It matches your eyes."

"Ouch, Abhi!" Carrie said pretending to be offended.

Paolo remained unconvinced regarding the boat's condition. "That outboard motor looks ready to . . . how do you say it? Give up the ghost? How do we know it's not going to break down and leave us stranded out there?"

"That long-tail diesel may be worn," Abhi said, "but it is solid. Trust me on that. I tested it myself. Took it apart and put it back together. It's old and tough, like me. And besides, the boat also has a set of oars, just in case. Nothing electronic in those, for sure."

"We might need them," Carrie admitted.

"I'm telling you this motor is sound."

"I believe you, Abhi. But so was the equipment on board the Novak, and we saw how well that worked."

"Yeah, that's true. So that's what's with all this analog stuff you had me get?"

Carrie nodded.

"Maybe it's time you told us what you know, Carrie," Paolo suggested.

"Okay," Carrie agreed, "but I want to check our gear first."

She opened the storage crates and took inventory of their contents—the underwater radios Abhi had mentioned, a toolbox, specimen scoops and sealed containers, two sealed wetsuits, dive weights, flippers, simple masks (in lieu of the analytical HUD helmet Carrie had dove with before), equipment belts, arm clips, two lengthy coils of dive line, two buoys, waterproof tape, a full case of phosphorescent torches, sunscreen, a case of bottled water, a large cooler packed with ice, two full twenty-gallon cans of diesel fuel for the motor, a first aid kit, a machete, and a Sudoku book. She frowned upon spying the last two items, and gave Abhi a quizzical look.

"That's for me." He shrugged. "I need something to do while the two of you go for a swim. I read in a magazine that people my age should do things like this to keep the dementia away. And I never cared for the Word Jumble."

"And the machete?"

Abhi shrugged again. "You never know. Better to have one and not need it than to need one and not have it."

Carrie smiled. "I think you've seen *Jaws* one too many times, Abhi."

"Perhaps you are right. But if Quint had done Sudoku, things would have ended much better for them, I'll bet."

They began to load the gear onto the small boat. The sun had risen higher and the day was starting to heat up. The stench of rotten fish and mildew that seemed to hang over the wharf grew stronger, but did nothing to dampen their spirits. Their laughter soon faded, however, as Carrie began to brief them on her theory.

"I saw something down there," she said. "I don't know what it was and I don't know how to describe it. The water was dark, of course. But this . . . thing . . . was darker. I think Peter saw it, too, before he . . ."

Pausing, she stared out at the water, unable to find the right words to explain what she had seen. "It's okay." Abhi nodded in encouragement. "Go on."

"I don't know what it was, but I know it was real. It wasn't my imagination. All I remember is a dark shape. But I think I know what's ruining our electronics. There was some weird effect in the water, below about eighty meters."

"What kind of effect?" Paolo asked.

"I'm not sure, but I experienced it myself when I left my suit. The same interference that shorted out our diving equipment played havoc on my body's own nerve function as I swam for the surface."

Paolo nodded, encouraging her to continue. "How so?"

"It's . . . hard to explain. My arms and legs tingled, and then started to go numb. And I think I was hallucinating. I can't be sure. But I definitely remember the numbness. It wasn't painful. Indeed, it was the opposite of that. It was almost . . . calming? It seemed to spread through my whole body."

"You weren't scared?" Abhi asked.

"No." Carrie shook her head. "That's the thing. I should have been afraid. I should have been fucking terrified, but I wasn't. I barely made it to the top, even with my background and training. And Peter? Well, Peter never stood a chance."

Paolo stared at her intently. "And you don't know what the source of it was?"

"No. I suspect it must be chemical. That seems to make the most sense. Some type of chemical that can impact both living beings and electronics."

"Or perhaps it was just a simple blackout," Paolo suggested. "Low oxygen in your brain. That seems more plausible to me."

"I know what shallow-water blackout feels like, Paolo! It wasn't that, or hypoxia, or any other bullshit excuse you want to suggest."

"You just said that you hallucinated—"

"I did. But the cause wasn't anything that I did. We did everything by the book. Peter was within an arm's length at all times. We kept visual on each other. Everything was fine until our equipment malfunctioned. And we were still fine, even after it malfunctioned. It wasn't until we slipped out of our suits that . . . we weren't fine anymore."

"Okay." Paolo held up his hands in surrender. "Okay, Carrie. I'm sorry. I did not mean to offend."

Seabirds squawked angrily overhead, swooping downward and bombarding the surface of the harbor, fighting over a school of tiny fish swimming near the surface. Occasionally, one of them flew back up, clutching a wriggling fish in its talons, and then greedily darted for the shore.

Carrie took a deep breath, calmed herself, and then continued.

"Obviously, we need equipment to truly study the collapse, but whatever this reaction is—it's shorting our equipment out. So, what I propose is very simple. You and I will use basic scoops and containers to collect samples from as deep down the wall of the collapse as we can."

"What sort of samples do you want to focus on?" Paolo asked.

"Whatever we can get—silt, rock, water, plants, even small organisms. We need enough to analyze in a lab."

"What lab? We can't use Alpinus, or they will know we did this without their approval."

"Then we'll enlist the NOAA," Carrie said. "Or another lab—Scripps, UNOLS, Woods Hole, AOML, Proudman. Between the two of us, we've got contacts at each of them, and more. We could even take it to the Globe Corporation if we needed to."

"I'm sure that would go over great with Alpinus. Hiring us to do the work and then we turn around and take it to their biggest competitor?"

"Consider it a last resort. And besides, at the very least this will allow us to determine how to proof our scientific instruments and electronic gear against whatever is contaminating the water. I have to think Alpinus and the NOAA will both be interested in that information, regardless of how we initially obtained it."

"Perhaps," Paolo agreed, rubbing his chin thoughtfully.

"It doesn't matter who the United Nations sends out here to investigate. The same thing will happen to their equipment that happens to ours. We've seen that already. Even the press corps were experiencing problems with their gear. You were worried about your reputation, Paolo?"

"Yes," he admitted.

"Well, then this is the best way to make sure your reputation remains in good standing. We collect samples, analyze them, find out for sure what's causing the interference, and then figure out a way to prevent it for further expeditions. We'll be heroes once again."

"I still am a hero," Abhi joked.

Paolo watched the seagulls circle and wheel and squawk for a moment. When he turned back to her, his expression was skeptical.

"I do not believe you are being entirely truthful with us, Carrie. You are a good person, yes, but I have never known you to be this altruistic. At least, not to this degree. And especially not when there's no paycheck forthcoming."

"You're right." She sighed, pushing the bangs from her eyes. She was already starting to sweat in the morning heat. "It's not my only reason for wanting to do this."

"Then why else?"

"Because of what I saw . . . or what I think I saw. And because I owe it to Peter. And because whatever this is—it nearly beat me. I don't like that."

Paolo's smile was smug. "So you intend to conquer it? This mysterious force of nature?"

Carrie shrugged. "You know me."

"I do indeed. You like to win."

"You say that like it's a bad thing."

"I don't mean it to be," Paolo replied. "Indeed, I have always admired your determination. It was one of the things that first drew me to you . . . back then. But this is different, Carrie."

"May I say something?" Abhi interrupted.

They both turned to him.

"What's up?" Carrie asked.

"I know I'm just a glorified boatswain's mate, but it seems to me that if something in that water is capable of interfering with top-of-the-line analytical equipment, robots, and gear—including, apparently, the central nervous system of human beings—then it might not be a great idea to swim there, no?"

Paolo laughed. "Have no worries, Abhi. You have procured two good wetsuits for us, and a good wetsuit will protect us from anything."

Out over the water, the sea birds continued to shriek and feed.

FIVE

With Abhi guiding the boat, they motored up to a location about five miles offshore and one hundred fifty meters above the collapsing ridge. The ocean here was full of silt and sand. Even the waves seemed choked with it.

"Are you sure about this?" Abhi asked, eyeing the surface. "It seems to me like you'd be swimming in sandpaper."

"We'll be fine," Carrie assured him. "Most of it sinks right to the bottom. It will impact our visibility, for sure, but that's all."

Paolo and Carrie drank several bottles of water each, determined to stay hydrated. Even though it was still early in the morning, the sun already squatted overhead, pulsating like a blister ready to burst. It reflected off the water, making them squint. All three were bathed in sweat. When Carrie licked her lips to moisten them, she tasted salt and brine.

Abhi killed the motor. The boat rocked gently on the waves, the hull creaking with the movement. The wind seemed to die off, suddenly, which only increased the brutal heat. Abhi busied himself by applying sunscreen to his nose and ears. It glistened on the fine hairs protruding from both.

"I'm glad I remembered to bring an umbrella," he said, squinting up at the sun. "It's going to be brutal today."

"Why don't you get it out?" Carrie asked.

"Maybe later."

Carrie frowned. "I know that look. What are you hiding, Abhi?"

Sighing, the older man rummaged through the gear, and then produced an umbrella. When he opened it, Carrie and Paolo erupted in laughter at the image of *SpongeBob SquarePants* emblazoned across it.

"I picked it up at the Dollar Store on the way here," Abhi explained. "All they had was this or Barbie."

"If you get too hot," Carrie said, "cool off in the water."

Abhi blanched. "No, thank you. I'm staying right here on the boat."

Carrie and Paolo prepped for their dive, slipping into their sealed wetsuits and flippers. Abhi and Paolo made an exaggerated effort to look away while Carrie changed, which made her smile. She and Paolo stored their clothes, phones, and personal items in a storage crate. Then, Abhi secured one end of each of the dive lines to the boat while the two divers strapped on their arm clips and belts.

"Shouldn't you hyperventilate or something?" Abhi asked. "Get extra oxygen into your bloodstream before you dive?"

"No," Carrie said. "That's the last thing we want to do. Hyperventilating can make you pass out, and anything other than normal breathing messes with the carbon dioxide levels in your blood."

With a grunt, Abhi unspooled the dive lines and watched them sink below the surface.

"That water is pretty murky," he said. "Even with the sunlight hitting it. How are you going to see anything down there?"

"Visibility will be limited," Carrie admitted, "like I said before. But we can carry the phosphorescent torches on our belts and then affix them to our arm clips as we gather the samples. And we'll keep each other in sight at all times. Right, Paolo?"

"Of course."

"We've got a full case of torches, so we should be able to make as many trips as necessary, to get everything of interest. If we need to, we can use a few of them at a time."

"What should I do while you're down there?" Abhi asked. "How can I help?"

"Keep an eye on our dive lines," Carrie said, grinning. "And have fun with your Sudoku."

"You can count on that."

"Don't go anywhere, *Gordo*," Paolo said to Abhi.

"Gordo?" Abhi frowned. "I speak Spanish, you Chilean jackass. I know what that means. And for the record, I am not fat."

Paolo shrugged. "Where I come from, it is a term of endearment."

"Where you come from," Abhi replied, "people still think electricity is a new invention."

Carrie handed a diving mask to Paolo.

"Make sure the seal is tight," she told him as she donned another for herself.

"This isn't my first dive, Carrie."

She bit her lip until the urge to reply sarcastically had passed. "No, of course it's not. I was just referring to exposure. The wetsuits are sealed, so our skin shouldn't be exposed, but if my theory is right, you don't want water getting through the mask."

"What about our mouths?"

"That can't be helped."

Nodding, he strapped weights to his belt, which would allow him to descend faster. Then, he took three more measured breaths, slipped the mask over his face, and slid into the water. Carrie sighed.

"Even this has to be a competition with him," she said.

"At least he didn't call you fat," Abhi said.

Carrie put on her mask and quickly followed Paolo beneath the waves.

Abhi pulled a small silver flask out of his back pocket, unscrewed the lid, and held it aloft in a toast.

"Salud," he said, and took a drink, grimacing at the taste. He shivered. "Best batch of paint thinner I've ever tasted."

He was struck by the silence. Feeling sheepish, he returned the flask to his pocket and picked up his umbrella.

And waited.

Carrie stuck to her dive line. It would be especially important farther down, where visibility would be extremely limited, even with their phosphorescent torches. Things could go wrong on a dive, even to one not already cursed with the problems their expedition had undergone, and even to experienced divers like Paolo and herself. She could get a cramp, inhibiting her ability to swim up. If she didn't equalize and the pressure damaged her eardrums, vertigo could set in quickly. She'd known a diver that had happened to. The hapless man had swam farther downward, believing himself to be surfacing the entire time. It could be even more dangerous ascending. When a diver was resurfacing and the pressure on them decreased, there was a risk of blacking out. That risk increased if they paused or exhaled. Staying close to the dive line could mean the difference between life and death in situations like those. As her instructor had said, all those years ago, "Don't think of it as a dive line. Think of it as a lifeline." It had been one of the most important lessons she had ever learned.

As she had expected, their visibility was poor, but she was surprised to discover it was even worse than it had been just a few days before, when she'd dove with Peter. Obviously, the collapse was growing worse, as more and more sand and silt were churned up into the water. Despite the debris, she saw Paolo a few meters below her, silhouetted in the glow of his phosphorescent torches. He followed his own dive line, headed toward the rim of the collapse. He paused, glancing up to make visual contact with her, and waved. Carrie waved back.

When they reached one hundred meters, Paolo paused for a moment. Carrie studied him closely, looking for signs of distress. He met her eyes, shook his head, and continued his descent. There was so much debris swirling around them that Carrie was reminded of a snowstorm. If the collapse continued, she thought, and the evacuation didn't happen, then Mauritius's tourist board might have to advertise an underwater blizzard rather than an underwater waterfall.

Her lips began to tingle, and for a moment, she panicked, remembering what had happened the last time she'd felt this. They grew numb, but the sensation didn't increase or spread. Still, the feeling left her unnerved.

The water grew colder as they descended. At one hundred fifty meters, they reached the spreading seafloor. While their visibility was still hampered, there was less debris in the water here, due to the currents. Carrie's eyes widened in surprise. The seafloor was littered with the dead bodies of fish, crabs, and other marine life. Most likely, all of them were victims of hypoxia, a condition that was probably spreading as the collapse continued to reduce the oxygen content in the coastal waters.

Reaching the end of their limits, both of them hurriedly

collected samples from the corpse-strewn bottom, and then, with air still left in their lungs, followed their dive lines back up to the boat. Because a diver's lowest level of oxygen usually occurred twenty seconds after surfacing, Carrie exhaled at the end of her ascent, and then inhaled immediately upon breaching the surface. She held that breath for a moment and clenched her stomach muscles, then repeated the process again, increasing both her oxygen and blood pressure.

"Are you okay?" Abhi called.

She nodded, blinking. It was hard to see him. The temperature change and immediate sunlight were both disconcerting. She waited a moment, letting her eyes adjust. Paolo surfaced next to her, hooking his breathing as she had just done. Carrie realized he was clutching something in his hand.

"What do you have there, Paolo?" Abhi asked, putting down his umbrella and moving to their side of the boat. "Dinner?"

Still focused on his breathing, Paolo held the object aloft. It was the corpse of a horseshoe crab. Carrie noticed something odd about it right away. It was stiff and rigid, rather than floppy.

"A scientific sample," he panted, shaking water from his eyes. "As you requested."

Assisted by Abhi, they clambered aboard the boat, removed their masks (which had fogged up from the temperature change) and unloaded their first haul of samples.

"Seriously," Abhi asked again, "what's with the crab?"

"Hypoxia," Carrie replied. "It's what happens when the water is low in oxygen. It's usually caused by agricultural pollution or jellyfish blooms. Or, in this case, the collapsing seafloor. The bottom around the trench is littered with dead stuff."

"Except it's not hypoxia." Paolo poked the dead crab with his finger. "I thought so at first, too, but look at this. You see?"

Carrie frowned. "No."

"It's frozen solid. Go ahead and inspect it for yourself."

She did, tentatively at first, and then with astonishment. The creature was indeed frozen, as if it had just been removed from the freezer of a supermarket, rather than the seafloor. Although they didn't have a thermometer on hand, it was obvious to Carrie that the crab's body was far colder than even the ambient temperatures Paolo had found it at, one hundred fifty meters below. Even now, after bringing it up through the warmer tropical surface waters, and exposing it to the sunlight and heat here on the boat, it hadn't begun to thaw.

"This isn't hypoxia," she said. "This is something else."

Paolo nodded. "Right, it looks like it at first blush but hypoxia isn't what killed this creature. And I bet if we go back down, we'll find that the other corpses are just like this one."

"So," Abhi said, "there's this hypoxia thing, but something else killed this crab?

Paolo and Carrie nodded.

"But if it wasn't hypoxia," Abhi asked, "then what was it?"

"I don't know," Carrie admitted. "Something . . . new. We need to get back down there and retrieve more samples. Abhi, can you put this in the cooler, so we can study it later?"

"You mean . . . touch it?" He paused, staring at the crab with concern. "It's not infected with something is it? I don't want to catch a disease."

"It's hard to say for sure," Carrie admitted. "I don't know of any sort of virus or bacteria that would cause this, but we should be careful all the same."

Abhi opened the toolbox, pulled out a faded red grease rag, and used that to pick up the corpse. His nose wrinkled. He carried the dead crab gingerly, arm outstretched, as if it were a live grenade. Then he placed it in the cooler, closed the lid, and shuddered.

Carrie turned to Paolo. "What happened down there? Was everything okay? I thought you were in trouble for a second."

"At about a hundred meters," Paolo confirmed. "Yes, I wanted to talk to you about that before we dive again. I think you're right about that weird neurological effect in the water. It hit me just past a hundred meters or so. My lips began to tingle, and get numb."

"I felt it, too. But I'm okay now."

"Yes," Paolo agreed, "it seems to have passed for me, as well."

"Well, just to be safe, let's use the tape to double seal the seams on our wetsuits."

She retrieved the roll of tape and began applying it to Paolo's suit. Then he did the same for her. Carrie shivered as his fingers brushed against her, but if Paolo noticed, he gave no indication.

"Ready?" he asked, when finished.

She nodded. "Let's go."

"Or," Abhi suggested. "We could just call it a day, head back right now, and find a bar. Surely this is enough of a sample to study."

"Come on, Abhi." Carrie smiled. "Where's your sense of adventure?"

"I left it behind in my forties."

Carrie winked at him. "Then do it for science."

She dived back over the side with a splash. Paolo followed her. Abhi moved to the side of the boat, and watched them vanish beneath the murky surface.

"They may be scientists," he muttered, "but I'm the only one smart enough not to go back down in that mess."

When they were gone from sight, Abhi fished out his flask and took another drink. Then he retrieved his meerschaum pipe and his tobacco pouch. The pipe had belonged to his father, who had bought it in Syria during World War II. His father had never smoked it, but when he died, Abhi had broken it in. He had realized too late that actually using the pipe would cause it to lose its ivory color, but it was still precious to him, and a source of comfort. He had been all over the world in his sixty years, and the pipe had accompanied him for most of those travels. He had smoked it in countless ports of call. He packed it now with aromatic tobacco—a mix of cherries and ginger scents, and lit it. It took him a few minutes to get it going, and he had to shield it from the wind with his hand.

"Ah, there we go."

Puffing thoughtfully, he leaned against the rail and considered how quiet it was. Even the waves seemed muted as they lapped against the boat.

Slowly, his gaze turned to the cooler. He thought about the horseshoe crab inside. Despite the heat, his skin prickled. He puffed his pipe more furiously, and rubbed his arms.

He stared out at the surrounding ocean, and noticed for the first time that they were the only vessel in sight. Usually, this area would be busy with nautical traffic, but sea lanes had been rerouted due to the studies of the collapse. Still, he thought there would be at least a few civilians or tourists daring to break the quarantine. At the very least, there should be some boats from the scientific flotilla about. But the ocean was deserted. It then occurred to Abhi that the sky was deserted, as well. Back at the harbor, it had been choked with squabbling sea birds, but they seemed to be avoiding this region. Even the water seemed lifeless. Except for the waves, it remained still. There were no fish jumping or curious dolphins coming up to inspect his craft. The latter could be attributed to the collapsing sea floor, but he didn't think that would deter the birds.

He smoked and stared for a while longer, until the ocean

and the sky merged into one endless, unbroken gray and white plane. Then he retrieved his flask and had another drink, shuddering as the molten liquid burned its way down his throat.

Eyeing the vacant horizon, Abhi suddenly felt very alone.

Puffing the pipe, he returned to his Sudoku book, but found it hard to focus. He kept looking up, and eyeing the cooler nervously.

"Any minute now," he whispered. "They can't stay down there forever."

SIX

Halfway through the second dive, while Carrie gathered a plant sample and placed it in a container, she noticed a sudden and drastically pronounced decrease in the temperature of the water around her—the equivalent of walking from the heat into a freezer. The ocean, already murky with the stirred up silt and sand, seemed to grow darker. Her skin prickled. Quickly sealing the container and securing it on her belt, she glanced around the gloomy waters for Paolo, to see if he'd noticed the temperature drop, as well. She spotted him, illuminated by the ambient light of his torch, as he hovered almost directly over the trench, collecting samples from an overhanging wall of broken coral. A sea anemone was perched nearby him, tentacles frozen in mid-wave. The anemone's usually vibrant body was uncharacteristically bland, to the point of being almost completely devoid of color.

The coldness and darkness grew more pronounced. They seemed to press against her like physical entities.

Carrie didn't panic, but she definitely felt unsettled. Her diver's directional sense of temperature told her that the steadily increasing cold was emanating from within the trench itself. This was something new, something she hadn't experienced on the dive with Peter. Or, if she had, she no longer remembered it, overcome as she had been by the other events from that fateful excursion.

Kicking hard, she swam out to the side of the chasm, above and to the right of Paolo. Yes, she was certain the cold was radiating from the chasm. It was easy to imagine it as an almost physical thing. She thought about the horseshoe crab Paolo had recovered—frozen solid. Curious, she pulled a torch from her belt, and dropped it downward.

Her lips began to tingle again, but this time, the sensation was much stronger, and the numbness occurred more rapidly. The water temperature continued to fall, along with the torch. Alarmed, Carrie watched the light descend. It seemed to slow, as the numbness crept into her cheeks and nose. The torch twisted and turned, and she had a flash of memory—her and her sister catching fireflies one summer and putting them in a mason jar with tin foil over the top. It had been a magical night. Their parents had let them stay up late, and they'd danced around in the backyard, laughing with delight, chasing after the diminutive and fleeting lights as they flickered from one blade of grass to another. They had caught them carefully, mindful of not squishing the fragile creatures. As the moon rose higher, and the evening grew darker, they had pretended the insects were fairies, just like Tinker Bell in Peter Pan. Later, they had poked tiny holes in the tin foil with a toothpick, and put the fireflies on the nightstand between their beds. All night long, they'd slept in the soft green glow emanating from the jar . . .

Carrie suddenly came back to herself, wondering just how long she'd been daydreaming.

What the hell is wrong with me?

This wasn't like her at all. This was the type of thing that got a diver killed. And why did Paolo seem oblivious to what was occurring? He was supposed to be her dive partner. He should have noticed her state. And surely, he could feel the temperature plunging? It was all around them now.

Her lungs ached. She was nearing her limits. She needed to start ascending now.

Panicked and disoriented, she focused instead on the spiraling light of the falling torch, just as something hiding in the darkness snatched it from the water. She couldn't tell what—the water was filled with too much debris—but she caught a glimpse of something spindly and knobby and segmented. Whatever it was, the thing broke the torch into pieces, extinguishing the glow. Then, the creature moved toward them.

Carrie felt the water shift as a massive, dark form glided from the trench. This must be it, this is what she saw with Peter. It was much closer than it had been on that previous dive. Then, it had been far away, a shadow amongst the other shadows in the trench. Now it was emerging. Indeed, it didn't seem to stop emerging. Like a long train, coming out of a tunnel, more and more of it appeared, flowing from the crevice. Terrified, she glanced at her partner. Paolo's attention was still focused on the coral, and he seemed unaware of the danger surging toward them.

With little air left in her lungs, she darted toward Paolo and caught his attention. He smiled as she approached, holding up one hand and giving her the okay symbol. Carrie grabbed his arm and pulled hard, kicking for the surface. Offering no resistance, Paolo immediately followed her.

Carrie couldn't see much beyond the light of their torches,

and the dim hue of the sun far above—indeed, the surface had never seemed farther away than it did now. But despite the engulfing shadows, she had a sense of something aggressively pursuing them, pushing both water and cold in front of it like a wall as it ascended. Paolo must have felt it too, because he suddenly paused and turned. Then, he lit a torch and dropped it toward their pursuer. As they watched, the shadows seemed to snap the light up. Then, the torch was gone.

Wide-eyed, Paolo swam upward again with renewed speed. Carrie braved one last glance, trying hard to catch a glimpse of the creature below them, but it was still indistinguishable— just a dark, monstrously big, amorphous mass, radiating cold.

Her ears began to ring, and she felt her pulse throbbing in her throat, as her oxygen ran low. The aching in her lungs increased, becoming a sharp, urgent, pounding pain. Kicking hard, she headed for the surface, following Paolo's wake. The coldness seemed to follow, nipping at her flippers. Carrie stared upward, focusing on keeping the bottom of the boat visible. It floated above them, a safe haven full of sunlight and shelter and most importantly, air.

Suddenly, her left leg seized up, as if she had been shocked. The numbness in her face grew stronger, and Carrie had to fight to keep her mouth from opening involuntarily. Her eyes felt droopy, and the ringing in her ears was now a siren. Her left leg was useless. She struggled to swim upward, using her other leg and arms to propel herself, but the paralysis crept up her side. Her other leg began to tingle.

Using her torchlight, Carrie hurriedly examined her leg, looking for evidence of a jellyfish sting or something else that would explain what was happening to her. As she did, she caught sight of the predator below. It began to take shape, but what she saw only confused her more. Her fear and desperation melted away as she watched, replaced with a calm, almost

Zen-like state. Why had she been so afraid? She couldn't remember. Then she decided that it didn't matter. The creature
was far more fascinating than her own foibles and insecurities.
The thing below seemed to simultaneously surge upward and
recede downward—an ever-changing, amorphous collection of
segmented appendages, tentacles, beaks, blubber, and eyes—
sharp-edged, spindly softness surrounded by an inky blackness
that moved with it. With what little strength she had left,
Carrie moved her torch, hoping to see it better. The creature
paused, as if fearful of the light.

Then, in the midst of the shifting blob, Carrie saw her dead
mother.

Mom . . . ?

"Hello, Carrie."

Something seized her arm, pulling hard. Still engulfed in
calm, Carrie glanced up and saw Paolo. His expression was
frantic. He tugged, urging her to swim. Carrie shrugged, trying to communicate that she was okay. When she attempted
to point at her mother, she found that the strange paralysis
that had now rendered both of her legs useless was creeping
into her arms, as well.

Paolo wrapped his arms around her mid-section and
strained, kicking for the surface. Still clutching her torch,
Carrie glanced downward. Her mother was gone. She opened
her mouth to call out for her, and then—

—they broke the surface, and Carrie coughed, gagging on
seawater. Paolo gripped her tightly. She coughed again, struggling to breathe. Waves crashed over them both as Paolo guided
them toward the boat.

"Is she okay?" Abhi's tone was alarmed.

"Help me pull her up," Paolo gasped. "I'm . . . losing
strength."

Abhi pulled her from the water and into the boat. Sputtering,

Carrie rolled onto her side, while the frantic boatswain's mate assisted Paolo in climbing aboard. Paolo collapsed onto the deck, panting. Abhi stared at them both in concern.

"I'm . . . fine . . ." Paolo waved him away. "Check on . . . Carrie . . ."

"I'm . . . okay . . ." she rasped. "My leg . . ."

"What's wrong with your leg?" Abhi knelt at her side in concern.

"Paralyzed . . ." Her voice was hoarse. Her lungs felt like they were on fire and her head throbbed.

"Was it a jellyfish sting?" Abhi asked. "Let me see."

It took all of her strength just to shake her head and feebly wave him away. "Just let me . . . rest a moment . . ."

Abhi's expression turned grim and decisive. He stood up abruptly, fists clenched at his side.

"Right. Both of you rest. That's an excellent idea. You rest up while I take us in."

Paolo nodded. "You'll get no argument from me."

"No," Carrie protested, rolling over to face them. "We're not . . . done out here."

"We most certainly are," Paolo said. "At least for today. That was too close."

"Abhi . . ." Gritting her teeth, Carrie forced herself to sit up. "I'm in charge . . . here. We need to . . . stay."

Shaking his head, Abhi tipped his still-smoking pipe over the side, dumping the tobacco into the water. "What we need is to get you to a doctor."

"I'm okay," she insisted. "Yes, I ran into trouble down there, and yes, something paralyzed me, but the sensation is passing. Feeling and movement are already returning. See?"

She wiggled her leg, and then lifted it up and down, offering proof.

Groaning with the effort, Paolo rose to his feet. "Let's take your wetsuit off."

"Oh no," Carrie joked. "You had your chance at that when we were at Scripps, buddy. That ship has now sailed."

Paolo offered a tight-lipped, humorless smile. "I see that you still make jokes when you are scared. But this is not the time for that. I'm serious. Take your wetsuit off and let me see what's going on with your leg."

Carrie didn't respond.

"Abhi is right," he continued. "We should leave. What if . . . whatever was down there . . . surfaces, or comes up under the boat?"

"It won't," Carrie said. "I don't think it will come to the surface. I think it's afraid of the light."

"Wait a minute," Abhi protested. "What thing? What are you talking about?"

Paolo ignored him. "How can you be sure?"

"You saw how it reacted to our torches. And when we neared the surface, and the sunlight was stronger, it stopped pursuing us. Call it a scientific hunch, but I don't think it will come up here, unless it absolutely has to."

"I hope you are right."

"What thing?" Abhi demanded again.

Still ignoring him, Paolo knelt beside Carrie and gently touched her leg. "Can you feel that?"

Swallowing, Carrie nodded. "Barely. But yes, I can feel it."

"Lean forward."

He began to remove her wetsuit. Abhi turned away, clearly uncomfortable.

"Paolo . . ." Carrie took a deep breath. "I'm telling you . . ."

"I want to look at your leg," he explained. "Just relax, Gatito."

His usage of 'kitten'—their old term of endearment—surprised Carrie. Paolo hadn't called her by that pet name since they broke up all those years ago. As he peeled the suit away, Carrie shivered, despite the sunlight and heat.

"I don't see any wounds," Paolo observed. "Where was the approximate origin of the paralysis?"

"Around my ankle, I guess. But it happened quickly. You know the sensation we both experienced earlier, on our lips?"

Paolo nodded.

"It was like that, but much quicker."

"But your leg and ankle weren't exposed like your mouth was. The wetsuit was sealed." Frowning, Paolo examined her ankle more closely. "I don't see any marks. Nothing to indicate a sting."

"You were thinking a jellyfish?" Carrie asked.

"Yes. It would make sense. Jellyfish blooms occur in the dead zones caused by hypoxia."

"But I didn't see any jellyfish. Did you?"

"No," Paolo admitted. "Certainly not a bloom of them. But we can't discount the possibility that we overlooked one. Our visibility was hampered, after all."

"And yet it was good enough that we both saw that thing."

Paolo started to reply, but then paused and simply nodded.

"What thing?" Abhi demanded a third time. "If the two of you don't start explaining what's going on here, I'm going to mutiny and take us ashore."

"I don't know what it was," Carrie said. "It was something big, lurking in the collapsing trench. A territorial predator of some kind."

"A shark?"

"No, not a shark. Like I said, I don't know *what* it was. I only caught a few glimpses. But I have a theory."

Both Abhi and Paolo stared at her intently, listening.

"I started to hallucinate," she explained. "At first, I just felt the numbness around my mouth. But then, when I felt the water temperature change, I dropped a torch down into the collapse, and I sort of . . . zoned out. I started thinking about something that happened when I was a kid."

"I had a moment like that, as well," Paolo confirmed. "It only lasted a few seconds, but I got distracted."

"Did you notice the temperature change?" Carrie asked.

"Not at first. Not until you got my attention. As I said, I was . . . distracted."

"When it started to pursue us—when it got closer—that's when the numbing sensation overcame the rest of me, starting with my leg. At the same time, I started hallucinating, again."

"What did you see?" Abhi asked.

"My mother. And she's been dead for almost two years."

"Oh, Carrie . . ." Abhi's voice was thick with emotion. "I'm sorry."

"Thank you, Abhi, but I'm fine. Really. It was just a hallucination, I know that. You didn't experience anything else, Paolo?"

"No."

"I think that's because you were closer to the surface than I was. I think that thing, whatever it was, sends out hallucinogenic neurotoxins through the water to pacify its prey. Similar to an Irukandji jellyfish. I knew it was there. I knew it was observing me. But I felt no fear. Just like when Peter and I dived. I wasn't scared. I wasn't concerned at all. If anything, I just wanted to surrender."

"Okay, then." Abhi strode toward the motor. "That sounds good to me. I vote we surrender."

"But," Paolo said, ignoring Abhi and turning to Carrie, "if it's a neurotoxin, why would the effects have been stronger this time? Why wouldn't it have impacted both of us like this on the previous dive?"

"Because I was closer to it this time. Because it turned aggressive. And in doing so, it flooded the water with a much larger dosage. Enough that it was able to somehow penetrate my wetsuit."

Abhi started the motor and raised his voice to be heard over it. "I'm glad that you are both okay. We've done a lot of science today. Hooray for science."

Carrie stood up. "What are you doing?"

"I'm driving," Abhi explained. "You did your science. Now it's time to go home."

"No," Carrie said, "now it's time we apply what we've learned and go back down there."

Abhi sighed. "I was afraid you'd say something like that."

Grinning, Carrie walked toward him. "And step aside, Abhi. This time, I'm driving."

"No," he insisted, gently but firmly pushing her away, "you are not. You may be in charge, Carrie, but I'm the pilot of this boat."

"You're serious," she said, surprised. "What gives, Abhi?"

He stared straight ahead, and hesitated before answering her.

"What gives is that I'm scared," he admitted. "I don't like being out here. Something about this area feels wrong. But, here we are, and if we're not heading back to land anytime soon, then I need something to do. Piloting our boat makes me feel better. It takes my mind off things."

"Okay," Carrie conceded. "Fair enough. I'm sorry."

"Don't apologize," Abhi said. "You have nothing to apologize for. Just promise me you'll be careful."

"I will."

"Good. Now, tell me where we are going."

SEVEN

Resolving to steer clear of the territorial predator they'd encountered in the collapsing trench, Carrie had Abhi motor themselves a few miles to the east, on the opposite side of the trench, where a coral reef was collapsing into the breach.

"We've already surveyed those effects," Paolo said.

"Yes," Carrie agreed, "but not at length, because that thing showed up. We need more samples. Plus, I want to test a theory regarding these supposed neurotoxins. We begin experiencing electrical interference, paralysis, and hallucinations below eighty meters. But the collapse of the reef in this location begins well before that. It's much closer to the surface. I propose we stay above the eighty-meter mark. And we're going to use those communicators Abhi brought along. If they begin to fail, it's an early indicator that the predator is in the area."

Abhi rummaged through the gear and produced the pair of radios. They were compact enough to fit in a diver's ear. He handed them to Carrie, who handed one of them to Paolo and the other back to Abhi.

"Okay. Now, Abhi?"

"Yes?"

"Since Paolo and I obviously can't talk underwater, you'll need to keep up a steady stream of chatter."

"About what?"

"About anything. Just make sure you keep talking. If the radio starts to fail, or if Paolo can't hear you, then we know the creature is in our proximity, at which point Paolo will warn me."

"Why do I have to listen to him prattling in my ear?" Paolo asked. "Why can't you wear it?"

"Because my eyesight is better underwater than yours," Carrie answered. "I'm going to be watching for that thing while you focus on collecting samples."

"And what if your theory about the communicators is wrong?"

"Then we'll need to stay aware. If either one of us begins to experience tingling or numbing, or if we start to hallucinate, or if the temperature changes suddenly, we need to let the other know right away."

Paolo appeared unconvinced. "I hope you know what you're doing, Carrie."

"I hope so, too."

"Just remember," Abhi muttered. "I voted that we all go back to shore."

The creature stalked the intruder, following it from below, safe in the comforting shadows of the trench. So far, the intruder had stayed above the surface, basking in the hated sunlight, while it sent the two little parasites out to steal the creature's food.

The creature experienced a new sensation—something it was totally unfamiliar with, until now.

Fear.

The creature was afraid. Afraid of the intruder who could withstand the light, and who ignored the creature's clearly designated claim on this part of the ocean. Afraid of the intruder's little parasites. Afraid of the small lights that came from them, disrupting the darkness. This new sensation was most unwelcome.

Despite its fear, the creature had let the parasites take the frozen animal from the web. The crab was only one of many. A single morsel. The creature had remained passive, content to allow the theft, lest the parasites bring more light into its domain, or discover what else was here.

Now, however, as the intruder crept along above, the creature's frustration and fear slowly gave way to anger and aggression. The intruder was approaching an important place—a place the creature would defend to the death, if need be.

Its agitation simmered as the intruder slowed to a halt far above. The water grew frigid as the creature seethed.

Steeling itself, the creature sank deeper into the shadows, where it watched and waited.

At just below eighty meters, Paolo reached the coral shelf and found it littered with more frozen sea creatures and plant life. He quickly gathered samples while Carrie hovered above him, nervously standing guard. It was hard for him to focus on the task at hand—especially with Abhi prattling like a maniac in his ear.

"And then, I remember we were in Rota, Spain. Or maybe it was Palma. Definitely one of those. The ship's boiler was broken, so our port stay was extended a full month, but I didn't mind. I had a girl there. She was . . . Damn, what was her name? Camila? Catilina? Carinna? Hell, I don't remember. It was so long ago . . . Anyway, I might not remember her name, but I remember her eyes, and her laugh, and the things she could do with her . . ."

The older man's voice sounded strange and tinny through the tiny speaker, distorted by distance and depth. Shaking his head in annoyance, Paolo scooped several tiny fish from the shelf and sealed them in a sample bag. All of them were stiff, and felt more like plastic than flesh. Abhi, meanwhile, continued.

". . . because they have iguanas in Cuba like America has squirrels. The damn things are just running around everywhere. Anyway, we were on our way back to the ship after a long night of drinking, and my friend, Miller—this crazy guy from Texas—catches one of these iguanas and tries to bring it on board. But the quartermaster catches him with it right away, because they searched our bags, and when he tries to take it away from Miller, the iguana scrambles up, bites the quartermaster on the nose, and starts scratching and clawing his arms. It was horrible, but also one of the funniest things I've ever seen."

Abhi's laughter made Paolo's head hurt. Trying his best to ignore it, he clipped the sample bag to his belt, and turned his attention back to the decaying reef. He noticed a large swath of broken coral that looked like it had been gouged, as if by enormous claws or talons. Then, below that, he spotted something especially curious—a nest of eggs that he could not immediately identify. They weren't tapioca pudding-shaped glob-like fish eggs, nor were they the distinct, oddly shaped mermaid's purse laid by sharks. Indeed, they seemed to embody characteristics of both jellyfish and octopus eggs, while simultaneously displaying mammalian traits, as well. They were polyp-shaped, like the eggs of a jellyfish, and strung across the overhanging coral like those of an octopus. But while an octopus's eggs were soft and translucent, these eggs had a hard, brown shell that looked almost rock-like. He poked one experimentally with his index finger, confirming its density.

"... and I had no choice but to admit I'd taken the wine—that was how I ended up going to Captain's Mast for the sixth time," Abhi continued. "After that, I decided to join the merchant marines, instead. They were a lot more easygoing when it came to such matters."

Confident that he still had enough oxygen in his lungs, Paolo signaled Carrie. She gave him an okay sign with her hand. Then, with Abhi babbling in his ear about an incident involving a dog and a one-legged man at a laundromat in Kenya, Paolo reached again for the nest.

Carrie watched Paolo dive down for the sample, and marveled at his stamina. She had to admit, however begrudgingly, that despite his arrogance, she was impressed with his abilities. Even amongst other free divers, she seldom encountered anybody else who could match her skills, but so far, Paolo had done so without complaint or struggle. She had also been taken aback by his genuine concern and the care in his voice earlier.

The years have been good to him, she thought. *He's grown up a lot.*

She found herself wondering if he was currently involved with anyone. She couldn't remember if he'd mentioned a wife or girlfriend. Her mind wandered back to when they'd been younger, caught in the rain on their third date, absolutely soaked to the bone, laughing, sputtering, blinking water from their eyes, and then he had pulled her close . . .

Alarmed, Carrie shook her head, aware that she had drifted off again. She looked for Paolo, noticing two things as she did.

Her lips were starting to go numb.

And the water temperature had plummeted.

Suspicious, Carrie glanced around nervously. Aware of the risk she was now under, she was just about to signal Paolo and head for the surface, when something else caught her attention. Her eyes widened in horror.

A large, dark, amorphous shape slowly emerged from the trench, scuttling up over the lip and heading for Paolo. With the low light and debris, she still couldn't see it clearly. She saw the same spindly, sharp edges alongside softer, fleshier appendages, and had a sense of a horseshoe crab crossed with a jellyfish and giant squid. She fought the crazy urge to open her mouth and scream a warning for him to get away. Paolo seemed oblivious to the danger, but he did pause, tapping his ear. Carrie realized that the radio must have started to fail, as the waters became flooded with the interfering substance emitted by the creature.

Her lungs began to ache as she ran low on air. Paolo turned toward her and caught sight of the threat surging toward him. Even from this distance, and despite the poor visibility, she thought she saw his expression register panic.

Clutching a specimen bag tightly, Paolo plunged into a crevice, hiding between outcroppings of coral and rock. Carrie watched with a stomach-churning mix of amazement and horror as the segmented creature ripped into the silt under the coral, furiously trying to dig Paolo out. The debris from the excavation obscured them both.

Her head began to pound and her ears rang, signaling that she was just about to run out of oxygen. More alarmingly, the numbing sensation was beginning to spread throughout her body. Concerned over what effect it might be having on Paolo, and how much oxygen he had left in his lungs, she swam upward, keeping the boat in sight. Although she couldn't see Paolo or the creature, when she reached a depth of twenty meters above the swirling cloud of silt, Carrie grabbed a handful of flares from her dive belt. Recalling how aggressively the thing had attacked the lights on the previous dive, she dropped the torches. The debris cleared as the flares neared the coral, enough that she spotted the enraged creature pause in its digging to attack the lights instead. She dropped another handful of torches and caught a glimpse of Paolo swimming hard, north and east along the reef, staying low and close to the coral.

Fighting against the sinister paralysis creeping through her body, Carrie made her way up to the boat. A roaring sound filled her ears, and her vision grew spotty. The vessel floated above her, surrounded by a halo of filtered sunlight. She was afraid to take her eyes off the hull. She surfaced, sputtering, years of training and instinct forgotten in a moment of panic, and gulped precious air. Waves slapped her face, yet she barely felt the sting.

The buzzing in her ears subsided, giving way to the churn of the surf and Abhi calling out to her in concern.

"Are you okay? Carrie? Talk to me! Where's Paolo?"

Paddling for the boat, Carrie spat water. "Drop . . . flares . . ."

"What?"

"Drop some flares! Hurry, Abhi! Just drop them in the water."

Without further comment, Abhi rushed to the torch crate and ripped the lid off the wooden box. Carrie clambered over the side of the craft, dripping water in her wake. With no time to explain, she hurried over to the crate and grabbed a hand-ful of flares. Abhi did the same. Then, they began dropping the lit torches into the water. Carrie hoped that it would be enough to distract the creature a little bit longer, and buy Paolo more time to escape.

Except that he's out of time, she thought. *There can't be much air left in his lungs.*

"Get ready to move," she gasped. "Take us north and east. But slowly."

"Carrie, tell me what's happening! Where's Paolo?"

"I don't have time to go into it, Abhi. The creature attacked us. Paolo escaped, but he's so far off now, he'll need the torches to relocate us."

Nodding, Abhi rushed back to the case and dragged it to the middle of the deck. They stood on each side, lighting flares and dropping them into the churning water. Carrie watched the lights as they descended into the depths, and was once again reminded of fireflies. She shivered in the heat. The torches continued to fall, but there was no sign of Paolo—or the creature.

Without taking her gaze away from the ocean, Carrie reached down, fumbling for more flares. Her fingers skittered across bare wood. When she glanced down, she saw that the crate was empty.

Paolo still hadn't surfaced.

"Come on," she whispered. "Come on, come on, come on . . ."

"Carrie," Abhi said, his voice low, "maybe we should—"

"We're not leaving."

"That's not what I was going to suggest."

Gripping the rail, Carrie stared at the water. The railing was scorching hot after sitting for so long in the sunlight, but she barely noticed. She chewed her lip, and tasted blood.

"Not like Peter," she whispered. "Not Paolo."

The lights continued to sink, getting smaller and smaller now.

Then, they started to go out.

There was a commotion off the starboard side, as something surfaced with a loud splash.

"There," Abhi shouted, pointing. "Over there!"

It was Paolo. He had come up a few hundred feet away from the boat. Abhi and Carrie called to him, but then Carrie glanced back down into the depths.

The falling torchlights continued to wink out, one by one, closer and closer to the surface.

"Shit! Abhi, motor over to Paolo."

"Are you sure? He seems okay. He's swimming toward us."

"So is that thing! We need to get to Paolo while it's still distracted by the torches."

Abhi raced for the motor and got it started. It sputtered, belching blue-gray smoke and diesel fumes, and then hummed. As he pointed the boat toward Paolo, Carrie rushed to the bow. The boat bounced up and down on the waves. Saltwater splashed her face, but this time, Carrie felt it, as the paralysis faded. She dropped a few more torches, flinging them as far as she could, hoping to distract the predator a little longer. Then, she turned her attention back to the surface and kept sight of Paolo, bobbing with the swells like a human beach ball.

"Slow down," she shouted over the roar of the motor. "Only about fifty feet!"

Abhi did as commanded, but rather than idling, the motor coughed again, releasing another plume of smoke, and then died. The ocean suddenly seemed very quiet.

"What the—" Abhi pounded on it with his fist.

Carrie cupped her hands around her mouth. "Swim, Paolo!"

Abhi removed his hat and wiped his brow. Glowering, he checked over the motor.

"You've got gas and oil," he said to the stubborn engine. "What else do you need?"

Paolo swam for them, closing the distance with seemingly no trouble, despite the length of time he'd been underwater.

Even alongside her terror, Carrie was filled with admiration for his abilities. Paolo reached the boat while Abhi cursed and pleaded with the motor. Carrie reached for Paolo's outstretched hand, and grasped it firmly.

"You okay?"

He nodded, too winded to speak. Then he smiled.

Carrie smiled back at him. "I'm glad."

Then, as she began to haul him aboard, something seized Paolo from below.

Paolo screamed. "My leg! It's got my leg!"

Yelling, Carrie pulled hard, but the creature pulled back—a horrifying game of tug-o-war, with the terrified diver as the rope. Paolo's eyes were wide circles, and his complexion turned alabaster from shock. His breathing came in short, panicked gasps.

"Don't let go," he pleaded. "Don't let go! Oh God . . ."

"Abhi," Carrie shouted. "Help me—"

He was at her side before she could finish, grabbing Paolo's other flailing arm and tugging. Abhi gritted his teeth, grunting with the effort, and cursed in three languages. Carrie braced her feet against the bow and renewed her efforts. Paolo's screams turned to unintelligible shrieks as the creature refused to let go. His wetsuit slipped in their grasp. Carrie shrieked as he slid away from her, but Abhi held on tight. Seconds later, Paolo's frantic cries were drowned out as something scraped against the bottom of the boat, denting the metal hull from beneath.

"Oh Jesus," Abhi breathed. "It's going to tear through . . ."

"Pull," Carrie screamed, grabbing Paolo's outstretched hand. "Pull, goddamn it!"

The boat rose suddenly, higher and more rapidly than any wave could have tossed it. Carrie's grip slipped again, and Paolo's hand fluttered away. Once more, Abhi managed to hold on. The boat's hull buckled behind them as something slammed against it. Metal shrieked torturously. Then, the boat crashed back down again, slamming into the water. Salt spray hit their faces. Abhi pulled, the tendons standing out in his neck. Carrie leaned forward, and managed to get her arms around Paolo's chest. The two of them yanked him from the ocean and onto the deck.

"Careful," he groaned. "The sample . . ."

Carrie looked to where he was pointing and saw a sample bag affixed to his belt, bulging with an egg of some kind, big enough that it barely fit inside the container. Then her attention returned to Paolo. Blood smeared the deck around him, streaming from a horrific-looking wound on his leg.

"Get us out of here," Carrie told Abhi. "Hurry!"

"If you know any prayers," he muttered, "now would be a good time to use them."

Ignoring him, Carrie knelt beside Paolo and tended to his wound. His wetsuit had been slashed open, and blood welled steadily from a gaping, tattered hole just above his ankle. Worse, his calf and ankle were both black from what appeared to be the beginning stages of frostbite. Before she could examine the injury further, the creature slammed into the bottom of the boat again. The hull rose and buckled directly beneath them. Gear and equipment crashed to the deck and rolled around.

"Abhi! Do something!"

"I'm working on it!"

Paolo whimpered as Carrie touched his leg. Despite the heat, his lips were chattering and his skin was covered in gooseflesh.

"You're going into shock," she said. "Try to relax, Paolo. It's going to be okay. I promise. Just hang on. You hear me? Hang on!"

She realized then that both of them were crying. She clasped his hand and squeezed. Paolo rolled his head back and forth in agony, but he squeezed back. He tried to smile at her, but could only grimace.

Behind them, Abhi began hitting the motor with a wrench, and swearing at it in several different languages.

"Gatito," Paolo sighed. "I . . ."

"Don't talk," she said. "Just hang on."

Carrie looked closer at Paolo's punctured ankle, and discovered why the blood flow was a trickle rather than a flood. There was something lodged in the wound. Something about the size of a golf ball. Frowning, she bent closer and squinted. She couldn't be sure what the object was, but it looked like a hard, ovoid mineral.

The boat shot upward again as the creature battered it from below, causing all three of them to scream. Then, as it slammed back down, the diesel long-tail motor roared to life.

"Go," she shouted, holding on to Paolo. "Go-go-go-go!"

Abhi teased the throttle, apparently concerned about the engine stalling out again. Carrie wanted to scream at him to hurry up, but she resisted, fighting down her panic by focusing again on Paolo's leg. Behind her, the motor grew louder as Abhi slowly increased their speed. He shouted, but Carrie couldn't be sure if it was from triumph or terror.

Paolo followed her eyes to his wound. Fading toward shock, he clasped her hand again.

"Get it . . . out. And . . . take care of . . . this . . ."

He let go of her hand and gently patted the scavenged egg. Then his eyes rolled up in his head, and he went limp, sagging against the dented metal deck.

Carrie stood up and glanced over the side, scanning the ocean for signs of pursuit. The ocean was choppy and clouded, and silt swirled in their wake, but the creature was nowhere in sight. She grabbed the first aid kit, and then hurried over to the toolbox and rummaged inside of it, searching for a pair of needle-nose pliers.

"How is he?" Abhi called.

"He's unconscious, and there's something lodged in his leg."

"What kind of something? You mean like a stingray barb?"

"I don't know what it is," Carrie admitted. She looked again. "It's organic."

"And that thing in the water?"

"I don't see it. Maybe it gave up. Just keep us steady."

"Petal to the medal," Abhi said, accentuating.

"I think you mean pedal to the metal, Abhi."

"That's what I said, Carrie. Now is not the time to—"

"Sorry. You're right. I'm just . . . scared."

"I am, too," Abhi admitted.

Returning to Paolo with the pliers and the first aid kit, she knelt down again and tilted his leg. Blood and water rushed over her feet as the boat rocked with the swells.

"Keep it steady," she yelled. "I'm going to try to pull it out."

"I'm doing my best," Abhi countered. "But it's getting choppier out here!"

Carrie noticed that her hands were trembling, as she first poured disinfectant over the pliers, and then over Paolo's wound. He moaned and twitched as the pink foam bubbled around the injury, but didn't wake. Carrie paused, using her breathing techniques to get her shaking under control. Then, she carefully tried to pull the object from Paolo's ankle. More blood welled around the pliers as she worked them around the object, pushing his flesh apart. Wincing, she finally managed to grip the ovoid. Then she pulled. Paolo groaned, clenching and unclenching his fists, but remained unconscious. She was glad for that. If he had been awake, there was no doubt in her mind he'd be screaming right now.

She felt like screaming herself.

Cursing, Carrie tugged harder at the mineral. Slowly, it cleared the ragged, blackened flesh of his ankle, but still refused to come entirely free. Then she saw why. The bottom of the ovoid was lodged deeper in his leg via a hook-like barb. She couldn't extract it without doing a lot more damage to Paolo. They needed a doctor. Or better yet, a surgeon.

She looked up and saw Abhi smiling sadly at her.

"Don't worry." His expression belied his reassuring tone. "We'll make it to shore."

Biting her lip again, Carrie nodded. She just hoped they'd make it in time.

EIGHT

"Any sign of it?" Abhi called over his shoulder.

"No," Carrie said, cradling Paolo's head in her lap. He still hadn't regained consciousness, and his skin was cold and pale. Carrie wasn't sure if that was from shock or the result of the creature's attack on him. She had used some shop rags and a length of rope to fashion bandages and a crude tourniquet above his wound. Paolo had whimpered during the process, but remained out cold.

She was worried about him, and also feeling unsettled by the emotions his condition had stirred up in her—emotions she'd long thought sealed away in a drawer, along with old cards and letters.

"What is it, anyway?" Abhi asked. "That thing that attacked us?"

"I don't know," Carrie admitted. "I still didn't get a good look. It seemed . . . it looked like some bizarre hodgepodge of a bunch of different animals. At first, I thought it might be a giant crab, but then—"

"A giant crab," Abhi interrupted. "You mean like a Clicker?"

At first, Carrie wasn't sure if Abhi was joking or not. It was hard to see his expression, since he was turned away from her.

"The Megarachne Servinei? That was just a hoax—a misidentification. It was never a real sea creature."

Carrie thought back to when Megarachne Servinei had first come to scientific light twenty years earlier, when a fossil was discovered in Argentina. It was thought, at the time, to be the biggest spider to ever walk the earth, and was even recognized in the Guinness Book of World Records as such. Plaster casts of the fossil were exhibited in museums around the world. But then Sinclair, a researcher from the University of Manchester had insisted that its origins be reclassified, writing for a scientific journal that the fossil was more of a cross between a giant crab and a sea scorpion. He had intended to offer proof that the Megarachne Servinei was an aquatic relative of the giant eurypterid and the Woodwardopterus, an invasive species from the Carboniferous Period. Unfortunately, Sinclair had died unexpectedly before he could ever finish presenting his findings. That hadn't stopped various Internet-based conspiracy theorists and cryptozoologists from speculating that he'd been right, however, and that the creatures, popularized by the nickname Clickers, still existed somewhere in the depths of the ocean.

"I don't believe that," Abhi said. "I know people who've seen one—or even heard one. In the North Atlantic, and off the coast of Maine, and another in the waters near Cuba."

"It wasn't a Clicker," Carrie insisted. "Maybe they saw or heard something they couldn't explain, but the Clickers were a hoax."

"The sea still has all kinds of secrets, even today."

"Maybe so, but that thing I saw wasn't a Clicker, either. It only looked like a giant crab at first. It's difficult to explain. It seemed to keep changing. There were tentacles, and a tail, and maybe a shell. I had a sense of it . . . flowing. That's not exactly the right word, but I don't know how else to describe it."

"And that thing he brought on board? Is that what I think it is?"

"I don't know. What do you think it is?"

"It looks like an egg to me."

Carrie didn't respond. Instead, she gently patted Paolo's cheeks, trying to rouse him. Her attempts were unsuccessful.

"Paolo? Can you hear me? I need you to hang on."

"I'm going to radio ahead," Abhi said. "That way we can have paramedics on standby at the dock to take him to Jeetoo in Port Louis. That's the closest hospital. Okay?"

Carrie nodded, blinking back tears. She was afraid that if she responded, her voice would crack.

Abhi steered with one hand and tried the radio handset with the other. But after several attempts at hailing the mainland, he frowned, staring at the radio in confusion.

"What's wrong?" Carrie croaked.

"The radio. There's some kind of interference. I don't understand. I checked the hell out of it before we left, and it was working fine. Now, it's acting up."

Carrie suddenly felt very cold. "What kind of interference?"

Abhi hung the mic back on the receiver. "Like what your radios were doing underwater. But you said that happened at a certain depth. I don't understand why it would be impacting us now, up here on the surface."

Carrie glanced behind them, scanning the waves. Then she turned back to Abhi.

"I think—"

Before she could finish, something slammed into the bottom of the boat, knocking them both to the deck. Carrie glimpsed the creature's broad shadow moving beneath the surface. Abhi screamed, flailing around wildly. Carrie grappled for a handhold as Paolo slipped away from her and flopped into a pool of bloody water. The boat spun in a wide arc, going off course and running parallel to the coastline. The motor whined like a wounded animal.

Carrie pulled Paolo from the water and checked to make sure he was still breathing. The creature rammed the boat again. The frame shuddered beneath them. She spotted Abhi clambering to his feet. Blood trickled down his face from a small gash on his forehead, but his eyes were clear and the panic and terror were absent from his expression, replaced with a grim determination.

"Hang on tight!" He struggled to right their course. "I just saw it go under. The size—I've never seen anything so big in these waters!"

Carrie was about to respond when something punched through the bottom of the boat, piercing the hull just inches from Paolo's leg. The segmented appendage was long and thin, brown in color, and covered with fine hairs and warty knobs. Its end tapered to a javelin-like point. To Carrie, it looked like some obscene cross between a crab and a spider. Spearing through the metal had wounded the creature. Blood streamed from several cuts around the joints. The beast incurred more injuries when it yanked its appendage back through the hole, leaving torn bits of meat dangling from the shredded metal. More blood spilled onto the deck, steaming in the sunlight.

Another appendage punctured the hull a few feet away from where Carrie crouched, and the creature further bloodied itself in the process. Given its reaction to their torches, Carrie had thought this animal was afraid of sunlight. But now it attacked them, seemingly without concern for the light or the damage it was doing to itself. The leg withdrew. It left behind a second hole, and the boat began to take on water. As a result, their speed slowed.

"Can't this fucking thing go any faster?"

"If it punches another hole in us, we're not going to be going at all," Abhi shouted. "I need you to bail!"

Carrie dragged Paolo over to the cabin, which was really nothing more than a raised platform with an awning to protect the pilot, controls, and the navigational and communications equipment. She shoved the ice-filled cooler aside and laid Paolo's still form on a bench, hoping he was out of reach from any danger below. Then she quickly returned aft, grabbed a bucket, and began to bail. The bloody water smelled sharply of brine, but there was another stench—an alkaline, chemical tinge that made her eyes water.

"I think its blood is toxic," Carrie gasped. "Try not to get it on you."

Abhi's eyes widened. "You mean like acid? Or poison?"

"Not acid. I think it probably could have the same effect it had on us underwater. If you start to feel numb, try to focus before the hallucinations begin."

"Wonderful," Abhi moaned. "That's all we need."

Crouched on her knees, Carrie dumped another bucket of red water over the side. As she did, she glimpsed a dark, massive shape disappearing beneath the boat.

"It's coming around again," she warned.

This time, instead of a segmented leg, the creature attacked with a tentacle. The appendage was thick as a telephone pole, and erupted from the water on their starboard side, weaving back and forth for a second before darting forward like a snake. It struck at Abhi, who, with a frightened squawk, side-stepped the flailing arm. He ducked low, grabbed his machete, and swung at the tentacle as it felt along the boat, searching for something. The blade parted the rubbery meat like margarine. Blood erupted from the wound, spraying the boat. The stench was horrific. Carrie took a deep breath and held it. Gagging, Abhi backed away. The injured appendage disappeared back into the ocean. The severed end curled and uncurled on the deck, jetting blood, and then lay still. The blood slowed to a trickle.

"I told you we should have gone back," Abhi complained, "but no. We couldn't go home. You had to do more science!"

Carrie's skin began to tingle. "Oh no . . ."

The boat rocked back and forth. The sea roiled and churned.

"Carrie," Abhi coughed. "I don't feel so good."

"It's the toxin. Get us ashore, Abhi. Hurry. While we still can."

"I don't think . . ."

A massive wave broke over the bow, flooding the boat. Carrie blinked saltwater from her eyes and then blinked again in disbelief. The wave had deposited hundreds of tiny seahorses into the boat. Each one was no bigger than the tip of her pinky finger. They wriggled around in the red-tinged water, brushing against her knees and ankles. Awestruck, Carrie forgot all about their peril. Instead of bailing, she dipped the bucket into the water and scooped up dozens of the little creatures. Smiling with delight, she tried to touch them. When she did, the wiggling seahorses turned into bursts of multi-colored lights. Carrie laughed, amazed by the experience. It was like a miniature fireworks display taking place inside the confines of the bucket. She wanted to share this joyous discovery with Abhi, but when she tried to call out to him, she discovered that her tongue had gone numb. She turned to him instead, slowly, and was surprised to see him staring at her in alarm.

"Carrie, the blood!"

She tried to say "seahorses," but instead could only slur. "Sheee . . ."

"Whatever you're seeing, Carrie, it's not there!"

Another wave crashed over them, drenching them both.

Sputtering, Carrie glanced down at the bucket. The seahorses and their kaleidoscope of colors were gone. She heard Abhi screaming at her to bail, but he sounded far away, and the matter didn't seem all that urgent. What she really wanted to do was sleep, or better yet, just dive into the ocean and slip beneath the waves. After all, that's where she'd always felt the most comfortable, wasn't it? Beneath the waves, she was in charge. She answered only to herself. Nobody could hurt her when she was down . . .

Something whipped by her head. She looked up and saw another tendril waving through the air. This one was thinner than the tentacle that Abhi had chopped in half, but the sight of it brought Carrie back to herself. She smacked it with the bucket. The appendage recoiled and then surged forward. Shouting unintelligibly, Abhi appeared at her side. He grabbed the tip of the appendage with one fist. The tentacle coiled and twisted, fighting him, but before it could break his grip, he pulled hard and swung the machete, cleaving it in half. Abhi stumbled backward, still clutching the squirming tendril. The tentacle's other half retreated, spraying blood like a fire hose all over the deck.

Carrie watched as Abhi tossed the severed appendage into the water and struggled to retain his footing. The boat rocked savagely from side to side, and the deck was slippery with blood and water. She stared down at a pink pool, and gasped as more little seahorses appeared, splashing and frolicking amidst the gore.

Then the illusion was shattered as Abhi grabbed her by the chin and tilted Carrie's eyes up to him.

"Listen to me, goddamn it. Whatever you're seeing, it isn't real. I'm seeing things, too. Remember, it's just the monster. We're hallucinating. Stay focused. Okay?"

Nodding, Carrie went back to bailing while Abhi lurched back to the controls. She noticed that he was moving stiffly, as if his legs and arms were sore. Of course, she wasn't moving as fast as she should be, either. A stiffness had crept into her bones, and the entire effort just seemed unimportant. So what if the boat sank? They could just swim to shore.

That's the toxin talking, she thought with a sudden burst of clarity. *Get back to work, girl, or none of you are ever going to reach land.*

The boat's motor coughed, sputtered, and then roared to life. Abhi pumped a fist in the air.

"Are you with me?" he shouted.

"I'm better," she managed to say. Her head was clearer, but it felt like her mouth was filled with cotton balls. "I'm okay. Just go."

More waves broke over them, then receded as Abhi leaned on the throttle. The motor roared as the boat shot ahead again. Abhi laughed, and then said something that Carrie didn't understand. He kept glancing to his left, and nodding, as if having a conversation with somebody else. She realized that while she was feeling more coherent, Abhi's hallucinations were intensifying. The only way to negate them was to clear the blood from the deck, but doing so meant bailing, which only put her in further contact with the toxins.

Why hadn't the creature given up after suffering such serious injuries? What did it want? This type of determination went beyond that of a predator simply hunting for food or an animal protecting its territory. This was obsession.

The egg, she realized. *It's after the egg. The tentacles were searching for the egg.*

The motor died with a small explosion of diesel fumes as the creature ripped the tail off the engine. Abhi didn't seem to notice at first. He kept them pointed at the shore, but their speed was failing. Carrie's pulse raced as she spotted the docks about one hundred twenty yards ahead.

That's the length of a football field. I can swim that. If my arms and legs weren't so sleepy, I could swim that.

"No, dear," her mother said, kneeling in the bloody water next to Carrie. "You'll never make it. It's better to just give up now. It will be easier that way."

"You're not real, Mom." Carrie felt like her mouth was stuffed with cotton balls.

"Stop being silly. Of course I'm real. You're the one who's being unrealistic."

"I can make it. Take the egg and let that thing follow me. Abhi and Paolo will be safe."

Her mother sighed. "You always were bullheaded, Carrie. Why can't you be more like your sister? She's so much more sensible than you ever were."

There was a screech of crushing metal as the creature battered and shredded the boat's aft end. More of the beast had emerged from the sea, but Carrie couldn't tell which parts of its bulk were a hallucination and which portions were real. It occurred to her that maybe the neurotoxins were what accounted for its seeming abilities to change shape. Maybe those shapes weren't real at all. Then, as if to spite her and prove her wrong, the creature seemed to solidify for a moment. Before she could take it all in, the monster sank beneath the waves again, as if fleeing the sunlight.

Abhi abandoned the cabin, grabbed the oars, and desperately tried to navigate them toward the docks. The engine continued to belch smoke and diesel fumes, which only added to the already toxic atmosphere on board.

"I know," Abhi shouted at someone who wasn't there. "I know, so just leave me alone. It was all my fault. I'll come back to her someday, if she'll still have me."

"Abhi?"

When he didn't answer, Carrie realized that she'd whispered his name. She smacked her lips together, working up enough saliva to speak. Then she tried again, summoning all of her willpower for a brief moment of lucidity.

"Abhi! We have to swim for it."

"I can get us there," he argued, even as the water surged over his lap. He didn't seem to notice that the boat's aft end was gone. He simply continued to heave on the oars as the boat's bow rose slowly into the air. "It's just a matter of putting our backs into it."

Taking care not to slip, Carrie crossed the precarious distance between them and squeezed his shoulder.

"Abhi, listen to me. We're sinking. We need to swim. You need to take Paolo and head directly for shore."

"What about Marissa?"

"There is no Marissa. We're hallucinating. Remember?"

"No." Abhi shook his head. Tears welled up in his eyes. "There was a Marissa. There had to be. I haven't seen her in so long. I need to tell her that I'm sorry. That it was all a mistake. That I should have told her what had happened. Why I did what I did."

"You can tell her when you get to the shore. They have phones there. We'll call her. Okay?"

"Okay." He sounded unsure.

A swarm of butterflies flitted around Carrie's head, arcing up toward the sun. She gazed up into the glare, shielding her eyes with her hand. The sun had grown impossibly large, seeming to fill the sky.

"It's not real," she said, and then glanced back down at Abhi. "Are you ready? Remember what I said?"

"I need to take Paolo?"

Carrie nodded. She glanced ahead of them, and saw that the boat had drifted another ten yards or so. Closer, but the shoreline still seemed so far away.

"What about you, Carrie? What are you doing? And what about the monster? It will get us as soon as we go overboard."

"No, it won't. I'm going to distract it while you get Paolo to shore."

"How?"

A giant claw burst from the water and sheared more of the hull in two as easily as a pair of tin-snips would cut through a soda can. The sound it made was horrendous.

"I'll dive in and try to lead it off while approaching the docks at an angle. You get Paolo to shore!"

Before Abhi could protest or try to dissuade her, Carrie snatched up the sample bag containing the egg, took a deep, shuddering breath, and then dove over the side. She cleaved the water and slipped beneath the surface, leaving behind the sounds of fury and destruction, and returning to the one place where she truly felt at home—at peace. Except she knew now that the peace she felt was just another hallucination, a by-product of the creature's neurotoxin, lulling her into complacency. The beast had ruined even this for her.

Despite the numbness that now engulfed her entire body, Carrie grew angry. Clenching her jaw until her teeth hurt, she swam hard. She spotted the monster behind her, so enraged and injured that it hadn't yet noticed her. She didn't stop to try and get a better look at its form. There was no time. The creature had been tearing itself to shreds while attacking the boat, and as a result, the water was even more shocked with toxins than their craft had been.

Carrie darted ahead, knowing all too well that this was the swim of her life. Indeed, this swim would determine if she'd continue to *have* a life. She focused on pushing forward, resisting the urge to glance behind her for signs of pursuit. She also struggled against the creeping passiveness that settled over

her again, fighting the urge to just give up and empty her lungs
of air.

Remembering that the creature had seemed to abhor the
sunlight, she arrowed toward the surface, hoping that would
give it pause. As she rose, the already murky water grew darker
around her. A frigid cold seemed to radiate through the ocean.
She glanced down and saw a dark shape rocketing upward.

Then her muscles began to seize up. Excruciating cramps
jolted her legs. It took every ounce of energy just to keep kicking. Her abdomen grew cold, and then numb. There was a roaring sound in her ears that belonged to neither the ocean nor
her pursuer. Her vision began to blur—kaleidoscopic flashes of
white and black dots danced and whirled.

"See?" her mother taunted, swimming along beside her.
"You should have listened to me. There's still time to. Just
give in, and stop this silly fighting. You were always so stubborn."

Carrie refused to look at her mother. Instead, she gritted
her teeth, fighting against the quickening paralysis.

Her mother clucked in exasperation. "I can't get through
to her. You try talking some sense in her, dear."

Carrie's father appeared in front of her, hovering just below the surface. A halo of sunlight crowned his head. Smiling,
he stretched his arms wide, offering an embrace. Still clenching her jaw, Carrie swam through him. Her father dissipated
like the seahorses, in a burst of colors. Then her head breached
the surface. Carrie tried to catch a glimpse of the shore, but a
wave smashed her back down before she could. When she surfaced again, her vision was blurry.

The numbness crept into her arms. She knew she could
cast the egg back—just let go of the sample bag and hope the
creature would pursue it instead. If she did, there was a chance

she could drag herself ashore with her half-paralyzed arms alone.

No, screw that. I didn't drag it this far to let go now.

Steeling herself, she fought for the bobbing shoreline, tapping into her last store of willpower and determination. Another wave pushed her below, and she realized the water all around her had turned black. The cold was an almost physical thing, seeming to envelop her. Carrie's legs stopped moving, and she began to drift downward.

There was a sudden, excruciating pain as something speared her forearm, ripping and tearing, trying to force her to let go of the egg. Carrie twisted away, catching a glimpse of a talon as she did. It was attached to a thin, spindly arm. The serrated pincer gouged her forearm, digging a ragged trench. She watched her blood flow from the wound in the dim light, mingling with the churning water. Her arm burned. Her veins felt like fire was pumping through them.

No way, Mom. I'm not giving up. I'm not . . .

The dark form surrounded her, moving as if to engulf her, and Carrie knew she could no longer resist its frigid embrace. She saw legs, tentacles, claws, scales, and something that looked like an eye, but couldn't have been, because no creature on Earth had an eye that big. It stared at her. Carrie stared back, refusing to look away.

The creature blinked.

Carrie grinned, ignoring the pounding in her lungs. Her heart hammered in her chest.

This is it. I'm sorry, Paolo. I'm sorry . . .

Her father appeared again, and smiled. She saw the creature behind him, surging forward with arms and tentacles outstretched, but she didn't care. Her father reached for her.

Then, the monster suddenly receded and her father vanished, as Carrie was flung upward, twisting and turning, caught in a tremendous, surging wave. The unexpected momentum forced the air from her lungs. Saltwater rushed in to replace it. The roaring in her ears was all-consuming now. All thought ceased. Nothing else existed. Not her injured forearm. Not her mother's dour recriminations. Not the beast or the cold that seemed to radiate from it. Not Paolo and Abhi. Not the egg. Her entire world was the roaring sound, rushing to meet her, eager to swallow her whole.

Still, even in this state, Carrie refused to go limp. Refused to surrender.

Then the wave tossed her onto the beach face-first, and the sound slipped away with her consciousness.

NINE

When Carrie opened her eyes again, she thought she must be back at the hospital in Chemin Grenier. It smelled like a hospital, and the drab décor was the same. She heard a machine beeping, and decided that it sounded like a hospital, as well.

Had the entire thing just been a dream—an oxygen deprivation-induced nightmare she'd suffered while recovering from the bends? Had she been here all this time, since the initial accident with Peter? Had Paolo and Abhi and the thing in the trench been nothing more than delirium? Then she felt something tug at her arm, which was still numb, and slowly became aware that there were other people in the room with her.

She turned her head to the left and saw a man stitching up her wounded arm. So, it hadn't been a dream. She should be so lucky. The injury was real enough, which meant that its cause had been real, as well. She remembered the beast, the way it had slashed her, determined to retrieve its egg. That had really happened. All of it. Her thoughts turned to Paolo and

Abhi. Where were they? Had her distraction worked? Had Abhi made it to shore? How was Paolo?

Her eyes drifted closed. They flickered open again as she felt another tug on her arm. She stared at the man, watching as he nimbly worked the needle and thread. No glue guns or medical adhesive for this apparent medical professional. He was old-school. He hummed tunelessly, seeming absorbed in the task at hand. He was obviously Mauritian, probably of Creole descent, and handsome. She assumed, given his clothing and the fact that he was sewing her up with some degree of expertise, that he must be a doctor. A nurse stood nearby, who Carrie judged to also be Mauritian.

Okay, Carrie thought. *I'm still in Mauritius. But where? And what happened?*

She tried to speak, but her mouth was terribly dry, and her lips felt chapped and cracked.

Finally noticing that she was awake, the doctor gave her a disarming smile.

"It's okay," he said. "I'm Dr. Barbet. Do you remember what happened, Miss Anderson?"

Before Carrie could answer, he nodded gently at the nurse, who approached Carrie with a small plastic cup filled with ice chips. She administered one, tracing it softly across Carrie's chafed lips before placing it in Carrie's mouth.

"Careful now," the nurse said. "Take it slowly. We don't want you to choke. Just let it melt in your mouth."

Carrie did as she was told, and moaned in gratitude. Ice had never tasted or felt so good. She sucked on the chip, feeling it grow smaller, and simultaneously feeling her strength return. She wiggled her toes, experimentally, and was relieved to see that the paralysis had passed. Only her arm remained numb, and she quickly determined that they must have given her anesthetic before attending her wound.

"I remember . . . the water. Paolo and Abhi . . ."

"Your companions are here, as well," Dr. Barbet replied. "Abhi is fine. He suffered only a few abrasions, and a case of sunburn. And Paolo is in surgery right now."

Carrie's full sense returned. She sat up, slowly, and reached with her good arm for the cup of ice.

"Carefully, now," Dr. Barbet cautioned. "The more you hold still, the better I can stitch you. We want to lessen the scar, yes?"

"I don't care about the scar." Carrie downed three more ice chips. "How's Paolo? His leg. That thing put something in his leg."

She paused, wondering if that had been part of the hallucinations.

"You said he was in surgery?"

The doctor turned to the nurse. "Could you inform them that Miss Anderson is awake, please?"

Nodding, the nurse left. The doctor waited until she had closed the door before answering Carrie's question.

"I don't know what his current condition is. I can tell you that we handled the frostbite, and there was very little permanent tissue damage. You got him here just in time to prevent that. We also removed the object from his leg. You'll be grateful to know that your wound had no similar object lodged in it."

"The ovoid." Carrie frowned, remembering the barbed mineral she'd been unable to dislodge from Paolo's wound. So that part, at least, hadn't been a hallucination.

"Yes. It turns out it is a kind of organic pod. It emptied a payload of toxin into Paolo's bloodstream. That's why you should be thankful you only got this gouge, Miss Anderson."

"Call me Carrie."

"Very well then, Carrie. Consider yourself lucky."

Finished with the stitches, he rolled his chair backward. Despite his calm demeanor, Carrie could tell from his expression that he wasn't telling her everything.

"The toxin. What's Paolo's reaction to it?"

Dr. Barbet sighed, hesitating. He drummed his fingers on his thigh, and when he spoke again, he wouldn't meet Carrie's gaze.

"I've never seen anything like it. In some ways, the chemical compound is similar to that of certain sea anemones, but there are also elements of jellyfish poison and other compounds. It's bizarre."

Pursing her lips, Carrie thought back to how the creature had seemed to have the characteristics and biology of different sea creatures.

"Whatever the toxin's origins," Barbet continued, "it's having crazy effects on him, I'm afraid. Killing him while manipulating his brainwaves. He swings between a state of lucidity and a brain state that I have no name for."

"Killing him? Oh God . . ."

"I'm very sorry, Miss Anderson. I'm sorry. I mean Carrie. But don't give up hope yet. We've sent for a specialist from Port Louis, and—"

"We're not in Port Louis? Where are we, then?"

"This is a special clinic. Quite isolated. The press will not bother you here. Indeed, I doubt they even know it exists. We're very exclusive. You're safe."

Before Carrie could ask him to be more specific, the door opened. The nurse entered the room, followed by two middle-aged white men in expensive suits. Each of them had an Alpinus Biofutures identification badge pinned to their ties.

"Doctor?" The first man, who wore glasses and had thinning blond hair, nodded at Dr. Barbet. "If you could excuse us for a few moments, please?"

Barbet looked like he was about to protest. Instead, he slowly rose from his seat.

"Certainly." He turned to Carrie. "Rest up, okay? And as I said, don't give up hope. I'll check back on you in a while."

Neither of the two new arrivals seemed to pay any attention to the doctor or nurse as they left the room and shut the door behind them. Instead, they focused on Carrie. After the staff were gone, they crossed the room, and stood at both sides of the bed. Now that they were closer, Carrie smelled cologne wafting off the blond. She couldn't identify the scent, but it certainly wasn't cheap. Despite its cost, the man wore too much of it. The second man had a thick, neatly-coiffed crop of gray-and-black hair. His large nose showed the telltale signs of having been broken at least once in the past, and his hairy, broad knuckles bore thin, white scars. He seemed uncomfortable wearing the suit. He did not smile, and when he stared at Carrie, she was uncomfortably reminded of a shark's emotionless, black eyes.

"Miss Anderson." The blond smiled, displaying perfectly capped teeth that were too large for his gums, and thrust out his hand. "I'm Mr. Ochse. This is my associate, Mr. Maberry. We're special investigators with Alpinus Biofutures' security division. We'd like to debrief you, if we may?"

Instead of shaking the offered hand, Carrie raised the plastic cup to her mouth and crunched an ice cube, chewing it slowly and with relish, enjoying the feel of it between her teeth and the effect it had on the two agents.

"Alpinus has a security division?"

"Well, of course," Ochse responded. "We're one of the biggest biotech companies in the world. A security division is simply responsible business."

"I see." Carrie crunched another ice cube, deliberately taking her time. "And I guess you're here to investigate me for unauthorized use of your equipment and your personnel, right?"

Ochse laughed, but Carrie thought it seemed forced and insincere. Maberry said nothing. His face was an expressionless slate, betraying nothing. He seemed almost bored, but Carrie also detected a hint of menace.

"On the contrary," Ochse replied. "We're quite interested in what occurred, and you're not in any trouble. We just want to know what happened. We're not interested in disciplinary action or charges."

"Really?"

"As I said, we're just here to debrief you. Shall we get started?"

Shrugging, Carrie indicated her consent. Ochse sat down in the chair Dr. Barbet had previously occupied, and scooted it up next to her bedside. The chair's feet made a screeching sound, and left black scuff marks on the floor. The still-silent Maberry remained standing, but he moved to the foot of the bed. His heavy-lidded eyes never seemed to blink. Ochse produced a small digital recorder from the inside pocket of his suit jacket, grinning as if he were a magician pulling a rabbit out of a hat, and sat it on the table next to Carrie. Then, he began to speak.

"This is Weston Ochse, AB Security, employee number eight-three-zero-niner. This is our initial interview with former AB freelance consultant Caroline May Anderson."

"Wow," Carrie murmured. "Nobody ever calls me Caroline."

He then stated the date and time, and asked Carrie to confirm her identity. When she had done so, they began a long, intense, and grueling debriefing that lasted a full hour. Carrie told them everything, starting with her release from the hospital in Chemin Grenier after recovering from the bends, her encounter with Jessamine, and later Paolo, her determination to further investigate the collapse, and ultimately, their encounter with the creature. She noticed that neither man seemed to scoff or display any disbelief at her story, even when she recounted the hallucinations in detail. They simply listened. Maberry remained a stone statue, impassive and unreadable. Ochse was more engaged, occasionally asked questions for clarification, but seemed mostly content to just let her talk. Carrie held nothing back. She could see no reason to do so, especially now that it seemed clear there would be no recriminations for her non-sanctioned expedition.

The only time she got a reaction out of the men was when she mentioned the egg. Ochse had glanced at Maberry at that point, and then informed her that no egg had been recovered when she was found in the surf. Carrie expressed her doubts about this, but Ochse assured her that nothing like what she was describing had been discovered. He suggested that it was a possibility the egg was still on the beach, or—more likely— it had slipped from her grasp when that final wave had tossed her ashore.

At the end of the interview, Carrie was exhausted, both physically and mentally. Ochse thanked her for her time, and offered his hand again. This time she shook it. All the talking had left her thirsty, but her plastic cup was long empty. Ochse assured her that he would notify the nurses and ask them to bring her some more ice.

Yawning and sore, she asked them if Abhi would get in trouble for helping her. After all, he wasn't a freelancer or a consultant, but a direct employee of Alpinus Biofutures. Smiling, Ochse gently assured her that they were debriefing him next, and while there might be some slight disciplinary action— perhaps a loss of pay or a written warning—the older man would most likely keep his job, as long as his account of the events matched her own.

The door clicked shut behind them. Carrie let her head loll to one side, and noticed that it was dark outside her window. She idly wondered what time it was as she fell asleep, waiting for the nurse to return with more ice chips.

When Carrie woke for the second time, she once again took a moment to remember where she was. After it all came back to her, Carrie's first thoughts were of Paolo and Abhi. She glanced around the hospital room, looking for a clock. One wall had a painting of a boat at sea that would have looked more at home in a cheap hotel room. Another wall held an emergency eye wash station and a fire extinguisher. A third had a plastic storage bin mounted on it, which was full of medical paperwork, and what Carrie assumed was her chart. But the room seemed to be devoid of clocks.

She heard birds tweeting softly, and turned to the window. Soft daylight filtered through the curtains. Carrie took a moment to lift up the corner of the gauze over her arm and examine her stitches. They seemed fine, although her arm was stiff and sore, and the flesh around the stitches felt taut and warm. Realizing that she wasn't hooked up to any monitors or IVs, Carrie slowly sat up and peeled the blanket back. Then she got out of bed. She shivered when her bare feet hit the cool linoleum floor. She waited a moment, making sure there were no lingering effects from the creature's neurotoxins. Then, when she felt more confident, she pulled her gown tightly around herself, shuffled over to the window, and drew back the curtains.

Dr. Barbet had mentioned that the clinic was isolated, but the full magnitude of that statement didn't hit Carrie until that moment. Rather than a medical complex with additional buildings, a parking lot, and well-manicured grounds, she found herself staring out into a thick jungle. She guessed, judging from the height, that her room was on the second or third floor of the facility. The grounds were deserted. The small, one-lane road leading to the clinic was empty, as well. She glimpsed what appeared to be a guard shack in the distance, as well as a high security fence, topped with razor wire. The sharp barbs glinted in the sunlight. Just looking at them made her shudder.

"Talk about the middle of nowhere. And what kind of clinic has fencing like that?"

Frowning, Carrie let the curtain fall back and stepped away from the window. Why had they been brought here, rather than one of the bigger hospitals or clinics? And where was here, exactly? Who were these people? She remembered Paolo's dire warnings from two days before—his paranoia that they were being followed and observed, that the Novak had been under some type of surveillance. Did that have something to do with their current whereabouts? Were Ochse and Maberry really working for Alpinus Biofutures? Maybe not. It was possible they had simply pretended to be—posing as security agents in an effort to convince Carrie to tell them what had happened. If so, then she had played right into their hands. But if they were actually working for Alpinus, that was equally confusing. Why would Alpinus Biofutures have a private clinic in Mauritius? And why was she just now learning about it? Why hadn't they taken her here after her ill-fated dive with Peter?

Peter . . . Carrie felt a sudden pang of guilt and regret. So much had happened, she had completely forgotten about him.

She began searching the hospital room, looking for clues. A check of the bathroom turned up nothing, and a search of the dresser next to her bed yielded no results either. She wondered where her personal items were—her phone and identification—and then realized that they'd been on the boat,

along with her clothes that she'd changed out of when she and
Paolo had donned their wetsuits. It had never occurred to her
to retrieve them when she and Abhi had abandoned ship. But
then again, why would it have? Both of them had been almost
overcome with hallucinations by that point. It was a miracle
she'd had the presence of mind to leave at all, let alone bring
the egg with her.

There was a cream-colored push button phone on the table
next to her bed. She picked up the receiver and tried it, but
there was no dial tone. She pressed zero and waited, but there
was only more silence. Shrugging, Carrie assumed it was one
of those interoffice systems where the user had to dial a certain code to get an outside line. Either that, or the clinic hadn't
paid their phone bill.

The room had a television mounted on the wall. Realizing
it was probably pointless, she decided to try it anyway. Maybe
there would be an interfacility channel that would shed some
light on where she was. Carrie grabbed the remote control from
beside the bed and clicked it on, flipping through the channels.
She found reruns of *Miami Vice, Grounded For Life,* and
Doctor Who, all dubbed in Creole, an old episode of Wheel of
Fortune dubbed in Khmer with Spanish subtitles, five infomer-
cials (two of which were also in Khmer), four cooking shows,
a soccer game, a horse race, a chess match, and three news
broadcasts, all of which were talking about the latest develop-
ments regarding the Mouth of Hell and whether or not a decision had been made regarding a nationwide evacuation. None
of this was any help. Indeed, it left Carrie feeling even more
helpless. Frustrated, she thumbed the remote, turning the television off once again.

"Shit."

Carrie was about to give up, admit defeat, and return to
bed when she suddenly became aware of voices outside her

door. She stepped closer, eavesdropping, and realized that it was Dr. Barbet and Ochse. She recognized the doctor's voice immediately, and Ochse's after a longer moment. While they were clearly doing their best to keep their voices subdued, their conversation sounded intense. Curious, she tiptoed to the door, pressed her ear against it, held her breath, and listened.

"—situation has not changed, unfortunately. The fact is, he's dying. Slowly, yes, but without an antidote, his fate is inevitable. I've got a lot of experience with toxins from both aquatic and terrestrial creatures in this region. The only way I know of to cure him is to retrieve a poison gland from the animal that attacked him. Once I have that, I can attempt to manufacture an antivenom. But I can't make any guarantees."

"You would do well to remember our arrangement."

"I'm not saying I won't do it or that I can't do it. I'm just saying it might not work. Remember, I still have no idea what we're dealing with. Maybe if you people were a little more forthcoming, I could be of more assistance."

"You're doing just fine, Dr. Barbet."

"Well, you'll pardon me if I don't see it that way. One of my patients is dying. What do you expect me to do?"

"We expect you to continue observing him and recording the scientific data."

"You don't care about his status?"

"Obviously, we'd prefer he live. We're not monsters, doctor. But there are bigger issues at stake here than the fate of one person."

Paolo, Carrie realized. *They're talking about Paolo. And that son of a bitch Ochse is treating him like he's some fucking statistic.*

"I see," Barbet continued. "And there's no way you could provide me with a poison gland from this . . . whatever it is that attacked him?"

"We've brought in a team to further engage the creature, but their scientific expertise is somewhat lacking. Our employer—your employer—didn't hire them to perform surgery."

"What sort of team?"

"A private security force, of sorts."

"Mercenaries?"

"Obtaining a poison gland isn't going to be their mission priority. I doubt they'd even know how to go about it."

"May I ask what their mission priority is?"

"You may not, Doctor. That's on a need-to-know basis. Is there any other way to treat the patient? Something you might have overlooked?"

"What about the egg?" Barbet asked. "The one Anderson brought to shore with her? When they first arrived, we performed an ultrasound on it. I'm no expert on this creature, simply because we still don't know what it is, but developmentally, the fetus seemed far enough along to have at least the beginning of a rudimentary poison gland. Perhaps we could begin with that?"

"I don't know what you're referring to, Dr. Barbet. There are no records of Anderson bringing an egg ashore."

"What? What are you talking about? You were there when we brought them in. The egg is down in the lab right now. You signed for it!"

"There is no egg, Dr. Barbet. Perhaps you're mistaken."

"I'm not mistaken! I performed the ultrasound myself. I'll take you down to the lab and show it to you right now. We've got it in storage."

"The egg doesn't exist. A search of your lab will confirm that, I think."

"You took it? Why?"

"I said no such thing."

Having heard enough, Carrie flung the door open hard enough that it slammed into the wall. She burst into the hall. Barbet, Ochse, Maberry, and another man, whose laminated identification badge indicated was another Alpinus security employee named Mariotte, all turned to look at her. Their expressions were startled, except for Maberry, who merely arched an eyebrow.

"This is such fucking bullshit," she exclaimed. "I can't believe what I'm hearing!"

"Ah," Ochse said, "Miss Anderson. I'm glad to see you're feeling better."

"Go fuck yourself, asshole."

Flinching, Ochse offered her a tight-lipped smile. "Hmmm. There's really no need for that kind of language. I just—"

"Save it. You're lying. You lied to me yesterday when I brought up the egg, and you're lying now."

Ochse held up his hands in mock surrender. "I assure you, Carrie, I'm not—"

"I said can it, asshole." She turned to Barbet. "Doctor, did you really perform an ultrasound on the egg?"

Shifting from foot to foot, the doctor glanced back and forth between Carrie and the Alpinus officials. He opened his mouth to speak, then closed it. With a sigh, he turned his gaze to the floor.

"Listen, lady," Mariotte said. He had the hoarse rasp of a longtime smoker, and glared at her through a pair of glasses that were smudged with fingerprints. "Before you say another word, you might want to pause for a minute, remember just what your situation is."

"What's that supposed to mean?" Carrie bristled. "Is that supposed to be some sort of threat?"

"It means—"

Ochse held up a hand, silencing him.

"Go outside," he commanded, his voice low. "Take a break. I'll handle this."

"But . . ."

"I said go, Mariotte. Smoke a cigarette. I know you're dying for one. Hell, smoke two of them."

"Actually," Barbet said, his tone sheepish, "there's no smoking in this facility."

"Oh yeah?" Mariotte took a step toward the doctor. "Who's gonna stop me?"

"Mariotte!" Ochse's ears turned red. "Go. Now."

Scowling, Mariotte stalked off down the hall. His footsteps echoed loudly on the tiles. Unlike the other agents, his suit was ill-fitting and wrinkled. The fabric seemed to cling to his body in all the wrong angles. Carrie fought to regain her composure as they watched him exit through a set of double doors at the end of the corridor. She realized that her hands were balled into fists at her sides. Her fingernails had dug into the flesh of her palms.

The color slowly faded from Ochse's ears after Mariotte was gone. The agent took a deep breath, exhaled, and opened his mouth to speak. Before he could, however, the door to another hospital room opened, and a familiar face stepped out into the hallway.

"Abhi," Carrie exclaimed. "Are you okay?"

"I'm fine," he grumbled. "Or at least I was until all this shouting started out here. The doctor told me to rest up. How am I supposed to do that with everyone yelling right outside my door? What's going on?"

"They're lying about the egg," Carrie told him.

"The egg?"

"The one we brought ashore with us. The one the creature was after. They're letting Paolo die to keep the egg whole."

"Why would they do that?"

"Who knows?" Carrie shook her head in frustration. "Who knows what reason?"

Abhi frowned. "They told me they never retrieved the egg."

"We didn't," Ochse insisted. "Now, I don't know what you thought you heard the doctor say, Miss Anderson, but you're obviously mistaken. I'm sorry if that upsets you, or if you think I'm lying, but I swear to you, it's the truth."

"Bullshit," Carrie mumbled.

"No," Ochse countered, "it's not. I assure you, there is no egg. It's understandable that you're confused. That you misheard things. You've been through a traumatic situation. Indeed, in the last week, you've been hospitalized twice. I think we all understand that."

Carrie stepped toward him, her eyes blazing with vehemence. "I know what I heard. And if I don't get some goddamn answers right now, the press will know what I heard, too."

Maberry stirred, his face still an expressionless slate, but his body was a tense mass of coiled muscle. Carrie glanced at him in disgust. He met her gaze with his creepy, emotionless eyes. Repressing a shudder, Carrie glanced at Abhi and winked in gratitude. Then she saw that he'd forgotten to tie his hospital robe in the back.

"Your butt is showing."

"Oh," Abhi turned red. "Sorry!"

Carrie returned her attention to Ochse.

"I know what I heard," she repeated, keeping her voice calm and collected. "Dr. Barbet said he examined the egg. He said there was a fetus inside. He also said it might be possible to extract a poison gland from the fetus."

Ochse shrugged. "Well, he's not saying that now. Are you, Dr. Barbet?"

Barbet kept his eyes on the floor, and didn't reply.

"We never received an egg." Ochse's tone was placating.

"But we are just as concerned about Paolo as you are, Carrie. We're concerned about all of you. Alpinus Biofutures values all of their team members."

Carrie snorted with contempt. "That's not what you said earlier."

Ochse held up his hands in surrender. "Will I jeopardize the lives of others strictly to save his? No, I will not. But I also see that you are adamant about this, and I respect your concern for your friend. We don't have this egg, but perhaps there is another way to help Paolo—a way to obtain this poison gland."

"I'm listening."

"We've hired another vessel and a team to go back out to the collapse. If you wish, you are welcome to accompany them, provided Dr. Barbet thinks you're well enough to be released from the clinic. He gives the okay and I'll clear you for travel. You can accompany the team and extract a gland from the creature, if you're able, and as long as it doesn't interfere with the team's main objective. Fair enough?"

Enraged, but seeing no way beyond the agent's stonewall, Carrie nodded in agreement.

"I'm going, too," Abhi said.

Ochse shook his head. "I'm afraid—"

"You will be," Abhi interrupted, "if you try to stop me. I go where Carrie goes. After all, I too can be in touch with chatty journalists."

Despite her anger, Carrie felt a deep sense of appreciation and gratitude well up inside of her for the older man. She repressed a smile, and blinked sudden tears from her eyes.

Then she realized that his robe was hanging open again.

"When is your team leaving?" she asked Ochse.

"They raise anchor tonight."

"That's good," Dr. Barbet said. "Given Paolo's condition,

there's no time to waste. The sooner you get a poison gland, the quicker I can attempt to manufacture an antivenom."

"Okay." Carrie nodded. "Then what are we waiting for? Get us on that boat."

TEN

As the sun slowly set, agents Maberry and Mariotte drove Carrie and Abhi to the port in a black, nondescript sport utility vehicle. Mariotte twitched for most of the ride, obviously in the throes of nicotine withdrawal, and, Carrie suspected, still angry about being reprimanded by Ochse in front of her. Maberry was his laconic, taciturn self. As a result, there was very little conversation during the drive.

Mariotte kept changing the radio stations, apparently dissatisfied with the various programs being offered. Most of the broadcasts were dominated with the latest news regarding the collapse and speculation on whether or not an island-wide evacuation would take place. Apparently, the government and the United Nations had finally drafted a proposal, outlining the logistics of such a massive endeavor.

While it didn't make up for the loss of their personal items, representatives from Alpinus had given Carrie and Abhi clothes to wear, as well as equipping Carrie with another wetsuit and diving mask, in case she needed them on this expedition. The clinic had also fed them well before their departure.

The cafeteria offerings had included seafood, chicken, pasta, and a fresh fruit and salad bar. Still unsure if she'd be diving or not, Carrie had limited her intake and focused on staying hydrated. Now, her stomach growled in complaint. Abhi, however, burped contentedly.

She stared out the window and wondered what her sister was doing right now, back home. She must be worried; they hadn't gone this long without touching base in years. Then her thoughts returned to Paolo. She made a point of focusing her worries on him, so that she wouldn't have to think about or examine the things she'd seen and heard while hallucinating. She had demanded to see him again, before they departed. He had still been pretty out of it, so there had been no opportunity for them to discuss anything, or the fact that she was risking her life to get this poison gland, but that hadn't mattered. For her, it was enough just to see him.

Carrie also kept looking for landmarks or street names that she recognized, but she saw nothing familiar. It had been her hope that once she and Abhi were outside the facility, she might be able to determine the mysterious clinic's location. Unfortunately, she had no such luck. Maberry almost exclusively stuck to remote, rural areas. It occurred to Carrie that perhaps this particular route had been chosen for that reason— to keep her and Abhi from learning more regarding their whereabouts.

It was almost dark by the time they reached the harbor. All that remained of the sun was just a dim red smear on the horizon. Carrie glanced around at the harbor, trying to figure out where they were, but again, she saw nothing familiar.

Abhi fidgeted nervously in the backseat.

"What's on your mind?" Carrie asked, trying to keep her voice low.

He glanced at the agents in the front seat and then shrugged.

"You suspected that the monster was afraid of sunlight."

"It's not a monster, Abhi. It's just a lifeform we haven't identified yet."

"Perhaps that is so. But whatever it is, it does not like the light. Correct?"

"That's my best guess, yes. It didn't surface to attack us until Paolo took the egg. And even then, it kept most of its bulk beneath the water."

"Well, now the sun has gone down, and we're going back out there. Probably not our wisest choice. Don't you agree?"

"It's not a choice at all," Carrie replied. "But you heard what the doctor said. Every minute we waste is one less minute Paolo has left."

"I'm not disagreeing with you," Abhi said. "I just wish the rest of my paint thinner hadn't gone down with the boat. I could do with a drink right now. Not to mention my father's pipe. That was irreplaceable, and it was on the boat, as well. I had always hoped to pass it on to my son, some day. Of course, in order to do that, I would have to have children first."

"I'm sorry." Carrie took his hand and gave it a squeeze. "When this is over, you can make all the hooch you want. And you can make all the kids you want, too. And I'll even buy you a new pipe."

"And a new Sudoku book? Because I never finished my other one."

Carrie laughed. "And a new Sudoku book."

"And don't forget, you still owe me money for the last boat."

"But the creature trashed it."

Abhi grinned. "That doesn't excuse your debt."

"You're a conniving old fart."

"Thank you, Carrie. I'm fond of you, too."

"Hate to break up your touching moment," Mariotte growled, "but we're here."

The vehicle slowed to a stop alongside a ship that looked so decrepit, Carrie's first thought was that it must be decommissioned. That notion was squashed when she saw all the activity onboard the vessel. She judged that it was approximately 160 feet long, with a beam of maybe twenty-five feet. The hull was a patchwork of different colors of paint, all various shades of gray or black, interspersed with clinging barnacles and cancerous-looking splotches of rust.

"Wait here," Mariotte said. "This isn't the type of place you want to go wandering off in. Especially after dark."

"I'm a big girl," Carrie said. "I can take care of myself."

Shaking his head, Mariotte got out of the SUV. A moment later, Maberry joined him. The two men hurried toward the ship.

"I'm a big girl, too," Abhi called.

Neither agent turned around.

"So," Abhi said, "what now?"

"They didn't lock us in," Carrie observed. "I don't know about you, but I'm tired of sitting."

"That's a good idea. My ass hurts."

Carrie opened her door slightly. When the two agents didn't turn around or react, she pushed it out the rest of the way.

A group of clouds passed over the moon, and the already shadowy pier grew even darker.

"Jesus," Carrie muttered to Abhi as they exited the vehicle and stretched. "And I thought that boat you got for us was bad."

Abhi nodded. "I'm not sure I've mentioned it lately, but I still haven't been reimbursed for that boat."

"You have mentioned it lately." Carrie snickered. "Two minutes ago, in fact."

He shrugged. "Dementia is common in men my age. Why else would I have agreed to go back out there with you tonight?"

"Because you love me."

Abhi chuckled. "Have I mentioned that you owe me money for the boat?"

"Stop it, Abhi! You're going to give me a complex." Carrie gave him a playful punch on the shoulder. "I'll add it to the list, okay? Sudoku book, a new pipe, and money for the boat. Maybe you can buy this thing. Although, I'm not sure you'd want to. It looks ancient."

"Aye," Abhi agreed, surveying the vessel. "She's old, for sure. I'd guess she was built in the fifties, maybe. Probably steam-driven at one point, but she's been retrofitted for diesel now. And that's not the only modern enhancement. See all those small arms mounted at various spots? And that big gun there is a Bofors."

"A Bofors?"

Abhi nodded. "Bofors forty millimeter auto-cannon. It's an anti-aircraft gun. First became popular back during World War II, but they're so reliable that they're still used today. That things got a range of over twelve thousand meters and can fire, if I remember correctly, three hundred thirty rounds per minute."

"Should I be impressed?" Carrie asked.

"I certainly am," Abhi replied. "Whoever the owner is, they're not here to fuck around. I guarantee you this ship has seen some combat more than once. It's a good guess the crew has, too. She's not a research vessel. It's a boat made for fighting. And notice something else?"

"What's that?"

"She's got no markings. No designation. She's flying a Japanese flag, but there's no number or classification on her hull. Not even a name."

Carrie frowned in confusion. "So what does that mean?"

"That she's not loved." Abhi sounded sad. "That she's just being used. She's just another weapon. Another tool."

Mariotte and Maberry approached the rusting hulk as a Japanese man descended the accommodation ladder clinging to the ship's side. He was short, stout, and somewhere in his sixties, Carrie judged. His greasy black hair was streaked with white, as was the goatee around his mouth and chin. A horrific, wide scar ran from the right side of his forehead to the lower left of his jaw, zigzagging at various junctures. The flesh inside the ragged mark was a sickly shade of pink. The contrast against his darker features was jarring. The scar was made worse by his general demeanor. His expression was like curdled milk.

The scarred man huddled with the agents at the bottom of the ladder. Although Carrie couldn't hear what was being said between them, it was easy to tell from his body language and his tone that he wasn't pleased about the inclusion of Abhi and herself. They argued for a few minutes, and then the man's demeanor suddenly changed. He seemed satisfied, if not happy. Turning, Mariotte motioned for Carrie and Abhi to approach. They did so with some trepidation.

"I don't like this," Abhi whispered.

"Too late to back out now," Carrie replied.

"This is Katashi Takenaka," Mariotte said, introducing the Japanese man. "He's the captain of this vessel, and in charge of this expedition. I've informed him of Miss Anderson's objective, and he is to give you his full cooperation while at sea, provided it doesn't interfere with his mission."

Well, Carrie thought, *now we know why he looked so pissed off.*

She stuck out her hand. "It's a pleasure to meet you, Captain Takenaka. This is my assistant, Abhi."

"Assistant?" Abhi frowned.

Carrie ignored him. "I'm sorry that we're meeting under these circumstances. I'm sure it must be an inconvenience for you, but we'll do our best to stay out of your way, and not trouble you or your crew any further."

Takenaka nodded curtly, his expression dour, but did not shake Carrie's hand. Instead, he turned his head, snorted, and then spat a wad of mucus into the water.

"Yes," he said. His English was almost flawless, if somewhat clipped, but his voice sounded like car tires crunching on gravel. "It is an inconvenience. My crew and I are not babysitters. But now I am being paid more money than was originally contracted, just for taking you both aboard, so . . . welcome aboard."

He swept his hand toward the ship, and smiled. It looked more like a grimace. Carrie had the impression that this was a man who was unaccustomed to displaying joy or happiness or good cheer. She noticed a long tattoo running along the inside of his left forearm—a series of Japanese letters. She had no idea what the translation was, but the tattoo had obviously been there for some time, judging by how faded the black ink had become. Another old scar bisected the tattoo's middle.

"You'll be the only vessel out there tonight," Mariotte informed them. "Our superiors made an arrangement with both the Mauritian government and the international research flotilla. No marine traffic is allowed in these waters until dawn."

"What about air traffic?" Takenaka asked.

"There's also a no-fly zone in effect until dawn, as well,"

Mariotte said. "Just make sure the job is completed before then."

"Make sure you have my money," Takenaka replied.

"You'll be paid the second half upon completion of the mission, Captain."

"I'd better be."

The two security agents didn't wish them luck or say goodbye. They simply returned to their vehicle and drove away. As their taillights faded into the darkness, Carrie and Abhi followed Takenaka up the ladder. When they reached the deck, a seaman approached the captain and said something in Japanese. While the two spoke amongst themselves, Carrie and Abhi observed the ship, taking it all in. The crew was a ragged, swarthy bunch composed of different nationalities and races. They seemed to emit a collective atmosphere of danger. She saw no other woman onboard. Despite the disconcerting vibe the sailors gave off, they obviously knew their craft, and went about preparing to get underway with a skill and efficiency that left her impressed.

"What do you think?" Abhi whispered.

She leaned close to his ear. "I feel like we just walked into the Mos Eisley spaceport."

Nodding sagely, Abhi tried to do an impression of Sir Alec Guinness. "We must be careful."

"You'll be dead," Takenaka barked, startling them. Then he attempted another smile, and failed once again. "Yes, I know Star Wars, too. And yes, it applies to these men. Most of them have worked for me for years. I know them all too well. They are hard men. But no harm will come to you. This is business and we are on the job."

"Do you get a lot of jobs like this?" Abhi asked.

Takenaka shrugged. "Until Alpinus Biofutures hired us, we were fighting pirates off the coast of Somalia. Protecting merchant vessels, mostly, for various companies and magnates. Before that, we fought sex-slave traders off the coast of Yemen. Before that, a militia in Sudan, and we also provided security after the tsunami back in 2004. But Alpinus offered us more money than any of these."

"I see," Carrie replied. "And what, exactly, did they hire you to do, Captain?"

"Ah, well. I cannot say. I signed a non-disclosure agreement. You understand? Legally binding and all that. I don't want to jeopardize my payday."

"I won't tell anyone."

"Neither will I. That's the point of a non-disclosure agreement. Things were much easier before we had those. I would like to find the lawyer who invented them and gut him like a fish."

Carrie ignored this, refusing to be dissuaded from her questions. "Were you paid to capture the creature?"

Takenaka's eyes shifted. "Not capture. No."

"To kill it then? They are paying you to do that?"

"As I said, I am forbidden to discuss the details of the arrangement. But we are not being paid to capture it."

"So you are being paid to kill it," Abhi said.

Something that could have been either a smile or a grimace crossed Takenaka's face. The scar on his face seemed to grow larger.

Carrie rubbed her forehead. "But why would Alpinus Biofutures want this thing dead? The United Nations already revoked their contract. It doesn't add up."

Takenaka's expression turned sly. "The only thing I care about adding up is the money. And now, we get a nice bonus for helping you. You need a poison gland from this fish, yes?"

Carrie nodded. "Yes. Although I don't know that fish is the right term, exactly."

"Does it need to be alive when you take this gland?"

"No."

"Then we can help you. There is no one better qualified."

Carrie realized that, despite his expression and gruff way of speaking, Takenaka was trying to put them at ease. She also realized that he had just confirmed, at least indirectly, what she and Abhi had guessed, and in a way that didn't violate the terms of his non-disclosure agreement. She was impressed.

"What exactly are your qualifications, Captain?"

"I am a mercenary. These days, I know the term is . . . how do you say it? Private security professional? I never liked that term. It was invented by the same men who invented non-disclosure agreements, I think. I fight for money."

"But how does being a soldier of fortune qualify you for this particular mission?"

His expression turned sour again. "Before I became this, I was a whaler for many years."

"A whale hunter? Isn't that illegal now?"

"It is now, except for scientific purposes. It was not when my father did it. And not when I started. I grew up in Osabe. Always, the people there were poor, except for the fishermen, and especially the whalers. So, I became a whaler, like my father. When they imposed the moratorium on commercial whaling in 1986, there was no more money to be made. Now, in Osabe, the only jobs are pouring concrete for the seawall they are building to keep out the tsunamis. There is no more whaling. No more fishing of any kind. So, I became a mercenary instead. It is better wages. Plus, my children do not hate me if I kill a pirate or a sex trafficker, like they do if I slaughter a whale. They want to be friends with the whales. I blame cartoons."

Carrie nodded again, unsure of how to respond. Abhi made a point of watching the crew bustle about.

"You may go up to the bridge," Takenaka told them. "Make yourselves comfortable. I must see to preparations before we raise anchor and get underway. Then, we will find your fish."

He walked away, laughing humorlessly. They watched him go. Carrie shook her head.

"He's . . . something."

"Aye," Abhi agreed. "He is something alright. Let's just hope he's right about that thing."

"What do you mean?"

"That we find it before it finds us."

There was a sudden commotion overhead. Carrie and Abhi both glanced up at the sky, in time to see a massive flock of seabirds, all heading inland and traveling fast. The noise they made was deafening. Even the mercenaries were momentarily distracted, all staring skyward as the squawking mass swooped by, blocking out the fading sunlight. Dollops of white excrement splattered the ship and the dock as they passed. A few unlucky sailors were also targeted.

"My God," Abhi gasped. "I've never seen so many birds at once. Not in all my years at sea. What could they be doing?"

"I don't know," Carrie admitted. "It's not a migration pattern. It's almost as if they're fleeing something."

Abhi stared at her, and then back up at the birds.

"I need a drink," he murmured as the flock was swallowed up by the dark.

They were barely two and a half miles out of port when the trouble started. The moon was just a dim sliver in the sky, and they sailed in blackness—the surrounding sea a rhythmically churning mass of shadows that seemed to envelop the ship. Takenaka had posted watchmen along the upper deck, and each was armed with a variety of weapons, ranging from antique whaling harpoons to fully automatic AR-15s and

Chinese-made SKS's. All of the sailors seemed to speak English, or at least enough of it to get by, which made sense, given the number of nationalities onboard the vessel. They most likely needed to rely on one common language to effectively communicate. But during the time it had taken to get underway, she'd heard snatches of Portuguese, Creole, Hindi, Russian, Pashtun, Somali, Vietnamese, French, and various accents ranging from Australian to Welsh to America's Deep South. They truly were an international crew.

Carrie and Abhi occupied the bridge, along with the captain and a half-dozen sailors, watching pensively as the vessel slipped through the darkness.

"I was told this fish can interfere with electronic equipment?" Takenaka asked.

"Yes," Carrie confirmed. "Electronics and living things, both. I'm not sure how, although I suspect it emits some sort of neurotoxins. The effect is also based on the target's proximity. The closer the person or electronics are to the web of neurotoxins, the better the chances of a disruption."

"We are up high enough," the captain proclaimed. "This is no little boat. Our equipment is beyond this web."

"I hope so," Abhi agreed.

Takenaka clapped him on the back. "We are, little man. Come, let me show you."

He guided Abhi over to a bank of equipment. Carrie suppressed a giggle as Abhi glanced over his shoulder and mouthed "little man" to her. He had at least three-inches height on the rumpled ex-whaler. She followed after them, still grinning. They stopped behind a sailor who was hunched over the sonar.

"You see?" Takenaka gestured. "Everything is working fine."

"Captain?" The sailor did not look up from the sonar, but his voice was tense. "I've got something."

"What is it?"

"I . . . I'm not sure."

Scowling, Takenaka leaned over the sonar operator and glowered at the screen. The backlight seemed to illuminate the scar on his face. Abhi and Carrie stepped closer, standing on tiptoe to catch a glimpse. When Carrie finally did, her breath caught in her throat.

Two massive shapes were hurtling toward the ship from the direction of the collapse. She couldn't judge their speed, but it was clear they were closing quickly.

"A school of fish, maybe?" the sailor suggested.

Without looking away from the screen, Takenaka raised his hand as if to strike the younger man. The sonar operator flinched, and backed farther away. Then, the captain turned to Carrie.

"A school of fish, alright. Two of them. Two big fishies. I thought there was only one?"

"I did, too," Carrie murmured.

"Well, you were wrong. This is unfortunate. If I had known there were two, I would have demanded more money."

Muttering in Japanese, Takenaka returned to the helm and grabbed a handset. He keyed the mic, and a squeal of electronic feedback echoed across the ship.

"Attention all hands, attention all hands. This is the captain speaking. General quarters, general quarters. This is not a drill. We have multiple targets approaching. All hands man your battle stations, on the double. I repeat, muster with weapons at your stations. Let's go to work. That is all."

The ship erupted with activity as hatches slammed open with metallic clangs and crewmen emerged from the decks below, hurrying to various positions on the main deck. Carrie and Abhi drew aside as the captain stalked the bridge, barking out orders to the other sailors.

"I don't understand," Abhi whispered. "The only time it left the trench before was when we had the egg. We're nowhere near the trench yet. And now there are two of these things?"

"Apparently," Carrie replied. "There's a mommy and a daddy."

"And we kidnapped their baby. That's just wonderful."

Carrie nodded, feeling a surprising sense of remorse.

"But why would they stray so far from the collapse?" Abhi asked.

"They've learned some things about us. If I had to guess, I'd say the creature—creatures—have no intention of letting any boats back into their turf. They're defending their territory. Their hunting ground and nest. They see us as just another predator. A boat came into their territory and stole one of their offspring. Now, a second boat is approaching. They don't intend to let that happen again."

"Shit . . ."

"Exactly," Carrie agreed. "We're going to have to warn the authorities. They need to shut down all traffic in these waters—commercial and private. And we'll have to make certain the research flotilla doesn't come anywhere near here until this situation is fully resolved."

Abhi's eyes widened in apprehension. "If these things are bringing the fight to us—if they've figured that out—then what else have they learned about us?"

"I think we're about to find out."

"Okay, men," Takenaka said over the intercom. "It's time to earn your pay. Let's do this like professionals, collect our money, and then we can all go home and spend it."

A chorus of cheers went up across the outer decks of the ship. Sailors raised boathooks, harpoons, and rifles in the air, cheering.

"Captain!" The sonar operator sounded frightened. "They're almost on us."

"Location?"

"One portside and the other aft."

"Distance?"

"Portside, three hundred meters and closing. Aft, four hundred meters . . . no, wait . . . three fifty. Jesus, these things are fast!"

Grinning, Takenaka hung up the microphone and turned to Abhi and Carrie.

"You will both stay here on the bridge, where you are safe. I can't be responsible for you if you venture outside. Yes?"

Abhi nodded. "Sounds good to me!"

"Two hundred meters," the sonar operator called. "One hundred fifty! Get ready!"

"Anderson?" Takenaka turned to Carrie.

Carrie shrugged. "You're the captain."

The ex-whaler's grin grew broader. "No, I am the hunter."

He turned and strutted off the deck, slamming the hatch shut behind him.

Sighing, Abhi leaned against the bulkhead. "I'll bet he's fun at parties."

Things escalated quickly as the pair of creatures attacked the large vessel in perfect unison. Carrie and Abhi watched from the bridge as the massive shapes emerged from the ocean, water streaming down their forms. Without the sun as a deterrent, they were much less cautionary than before. Despite this, Carrie still couldn't get a clear look at their structure because of the pervasive darkness. She caught only glimpses as spotlights flashed over their bulk. Pressed up to the window, she pushed her fist against the glass in frustration.

Despite their proximity, the ship's electronics still seemed to be functioning normally. The same could not be said of the mercenary crew. While only minutes earlier they had been cheering with bravado, now, most of them stood motionless, gaping in horror as the sea vomited up these monstrosities, the likes of which none had ever seen before. These men were used to fighting other men, Carrie realized. The foes they now faced were something else entirely.

Dozens of black-and-brown tentacles burst from the water. They varied in size, from the circumference of a sewer pipe to no thicker than an extension cord. As the swiveling spotlights trailed over them, Carrie noticed that some of the tentacles were lined with suckers, while others were not. As the night exploded with rifle fire and muzzle flashes, the flailing appendages whipped across the main deck, seizing anything they came in contact with. One curled around the antenna mast, and with a tremendous yank, snapped it off. Debris plummeted to the deck, sending sailors scrambling out of the way. Metal barrels, gear lockers, and even a mop were snatched up by the questing tendrils and yanked into the black ocean.

Abhi's hand fell on her shoulder, clutching.

"Oh my God," he moaned.

Carrie followed his terrified gaze and gasped. A helpless mercenary struggled and kicked, hovering ten feet off the deck, caught in the grip of a thrashing tentacle. Shrieking, he punched it ineffectually as it hauled him overboard.

The ship lurched suddenly, slamming Carrie and Abhi against the glass. For one terrifying moment, Carrie was certain that the window would break, spilling them both onto the deck below, but the glass held. Abhi screamed, but his face was still smooshed against the window, and the sound was just a muffled wheeze. When she tried to regain her balance and right herself, Carrie found that she couldn't. The boat's entire aft end was sticking up out of the water, and slowly rising into the air. When she looked forward, she saw why.

One of the creatures had heaved its amorphous, streaming bulk over the bow of the ship and was slowly, laboriously crawling on board. The crew was in panicked disarray. Most tried to flee, but many of them fell as the ship tilted higher, sliding down the wet deck toward the creature. Something that resembled a giant crab claw darted forward and seized the closest victim, gripping him around the waist. The soldier of fortune fired his weapon into the appendage, but the creature didn't relent. Seconds later, the black pincers squeezed, their serrated edges slicing through flesh and cracking bones. It waved the helpless mercenary back and forth in the air, and then his body split in half. His legs plummeted into the churning sea, while his upper torso splattered onto the still-sloping deck, splashing innards and blood across his hapless comrades. Horrifically, Carrie realized that the sailor was still alive, despite missing his lower torso. He dropped his weapon and tried to crawl up the deck, his face frozen with anguish and shock, as his organs spilled from him and slipped away. Then he lay still.

Another sailor had braced himself around a pole, using it to keep himself balanced. He fired an automatic rifle into the creature's bulk, spraying indiscriminately. Empty brass shell casings flew from the gun and fell at his feet, rolling forward on the sloping deck. Part of the creature seemed to flow toward the determined mercenary. A spindly, pointed leg, much like the one that had stabbed Carrie when she'd fled with the egg, hovered above the gunman. He kept firing as the javelin-like appendage slammed downward, spearing him through the top of his head. His body jittered and the weapon slipped from his hands. The leg withdrew. The man remained standing, even as his brains leaked out of his gaping mouth.

"That thing is going to capsize us if they don't do something!" Abhi pushed himself back from the window.

"That big gun," Carrie said. "What did you call it?"

Abhi blinked, momentarily confused. "The Bofors?"

"Yeah, that's it. Why don't they use that?"

"The range is all wrong. Those are for targets at a distance. Fighting pirate vessels and such. These things are way too close. Even if they could hit them where they are, the blast would sink the ship."

"We're going to sink anyway," Carrie muttered.

"No," Abhi said, feigning cheerfulness. "I'm sure we'll be dead long before the boat sinks into the trench."

Out in the darkness, Carrie caught a glimpse of a massive beak, and three baleful eyes the size of manhole covers. Despite her overwhelming terror, she paused to consider the beast's mystifying biological origins. It was seemingly unlike anything on record, either living or extinct—a bizarre, distorted amalgam of various sea creatures, all of which had grown to hellish proportions.

"That's not the same one," she murmured. "The one that attacked Paolo and I was smaller than this."

"So is this Mommy or Daddy?" Abhi asked, trembling.

"I don't think it matters."

Behind them, there were numerous crashes and clangs as gear and equipment that hadn't been properly tied down or stowed fell to the floor. A sailor cried out in pain. Several others cursed in a variety of languages. Alarms rang on the bridge, and a claxon sounded throughout the ship, nearly lost beneath the rifle reports and screams of panicked seamen.

Abhi teetered, pin-wheeling his arms to keep his balance. His eyes were wide and his face was lathered in sweat. Worse, his complexion reminded Carrie of wet cheesecloth. She worried that he was having a heart attack. She grabbed his shirt with one fist. The cloth was damp, and his deodorant had failed.

"Are you okay?"

Swallowing, Abhi nodded.

"Are you sure?"

"I'll be fine, Carrie. I just have some pain . . . in my chest. But it's not a heart attack. I've . . . had it before. Anytime I get stressed."

Carrie smelled a whiff of smoke—sharp and acrid, indicating an electrical fire. She glanced around, looking for the source, but its location was undetermined. Then, something out on the main deck caught her attention, instead. Carrie slammed her palm against the glass and pointed in disbelief, transfixed by what was occurring.

"Abhi . . . look!"

Captain Takenaka and a shirtless, heavily tattooed crewman had positioned themselves between a mounted footlocker and a bulkhead, using the former as leverage as the rear of the vessel continued to rise from the water. Despite their precarious balance, the two struggled to mount a counter-attack against the amorphous, multi-limbed monstrosity. The seaman was armed with a shotgun. The old whaler hefted some sort of rifle that Carrie couldn't identify at first.

A swarm of tentacles wriggled toward them. The bare-chested sailor lowered the shotgun and fired into the midst of the cluster, reducing the appendages to a shower of red-and-pink mist. Fleshy pulp splattered all over the bulkhead, and dripped from his and Takenaka's faces. Neither man seemed to notice. The sailor pumped the weapon's slide and fired again as another, larger tentacle snaked toward them. The appendage retreated.

Beyond them, in the darkness, the beast's form shifted. Water and foam rushed over the bow, swamping the boat.

Carrie even noticed a few small fish flopping about the deck, suffocating on oxygen. The monster clambered forth, heaving more of its body out of the sea. A deep, sonorous groan rocked the ship, and the bulkheads shuddered. All around her, Carrie saw mercenaries bracing themselves any way that they could, in an effort to remain upright. The tattooed sailor next to Takenaka dropped his weapon as he lost his balance. Screaming, he clawed frantically at the deck as he slid forward. Then, a segmented, pincer-like leg slammed down, spearing him through the chest. It withdrew, taking the still-squirming seaman with it.

The captain seemed oblivious to all of this. Carrie watched as he mounted what looked like a harpoon into the barrel of his rifle. Then, using a roll of duct tape that he tore with his teeth, Takenaka affixed what looked like a plastic jug to the missile's tip. The top of the jug had something sticking out of it that flapped in the wind. She realized it was a makeshift fuse of what appeared to be old rags.

Several things occurred to Carrie as she watched Takenaka ready his perplexing weapon. The first was to wonder what the second beast was doing. She'd been so preoccupied with the one off the bow that she'd almost forgotten about its mate. The second thought that occurred to her was that not once had either creature made a sound. Despite their clear rage, they attacked in total silence.

The ship rolled violently, and a thunderous boom echoed from somewhere below deck. Carrie felt the tremors through her feet. Nearby, a mercenary reached for the handset, which dangled by its cord, swaying back and forth. His efforts were compounded by the fact that he needed one arm to hold on tightly to the equipment in front of him, lest he tumble into the window. Finally, after what seemed like an excruciatingly long time, he succeeded in snatching it and keyed the mic.

"Engine . . . r-room," he stammered. "T-this is the . . . bridge. Report!"

A response came over the speaker, but it was garbled. The only thing they could understand was that whomever the speaker was, they were terrified. Screams echoed in the background.

"Say again," the sailor urged. "Engine room? You're breaking up. Can you repeat?"

There was a brief squall of electronic feedback, which dissipated into static. Then that, too, faded.

"The goddamn radio's out," he shouted. "I can't reach anyone!"

"Someone on the mainland must have seen all this," Carrie said. "Heard the gunfire?"

"We're too far out," another mercenary replied. "And even if we weren't, it's too fucking dark outside. They couldn't see shit!"

Carrie was about to suggest that maybe a passing airplane might have seen their muzzle flashes, but then she remembered the last thing Agent Mariotte had told them before departing— about the temporary restriction on air traffic and nautical vessels—and her stomach sank even lower.

"And we're alone out here. All alone." Hanging her head, she thought for a minute. "Does this thing have lifeboats?"

One sailor's short, sarcastic laugh was the only response.

Another boom rumbled beneath them. Smoke was visible now, drifting through the bridge. The air stank of diesel fumes.

"Carrie," Abhi said, crawling closer. "Carrie, you need to abandon ship."

"What?"

"You need to get out of here. This thing is going down."

Carrie was bewildered. "You heard them laughing. If the

ship can't make it out of here, what chance does a lifeboat have?"

"Probably none," Abhi admitted. "But you don't need a lifeboat. You're Carrie fucking Anderson. You can swim for shore. And you can make it."

"No, I can't. Not with two of those things out there. And I'm not abandoning you."

"It's the perfect time. The creatures are distracted with the ship. They won't even notice you slipping away, especially if you dive down far enough."

"Abhi, that's insane."

"You have to," he insisted. "Somebody needs to be able to tell what happened out here. That person is you. You have to dive. And it has to be now, while there's still time. Once this thing starts to sink, it's going to suck everyone in the vicinity down with it."

She shook her head forcefully. "No, Abhi. I'm not running, and I'm not leaving you behind."

"You just left me behind yesterday, Carrie."

"That was different. That was to save your life. And Paolo's."

"I'm old," Abhi said. "I don't need my life saved. There's nothing left that I need to do."

"Oh yeah? What about Marissa?"

Abhi's expression reflected his surprise. "H-how do you know about Marissa?"

"You mentioned her when you were hallucinating. I got the idea maybe there was some unfinished business between you and her."

"It is too late for that."

"Bullshit, Abhi. It's never too late."

Abhi opened his mouth to reply, but the ship lurched again, even more violently. To their left, a sailor plunged forward, slamming against the window. The glass shattered and he fell, screaming, to the deck far below.

"Oh God," Carrie closed her eyes and held on tightly as the deck continued to rise. Her stomach rolled. "Oh God, oh shit, oh God, oh . . ."

"The captain!" One of the sailors shouted, his eyes manic. "Look, all of you! It's the captain!"

Carrie turned in time to see Takenaka take aim at the beast and fire. The harpoon soared through the air, trailing flame in an arc as the fuse burned. Then, the missile struck the side of the blackish-brown hulk, and there was a searing explosion as the creature was instantly engulfed in fire. Flaming body parts rained down—splintered claws, severed tentacles, broken fragments of shell, and seared scales. The force of the explosion knocked the fiery monstrosity backward. It plunged back into the ocean, sinking beneath the churning waves. Dropping his weapon, Takenaka wrapped his arms and legs around a pole and hugged it tight, eyes closed.

The ship seemed to hang suspended in the air for a moment, and then—

"Hang on," Carrie bellowed. "Hang on, Abhi!"

ELEVEN

Gripping the rail, Abhi threw up over the side again while Captain Takenaka stood on the gore-stained deck, surrounded by spilled blood and slashed flesh and pulped innards and brass shell casings, laughing heartily.

"I'm really starting," Abhi gasped between retches, "to dislike that man."

Carrie patted Abhi's back and didn't respond. Her feelings regarding the ex-whale hunter were conflicted. On the one hand, he'd just committed one of the bravest, most determined acts she'd ever seen. But despite that, the callousness and arrogance he seemed to display, now that his payday was almost assured, repulsed her. He seemed to have no regard or thought for the sailors who had perished—sailors who had been a part of his crew. His taunting of Abhi, which had been playful when they disembarked, had now turned scornful and mean-spirited.

Shock, she thought. *Maybe he's in shock. Hell, we probably all are. He's coming down off an adrenaline rush. Maybe he doesn't realize he's being such an asshole.*

Abhi leaned out over the railing and vomited again. The wind blew the smell of it back to Carrie. She winced, trying to hide her disgust.

"Hey, little man," Takenaka called. "Make sure it all goes in the ocean, or I'll have you shoveling it up along with the rest of this mess."

"You're right," Carrie muttered. "He's an asshole and a bully. I hate bullies."

"That's right," Abhi croaked. "Defend my honor."

"You don't have any honor to defend, Abhi."

"Thanks. That makes me feel much better."

"Are you sure that you're okay? These chest pains have me concerned."

"I'm fine, Carrie. Honestly. Now go defend my honor and let me puke in peace."

She gave him one more reassuring pat, and then stalked across the deck toward the mercenary captain, taking care to watch her footing, as it was slick with seawater and blood.

The second creature had relented its attack in the wake of the explosion and—apparent—death of its companion. The combat and the ship's subsequent plunge had resulted in some damage to the vessel. They were now limping through the water rather than racing, but the sonar and other electronic gear was still operable in the aftermath, and there was no sign of either creature, either visually or through more technological means.

"That was some fight, eh, Anderson?" Takenaka called to Carrie as she approached.

"It was something alright," she agreed. "But it doesn't excuse you from being a jerk, Captain."

"What is . . . the word you said? A jerk?"

"It means you're an asshole."

"Ah, asshole. That word I know. I apologize if I have brought offense. I am just happy to be alive. You and your assistant should be, too."

"Not everyone was so lucky," Carrie pointed out to him. "What about your men who died?"

"What about them? It is not the first time we have lost people. In Somalia, we lost thirteen men in a single night. In Libya, six of our crew were captured by extremists. Two of them were crucified. The others were beheaded, and their bodies were used to fill in potholes in a road."

"That's horrible."

"Yes, it is. But these men know it could happen. They know the risks when they sign on with me. And the risks are one of the reasons they sign on." He paused, gesturing at the crew, all of whom were engaged in various tasks. "These men, they are not happy at home. Indeed, most of them do not have a home. No families. No wives or children. And even if they did have them, they wouldn't be satisfied with it. They long for something else. These men fought in wars. Sometimes— for some people—you can't leave that behind. It gets in your blood, and you want more. With me, they get that. They get more. And they also get paid."

"So that's really all it's about for you, Captain Takenaka? The money? Are that and the thrill the only things you care about?"

The ex-whaler studied her for a moment, glowering. His scar seemed brighter in the darkness.

"I used to care about other things. But yes, these days, it is the money. And the thrill. The thrill is nice. But mostly the money."

"Well, at least you're honest about it."

"Yes, I am honest about it. And you should not be so quick to judge. I have seen you on the television, you know? I think you care about similar things. Fame, perhaps? And with fame comes money. We are not so different, you and I."

Carrie kept her voice steady, so as not to betray the fury welling up inside of her. She was so angry that her lips, hands, and feet had begun to tingle, and her skin felt flushed.

"All I care about right now is retrieving a poison gland from one of these creatures and helping my friend. Something which you've just made more difficult by blowing up our best chance at securing one."

"Yes, well, it was attacking my ship at the time. I did not hear you complaining then."

"What was that, anyway? That bomb you made?"

Takenaka laughed. "I used a little homemade recipe my father taught me years ago. It worked on whales. It worked on your big fish."

"It worked a little too well, I'd say."

"We are still alive and the ship is still seaworthy. I'd say it worked fine. And I did not blow the fish up. Not completely. If it had been a whale? Yes. But not this thing. I only knocked some limbs off. The rest of it sank to the ocean floor. You should be able to find its carcass easily enough, if you need to. The trench is still three miles out. The current probably dragged the corpse there, rather than to shore. There is a powerful undertow here."

"I know," Carrie admitted. "I've swam in these waters before."

"Then you know I am right. Find the corpse, and you'll find your . . . what did you call it? Gland?"

Carrie dreaded the idea of a nighttime dive, especially now, when the water was filled with neurotoxin from the mortally wounded creature and the whereabouts of the other beast were still unknown. Visibility would be near zero. But the longer they delayed, the worse Paolo's prospects became. Sighing, she nodded.

"You'll need to drop anchor so I can dive. And I'm going to need the strongest underwater torches you have."

Takenaka threw back his head and laughed.

"What's so funny?" Carrie bristled.

"I said the carcass was there if you still needed it. But I do not think you will."

Carrie frowned in confusion.

"I was playing a joke on you," Takenaka explained. "I wanted to see if you would really go down there. I have to admit, I am impressed. But I am happy to say, you won't need to do anything so extreme."

"Why not?"

"Remember, Anderson, I only care about my payday, and there's still the matter of the bonus I was promised for helping you obtain what you seek. While you have been here with your friend, my men have been hard at work, making sure that will happen. Follow me."

He led her to the portside of the ship. Abhi trailed along behind them, rushing to catch up. As they walked, Carrie noticed Takenaka flexing his hands and occasionally shaking his arms at his sides, as if they'd gone numb.

"Are you working on a heart attack, Captain?"

"Eh?" He turned to her, frowning. "No. My arm is just a little numb. That's all. I think it was the recoil from my harpoon gun. It's a heavy weapon."

As they walked, Takenaka paused several times to quickly confer with members of the crew, listening to damage reports and estimates. This allowed Abhi time to catch up with them, as well. His complexion was gray, and he seemed subdued.

"Are you okay?" Carrie whispered to him.

He nodded, but she noticed that his expression was slack, and his eyes had a faraway, hollow look.

"I'll be fine," he assured her. "Stop worrying about me. I'm just tired. In the last two days I've been on two separate boats that got attacked by monsters. It leaves an old man winded."

"Well," Takenaka said, dismissing a sailor and turning back to them, "we won't be winning any races. One of our engines is blown. The communication system also seems to be down, along with a few other things. But we'll make it to shore."

"That's good," Carrie replied.

"Of course, the repairs this job cost me are going to eat up the pay I earned, so, lucky for us both we have your bonus."

Carrie's eyes went wide in surprise. "You have a poison gland?"

"Not quite, but . . ."

He motioned to the side of the ship where a group of mercenaries was raising a massive net they'd used to trawl the surface with, grabbing debris. The net bulged, full of pieces of the dead creature. Arms, legs, tentacles, and more jutted from between the netting, dripping onto the deck. When they had maneuvered it into position, the sailors released the contents, spilling assorted body parts into a great, steaming pile. The stench was horrific.

"Perhaps what you are looking for is in there?" Takenaka asked.

Carrie nodded. She had to admit to herself, however begrudgingly, that he was probably right.

"Yes," she said, "I suspect it might be."

"Good. This pleases me." He flexed his hand again, obviously still feeling some discomfort.

"Do you have a pair of work gloves?" she asked.

"No." Takenaka shook his head. "But I can have one of my crew muster a pair up for you. It might take a few minutes."

"That's okay. I'd rather get this done quickly. I can impro-
vise." She turned to a nearby mercenary. "Give me your shirt."

Grinning, the man did as ordered. A few other sailors
watched, clearly bemused, but none of them dared to comment
or joke about it. Perhaps it was the expression on her face, or
maybe they were just still shook up from the battle. If they had
made a snide comment at that moment, Carrie was fairly certain she'd have knocked the offender overboard. She stretched
the shirt out over her hands, noticing as she did that they were
still tingling. Then, using the cloth for protection, she began
sorting through the limbs, searching for what she needed.
After a few moments, she found a segment of one of the thing's
arms with barbs that looked just like the poison pod that had
been in Paolo's leg. She tugged, trying to free it from the pile,
but the cracked limb held fast, leaking noxious fluid onto the
shirt. Bracing her feet, she gritted her teeth and pulled harder.

"Here," Abhi said, taking hold alongside her. "Let me help
you, Carrie."

They started to pull again when Abhi gasped.

"What's wrong?" Carrie asked. "The smell?"

"No, not that. Look. There's a man in that pile, and he's
still alive!"

Carrie looked at where he pointed, but all she saw were the
creature's burned and battered appendages.

"I don't see anything, Abhi."

Blinking, he shook his head. "Oh . . . Oh, I . . . I must
have . . ."

Carrie glanced down at the blood on her shirt and on
Abhi's hands. More blood covered their shoes. And the deck. And
the captain's clothing. And the crew. The entire front end of the
ship had been splattered in blood and gore.

Takenaka stood with his back to the rail, watching them
disinterestedly. A group of mercenaries approached him. One

of them carried an open bottle of rum. He handed it to the captain. Smiling, Takenaka tilted his head back and took a big swig, leaving bloody fingerprint smudges on the glass bottle.

His hands, Carrie realized. *Takenaka's hands and arms were numb. He thought it was from the harpoon gun, but it wasn't. My hands are going numb, too. And his behavior since the explosion. He's not just being a dick. It's the blood. The ship is covered in neurotoxins.*

"Jesus Christ," she muttered, and clambered to her feet. "Abhi, listen to me very carefully."

"Hang on," he whispered, rolling his eyes. "El Capitán is about to say something. I'm sure we don't want to miss this."

Still leaning with his back against the rail, Takenaka raised the bottle, addressing the assembled crew members.

"Good job tonight, men! Most of you have been with me a long time, and because of that, you know we've been in some tough situations before. I don't think any of us ever expected what we saw here. I certainly didn't. But despite that, you handled yourselves well. Most of you did, at least. Sanderson, you shit your pants, judging by the stain on your rear end."

The mercenary crew erupted in laughter, except for the unfortunate Sanderson, who, Carrie noticed, had indeed soiled himself.

"Anyway," Takenaka continued with the bottle still raised, "we beat those things back into the water. We were contracted to kill one, and we killed one. Nobody said anything about a second target, so I'm not concerned that it's still out there. If our employers wish, they can pay us double and we'll come back for it. I'll meet with them in the morning. Each of you have been given your advance, so have fun when we hit port, but not too much. We may have to go back out tomorrow. I want each of you ready to muster at oh-nine hundred. In the meantime, here's to—uck"

His body stiffened, his mouth gaped, and his eyes went wide. The bottle of rum slipped from his hand and shattered on the deck, spraying the crew's boots with broken glass. Takenaka glanced down as a red splotch appeared in the center of his shirt and rapidly expanded. A second later, the tip of a barbed claw burst from his abdomen, flexing and swiveling around, sawing back and forth, making the wound wider.

Shouting, the mercenaries backed away in horror as the captain was lifted off the deck. Takenaka opened his mouth to shout, but a great stream of blood bubbled from his lips. He tried grasping the jutting appendage with his blood-slicked fingers, but to no avail. Screaming, he pounded at it with his fists. The scar on his face seemed to turn crimson for a moment. The claw flexed, and then opened, ripping Takenaka apart. Part of him fell into the ocean. The other two sections slopped onto the deck with a wet thud. His eyes seemed to stare directly at Carrie, and for a brief moment she wondered if he was still alive.

As if in answer, Takenaka's lips moved. A bubble of blood formed on them.

Carrie screamed.

Then, pandemonium consumed them all.

The mercenaries scattered in all directions. Some returned with weapons and took up defensive positions. Others fled beneath decks or ducked behind equipment, cowering and shouting in blind panic. Carrie realized that their reactions were exacerbated by the toxic effect the creature's blood seemed to be having on them. While it was diluted enough to not impact them with its full, hallucinatory and calming effects, it had altered their behavior nevertheless, as had the fear that now drove them.

The creature splashed back down into the ocean, drenching Carrie, Abhi, and the few mercenaries who had remained at their side. Takenaka's remains ran in bloody rivulets across the coarse, pitted deck. Abhi turned to run but slipped on a loop of intestines and fell, sprawling. Gritting his teeth, he sat up. Carrie noticed that he'd scraped his cheek and one of his palms, but Abhi seemed unconcerned.

Noticing that her arms were growing more numb, Carrie helped Abhi to his feet and held him by the shoulders, shaking him slightly.

"Are you with me, Abhi?"

He frowned in confusion. "I'm standing right here."

"No, I mean are you hallucinating? Are you with me?"

He nodded slowly. "I'm okay."

"Good. Do you think you can pilot this ship?"

He stuck out his chest and drew himself up to his full height. "You should know better than to ask me something like that. I can pilot anything."

"Then get up to the bridge and take the helm. Head inland, while we still can."

"It's going to be tough with only one engine left. If I push it too hard—"

"Figure out a way," Carrie interrupted.

"What about you? What are you going to do?"

She pointed at the pile of severed, burned limbs. "I still have to get that poison gland, or all of this is going to have been for nothing. Soon as I have it, I'll find you. I promise. Now go!"

Nodding, Abhi turned and ran for the ladder leading up to the bridge. He weaved back and forth, teetering a few times as the ship rolled, but managed to keep his balance.

Carrie glanced around the rocking ship, looking for a weapon or tool she could use to cut into the body part. She found a discarded screwdriver and a hacksaw within reach.

"Perfect."

She retrieved them both, noticing with distaste that the

screwdriver handle was sticky with blood, and then went to work on the appendage, cutting and prying the section with the barbs and the poison gland from the rest of the meat and shell. It was hard, disgusting work, made more difficult by the side effects of the toxin and the chaos all around her. Steam rose from the pile, seeming to glitter in the air. Carrie squeezed her eyes shut. When she opened them a second later, the sparkles were gone.

"Well, at least it's not butterflies or exploding seahorses this time."

She felt the ship roll slowly, and then settle, and knew that Abhi had reached the controls. She wondered then where the creature had gone. Judging by its smaller—but no less formidable—size, she figured it was the one she and Paolo had previously encountered. It probably wasn't big enough to swamp the boat the way the other one had attempted to do, but obviously it could reach the upper decks with its multiple appendages. But it seemed to have disappeared. All around her, the sailors appeared to be slowly coming to the same conclusion.

Several mercenaries of various nationalities approached her curiously. They were armed with an assortment of harpoons, boathooks, and edged weapons—hatchets, fire axes, and even a tarnished meat cleaver.

"What are you doing, lady?" The sailor spoke with a thick Nigerian accent.

"I'm operating." She continued prying at the leg with her screwdriver. "This thing is why we came out here."

"I thought we were hired to kill the monster," another man said.

"You were," Carrie admitted. "And you did. But this little thing right here is what they were paying you the bonus for."

"Bonus?" The first mercenary frowned. "The Captain said nothing about a bonus."

"Maybe he was going to keep it for himself," Carrie suggested, working the tip of the screwdriver beneath the gland. She saw that it was protected by a pink, leathery sheath. "But he's gone now, so I don't see why the rest of you shouldn't keep the bonus for yourselves. Right?"

She looked up at them and casually blew a lock of hair out of her eyes. The mercenaries glanced at one another. Slowly, they began to smile.

"You should come work with us," a man said, grinning. Two gold teeth glinted in his mouth. "You think like we do."

Carrie returned the smile. "Maybe I will, if this job doesn't work out."

"Do you always go around without your shirt on?"

Groaning, Carrie rolled her eyes. "See? You had to go and ruin it, didn't you?"

The engine suddenly made a grating noise that reminded Carrie of when she'd been a kid, and would roll up a sheet of paper and thrust it into the blades of the fan in her bedroom window during the summer. The ship's speed, already sluggish due to having only one operable engine, noticeably slowed.

The bridge hatch slammed open and a crewman emerged, waving his arms and shouting something. Carrie couldn't hear him from this distance, but the man was clearly agitated.

"The engine," his cry echoed. "The engine!"

She realized immediately what had happened. This new attack on the boat had taken on a different complexion, as if the creature had learned what the ship used to propel itself through the water. It was going after the remaining engine. And given their previously displayed heedlessness for injuries to themselves, she could only imagine that the creature wouldn't stop until it—or its prey—was dead.

Carrie jumped to her feet, and got the mercenary crew's attention.

"Anyone with a boathook or a harpoon, or rifle, get aft and protect that engine! The creature is trying to damage it. If you have a rifle, be careful where you aim. You don't want to do the creature's job for it. Go!"

They hesitated for a split second, and Carrie held her breath. Then, as one, they rushed off to defend the engine, following her orders without question.

"Carrie Anderson," she muttered, blowing a lock of hair from her eyes. "World-class free diver, respected oceanographer, and now captain of a mercenary pirate crew. I bet Mom would be proud."

"You think you're so smart," her mother sneered.

Carrie closed her eyes. "She's not there. She's dead."

When she opened her eyes again, the hallucination was gone.

She knelt back down, grabbed the hacksaw, and started cutting. She cringed as the sounds of the creature's attack on the engine rumbled across the ship again, but then that noise ceased, replaced by the sounds of sailors shouting, and a few gunshots.

The hacksaw blade chewed through the other side of the shell, and with a grunt, Carrie wrenched the poison gland free. Glistening strands of tissue hung from it. She sliced them away, but they stuck to the blade like spider webs. Grimacing, she dropped the tool on the deck. More gunshots rang out, followed by more screams. Carrie looked around for something to protect her prize, found an empty five-gallon bucket that had once held detergent, wrapped the gland in the sailor's bloodied shirt, and then carefully placed it in the bucket.

She saw distant lights glinting ahead of them, as Abhi piloted the boat toward shore. She couldn't be sure, but she suspected they were way off course. She saw nothing that looked familiar, and certainly not the harbor they'd departed from.

Grabbing the bucket by the handle, she began to run for the bridge. But another round of shouts from the aft end of the ship made her change course. She ran as fast as she could toward the sounds, careful not to slip as the boat rolled and rocked on the swells. She saw a cluster of mercenaries spread out along the tail, thrusting and stabbing at the ocean with their weapons. Another man stood to one side, reloading a rifle magazine. Carrie was almost upon them when a dark shape snaked up behind the man with the rifle, looming over him. The sailor didn't notice. Before she could shout a warning, the shape darted forward, and one of the creature's spear-like arms impaled him through the throat. With a tremendous flick, it tore his head from his body. His corpse plopped onto the deck. Then the arm flicked his head up into the air and out over the side of the ship.

Frenzied and enraged, the mercenaries renewed their defense, stabbing at the creature without mercy. Their desperate efforts were successful. After a moment, it sank beneath the waves, apparently giving up this mode of attack.

"Stay here," she shouted, "in case it comes back. We need to protect this engine."

"Where are you going?" one asked.

"The bridge!"

They nodded, seeming to accept her plan, and then returned their watchful attention to the churning waves.

Without pausing to consider her new, unexpected position, Carrie ran for the mid-section and charged up the ladder. The ship tilted again, nearly dislodging her. Carrie gripped the handrail tightly. The bucket smacked against her leg. When the ship righted itself again, she reached the top of the ladder. She yanked open the hatch door and stepped inside the bridge, where she found Abhi at the controls, assisted by two other crewman.

"Are we going to make it?" she asked.

He shrugged, not meeting her eyes. "We don't dare go any faster than this, but yes, I think we'll make it. Did you get what you needed?"

"Yes. Let's just hope we get it back to Paolo in time."

"I'll do my best."

Shouts echoed from below as a new commotion broke out, this time from the front of the ship. Carrie moved to the window and saw that the creature had moved to the bow. Like its mate, the thing was trying to climb aboard the ship, or at least capsize the vessel with its bulk—a task made more difficult by its lesser size. Several sailors charged forward into a fury of writhing tentacles and snapping claws, desperately trying to dislodge the beast. Carrie watched in horror as the creature slaughtered them one by one, severing arms and legs, bisecting others, or simply plucking them from the roiling deck and flinging them, shrieking, into the sea.

"How close are we to shore, Abhi?"

"About a half mile. But we're nowhere near a dock. The port is a good three miles away. All that's out there right now are rocks. I was just turning us."

"Floor it," she said, "and take us straight ahead to shore."

"Carrie, maybe you didn't hear me correctly. It's a rocky shoreline."

"I heard you. Head straight toward it. We don't have time to make the port."

Abhi blanched. "I think you must be hallucinating. You've got the creature's blood all over you, and—"

"I know exactly what I'm saying, Abhi."

As she watched, the last of the mercenaries in the ship's forward section was snatched from the deck by a large tentacle and squeezed until his midsection exploded. The man's intestines slithered through the rupture like steaming snakes.

"Carrie, even at this speed, we'll crash into the shore."

"If you don't do it, Abhi, we're never going to make it to shore."

"It's suicide," he insisted. "The chances of us surviving are slim. Some of those rocks are bigger than we are."

"Good. Aim for them."

Abhi shook his head in resignation. Then he grinned.

"It's always an adventure with you," he said. "You never do things the easy way."

"That's why you love me."

"Keep telling yourself that."

He opened the throttle and grabbed the controls, focused on staring straight ahead. His eyes widened when he saw the beast clinging to the bow. The one remaining engine whined, and a tremor ran through the deck as the vessel shuddered.

"Faster," Carrie shouted.

"It's weighing us down," Abhi told her. "And you hear that sound? That's the sound of our other engine failing. This is as fast as we go."

"How close are we?"

Abhi clenched the controls tightly. "About another three minutes. Maybe less."

Carrie turned to one of the crewmen. "Does the intercom still work?"

"No, ma'am. Are you really going to crash us?"

"Yes. What about the collision alarm? Does that work, or did the creature short it out, too?"

"I don't know," the mercenary said. "We can try it."

"Good idea," she said. "I think you might want to do that, and quick."

She glanced back out the window as the collision alarm began to sound, and saw the creature still clinging to the bow. She still couldn't get a distinct look at its flowing, ever-shifting mass, but it was clearly trying to clamber onto the deck, and all of its bulk seemed to now be out of the water. She was stunned, amazed that it had fully left the protection of the sea.

An explosion jolted the ship. The bridge shuddered as if it were about to fall apart.

"There went the engine." Abhi fought with the controls. "Got to keep it steady . . ."

One of the two mercenaries assisting Abhi glanced out the aft window. "The fire?"

"Forget about it," Abhi snapped. "It doesn't matter at this point."

"One minute," the other mercenary shouted, pointing at the dark shoreline.

"All hands brace for impact," Abhi shouted. "And Carrie?"

She turned to him, and saw that his cheeks were wet with tears.

"Just in case," he said with a smile, "it's been fun, being your sidekick."

"Abhi . . ."

"And don't forget," he yelled, as the ship's hull groaned, "you still owe me a new Sudoku book!"

The creature continued to cling to the bow as the shore loomed up out of the darkness. Rocks towered over them, jutting from the shallow water. The ship shuddered and shook as it scraped along the bottom. Explosions rang out, wrenching them back and forth, and the bridge filled with smoke. Coughing, Carrie curled into a ball on the floor, pulling her knees against her chest and tucking her head low. Something crashed behind her, and a crewman yelped in pain.

Abhi shouted something, but it was unintelligible. Carrie could barely hear him above the noise. There were so many people screaming, it was hard to distinguish one from another. The cries seemed to merge into one long, unending shriek of panic and distress. The cacophony was overwhelming—so loud that Carrie trembled.

The ship hit the shore bow first, pulping and grinding the creature into the rocks. Then, with an ear-splitting squeal of rending, twisting steel, the hull followed, as the front end of the vessel was dashed to bits.

Carrie was thrown forward, and slammed into a bulkhead. Her teeth snapped together on her tongue, and she tasted blood. Another explosion rumbled all around her. Smoke blinded her eyes and seemed to fill her throat. Someone was screaming, but once again, she couldn't tell who it was. It sounded very small and indistinct amidst the other noise.

Then, Carrie realized it was her.

PART TWO

SO ABOVE

TWELVE

"How do you feel, Paolo?"

"I feel like I've been run over by a ship."

"Trust me," Carrie replied, giving Paolo's hand a gentle squeeze, "I know what being run over by a ship feels like. You got off easy."

It had been nearly a week since the final confrontation with the creatures and the shipwreck that had followed. In the aftermath, both Carrie and Abhi had been brought back to the clinic—which they learned was privately owned and operated by Alpinus Biofutures—and treated for their injuries. Luckily, despite the violent and tumultuous crash, neither of them had been hurt too badly. The same could not be said for many of the other members of Takenaka's crew, all of whom had also been transported to the remote facility, rather than the other hospitals on the island. Apparently, officials at Alpinus Biofutures were taking full responsibility for the care and recovery of anyone involved in the expedition. Carrie had to give them credit for that. She was also in awe of how the company had managed to control the media coverage of the crash, relegating it to nothing more than two days' worth of mentions in the local press, despite the loss of life, the environmental impact from spilled oil and diesel fuel, and the wildfire on the shoreline. Granted, Takenaka's vessel hadn't been a giant cruise ship or an oil tanker, but it hadn't been a tiny schooner, either. Despite the fact that they'd run ashore in a rural, remote part of the island, people had still noticed.

"I don't feel like I got off easy," Paolo rasped. "My stitches itch, I can barely move, and my head hurts all the time."

"Well, the doctor says you seem to be recovering since he began administering the makeshift antivenom. We'll just have to give it more time."

"Thank you, Gatito." His voice was warm with gratitude. "What you did for me . . . it means a lot."

Carrie wanted to respond. She wanted to tell him how much he still meant to her, and how scared she had been when it looked like they might lose him. She wanted to tell him about her feelings for him and how good and simultaneously terrifying they felt. She wanted to voice her desire that they give it another try, even though she was certain any such effort would be doomed. But she couldn't bring herself to tell him any of these things.

"What are you thinking?" Paolo asked, sounding sleepy. "I can tell you are thinking something. Your eyes—those beautiful eyes—they always give you away."

"I'm thinking that I'm glad you're okay."

"And what are you *really* thinking?"

Instead of replying, she smiled, and gave his hand another squeeze. They sat in silence for a few minutes.

"It's cold in here," Paolo said, finally.

"Still? The heat is turned up all the way. Want me to get you another blanket?"

If Paolo heard her, he didn't respond. A second later, his eyes closed and his breathing slowed. Then he was asleep again. He'd been sleeping a lot, something Dr. Barbet had said was normal, but it concerned Carrie nevertheless.

A lot of things about Paolo's condition had her concerned.

Carrie listened to him wheeze, and watched his chest slowly rise and fall as he struggled to breathe, and wondered if the doctor was right. Despite Barbet's assurances, Paolo did not look like he was recovering. Stabilizing, maybe, but certainly not recovering. He was still bedridden, still too weak to move on his own. He could barely lift a glass of water by himself, let alone get up and walk around. His eyes had a sunken, hollow look, and there were dark circles beneath them. His skin had a sallow, yellow tone, as did his teeth and fingernails. He slept all the time, and when he wasn't asleep, he lay there battling to stay awake. He shivered constantly, which seemed to exhaust him even more, and insisted that the room was too cold, even with the thermostat cranked up to the point where anyone visiting him was uncomfortably hot.

Perhaps worst of all was the mental and emotional distress his condition seemed to be causing. Paolo complained of a constant, all-consuming headache, and sometimes he saw things that weren't there. These incidents were just like the hallucinations all three of them had experienced on the water, but while Carrie and Abhi no longer suffered from them, Paolo's visions seemed to be getting worse. His hallucinatory spells also seemed to come with olfactory and tactile components now. He didn't just see and hear things that weren't really there. He claimed to be able to smell and touch them now, as well.

If this was Dr. Barbet's idea of recovering, Carrie hated to think what his definition of a cure might entail.

She got up quietly, so as not to disturb Paolo, and got another blanket out of the dresser next to his bed. She covered him carefully, and then, after a moment's hesitation, she leaned over and kissed his forehead. His skin was warm.

"Get better," she whispered.

Paolo didn't stir.

Carrie left the room. The air conditioning in the hallway was a relief after sweltering at Paolo's bedside for the last half hour. After receiving clean bills of health, Carrie and Abhi had both been given permission to come and go freely around the clinic, provided they didn't leave the grounds, and stayed clear of certain restricted areas. Agent Ochse had explained that this was done for their protection and privacy, as well as the protection and privacy of the mercenary crewmembers who were still recovering, and of Alpinus Biofutures itself. Carrie had bristled at these restrictions at first, but she soon admitted that it was nice not having the media poking around. Plus, she understood the company's plight. They were ultimately responsible for what had happened to Takenaka's ship and crew, and their response to the aftermath required a degree of caution. She didn't like it, but she understood it. Even though she knew they would have been out there to kill the creature—creatures—even if Paolo didn't need the poison gland, she still felt responsible for their deaths and felt deeply the accompanying guilt. Why had she let him convince her? She'd chided herself since then, examining her motivations, and discovering only that—when it came to her ex-boyfriend—she didn't understand herself very well. Where Paolo was concerned, Carrie's emotions and thoughts seemed to betray her at every step, like they belonged to someone else.

The remains of both creatures had been recovered and brought back to the clinic in two dump trucks. Both were now on ice in one of the sub-basement levels. For the past few days, Carrie had been assisting Dr. Barbet in studying and analyzing numerous specimen samples. While it wasn't exactly her field of expertise, it was close enough that she'd been helpful. Barbet seemed genuinely pleased to be working with her. More importantly, she welcomed the distraction, and was eager to learn more.

Abhi, meanwhile, had spent his days watching television and playing checkers with the nurses and some of the mercenaries. He had also, much to his delight, obtained a new book full of Sudoku problems.

Neither Carrie nor Abhi nor the mercenaries had been allowed to leave the facility or to contact the outside world. The clinic's phones and Internet service were password protected, but Ochse had assured them all that Alpinus had informed their loved ones of their status.

Carrie turned down another hallway and stopped at a small alcove lined with a row of vending machines. Because neither she nor Abhi had any money after the creature's first attack, Ochse had arranged through Alpinus to get both of them some cash. Since they were confined to the clinic, there wasn't much to spend it on other than items from the vending machines and meals in the cafeteria. She knew Abhi was using at least some of his money to gamble with the nurses and the sailors late at night, but she hadn't asked him for confirmation. She had been invited to join the games once, but had instead been spending most of her free time watching over Paolo.

She ignored the two machines filled with candy and junk food, and the coffee dispenser which usually just took her money and gave nothing in return, and settled in front of the soft-drink machine. Carrie put her money in the slot, made her selection, and retrieved a bottle of water. She placed the cool plastic against her forehead and sighed, enjoying the sensation. Then she continued down the hall, heading for the elevators. She passed by an empty nurses' station. A Creole-dubbed

British soap opera played on a small black-and-white portable television, but no one was there to watch it.

She noticed offhand that the two hospital rooms she passed before reaching the elevator were both empty. Yesterday, they'd been occupied by two injured mercenaries. Now, they sat vacant, the beds made up with crisp, clean linens, and the blinds open to let in the sun. Maybe the patients had been discharged? But why would they be allowed to leave the facility while she and Abhi still had to remain behind? More likely, they'd been given partial rein of the facility, as well, and were just occupied somewhere else right now.

It occurred to Carrie that she still didn't have a clear idea of how big or small the Alpinus Biofutures clinic really was. She knew from riding the elevator that there were three stories above ground, plus a basement level and several sub-levels below it. There was a helicopter pad on the roof, which was how she and Abhi had been transported back to the facility after the shipwreck. The outside grounds appeared to be expansive but very secluded. She'd seen more razor-tipped security fencing in the distance, and security guards on patrol. Still, despite all that, she didn't feel like a prisoner. True to their word, the company had done their best to accommodate their patients, and make them feel comfortable. But even with all the amenities, Carrie was anxious to go home. She hoped Paolo would get better soon.

She was determined not to leave without him.

She took the elevator to the basement, shaking her head in disbelief at a Muzak rendition of Depeche Mode's "Enjoy the Silence." Was she really old enough that one of her favorite bands was now eligible for elevator music covers? What was next? Morrissey over the speakers at the grocery store? Yes, Carrie realized. She really was old enough for that to happen now.

If Mom were still alive, I bet she'd point that out, and then wonder aloud why I'm not yet married.

Carrie grimaced.

The doors hissed open, and she nodded at the guard—a man named Legerski.

"Miss Anderson."

"Mr. Legerski. Is Dr. Barbet back from lunch?"

"Yes, ma'am. Go on in."

Like Ochse, Mariotte, and the ever-laconic Maberry, Legerski worked for Alpinus's security division. She'd seen others like him over the past week—perhaps two dozen total. All of them were men. Though there were plenty of female nurses. The agents were all polite enough, but other than Ochse, she'd had no real interaction with any of them other than perfunctory conversations. Ochse had actually been trying to make an effort with her, engaging Carrie in conversation and trying to meet her requests, provided they were in his power to grant. That was how she'd gotten permission to assist Barbet with his work.

He still insisted that she was mistaken about the egg— that she'd misheard the conversation. Barbet had backed him up on this, telling Carrie that it was probably a mild hallucination, an aftereffect of the neurotoxins that had still been in her system. Carrie thought the doctor was being naïve, or perhaps even willingly misleading, but she didn't press the issue, even though it was in her nature to do so. Her hope was to establish a deeper rapport with the doctor first. Whatever the real truth was regarding the egg and its whereabouts, Paolo was now receiving treatment. That was what was important. And the men who had died during the last expedition?

Well, she was sure that Ochse had a conscience, too.

She walked through a set of automatic double doors and entered the lab. The first room was a foyer of sorts, complete with lockers. Carrie drained her water and tossed the bottle in a recycling bin. Then she stripped out of her clothes, placed them in a locker, and donned the necessary sterile protective gear that was required for dealing with these still unidentified specimens. Dr. Barbet had insisted that one of the conditions for her assisting him was that she adhere to these guidelines. Their superiors at Alpinus had dictated that all personnel who had contact with the specimens were to use these cautionary measures. As far as Carrie knew, Barbet, Ochse, and herself were the only ones who had actually been exposed to the corpses since their arrival.

She first put on a pair of purple scrubs, and then an ill-fitting white lab coat. She slipped a rubber vest and apron over the coat, cloth coverings over her shoes, and then snapped on a pair of latex gloves. Finally, from a dispenser next to the box of gloves, she pulled out a surgical mask and fitted it over her nose and mouth. Then, finished with her preparations, she moved stiffly toward another door. She pressed a button on the wall and the door hissed open. Carrie entered the lab itself, and saw an identically attired Dr. Barbet already waiting for her.

"How was your lunch?" His voice was slightly muffled by the surgical mask.

"Good," she replied. "Yours?"

"Okay. Although the shrimp were a little rubbery. I didn't see you in the cafeteria, though."

"I spent my lunch break visiting with Paolo. He said his head still hurts, but his leg is healing."

It was hard to read Barbet's expression, given that she could only see his eyes, but Carrie sensed something in his reaction, or rather, his lack of a reaction.

"Do you think that will pass?" she asked. "His headache?"

"Oh, I'm sure it will, over time. You have to understand,

Carrie, despite the work we've done here, I still don't have an understanding of what these animals really are. And because I don't yet have a full understanding of them, I also don't have a full grasp of Paolo's condition. But the antivenom seems to be working, and I'm confident his condition will continue to im prove. We just have to give it time."

He said this last part a little too emphatically, Carrie thought. She wondered if Barbet was trying to convince her— or himself.

Over the last few days, they'd done a number of procedures on various specimens from both creatures. They had conducted a necropsy, and then ran various tests on the exoskeleton, the tentacles, the claws, and internal organs. They had measured and weighed, done density tests, and gotten a closer look at the thorax, reproductive organs, digestive tract, and poison sacs. It had been a slow, laborious, and painstaking process, and each new discovery only left them with more questions. The creatures seemed to possess biological traits of a variety of sea creatures, and so far, it had been impossible to determine their true genus.

The one thing they had successfully solved was the nature of the creature's poison, and how it affected both electronics and neurons. When electrical current was conducted through a material, any opposition that the flow of electrons encoun- tered resulted in a dissipation or disruption of that energy. In normal circumstances, this process generated heat. However, in the case of electronics exposed to the creature, the end result was a lowering of the temperature. It had the same effect on the nervous system of living creatures. The toxin overrode the nerve cells, shutting down the electrical signals and neu- rotransmitters that regulated the body's functions, thus induc- ing a slow-acting paralysis. Barbet had described it as similar to shock-induced tetanus—the involuntary muscle contraction and paralysis induced by an electrical shock, like from a Taser. But in the case of living beings exposed to the creature's neurotoxin, the electric impulses within the body were slowly frozen to the point of paralysis. A similar thing happened to any electronic devices exposed to the creature's web—they were unable to generate electricity and became inoperable.

Or, at least, that's what Carrie had understood. She couldn't be sure she'd heard it all correctly, because the events of the last week had left her tired, and much of the science involved wasn't even remotely near her field of expertise. Still, Barbet had seemed pleased with the results. The one thing he still hadn't figured out was what caused the vivid hallucinations. He'd told Carrie that he suspected it had something to do with the human brain's neurotransmitters shutting down—synapses misfiring as the victim's temperature dropped, but he also admitted that was purely conjecture at this point.

Carrie's ruminations were interrupted by a loud yawn from Barbet.

"I'm sorry," he apologized. "That was rude of me. I'm afraid I'm more tired than I realized."

"We're both tired. We should knock off early today. You can go home and catch up on your sleep."

"Oh, I'll be here at the clinic. I have a room on the third floor."

Again, it was hard for Carrie to read his expression beneath the surgical mask, but she detected a hint of . . . nervousness, perhaps? Curious, she decided to gently press him further.

"Oh, really? I figured you for a local. I just assumed you'd live nearby."

"I . . . I do." This time, the stammer was definitely noticeable. Barbet was clearly uncomfortable with the discussion. "My home is just a few miles away, actually. But I've been staying here this week, so that I can monitor your friend. And there's just so much yet to be done . . ."

He trailed off, gesturing with a sweep of his hand at the pile of thawed specimens in front of him.

Carrie's eyes flicked down to the white gold wedding band on his finger, the bulge of which was barely visible beneath his latex gloves.

"Your wife must not think much of that—you staying here instead of going home. Hope she's not the jealous type."

"My husband, actually."

"Really? I didn't know Mauritius recognized same-sex marriage."

"They don't. At least, not yet. We got married in France on holiday."

"That's awesome. France is beautiful."

"It is, indeed." Barbet seemed to visibly relax again. "Don't get me wrong. It's not specifically against the law in Mauritius, but it's not exactly legal, either."

"Well, that's still better than some countries, I guess."

Barbet nodded. "Anyway, we got married in France but it's recognized here, for the purposes of benefits and such."

"So, what does your husband do, if you don't mind me asking?"

"Paul is an architect," Barbet said, and the pride in his voice was noticeable. But then the sadness and nervousness returned. "We were getting ready to adopt . . ."

"That's wonderful! A boy or a girl?"

"Well . . . neither, right now. There have b-been some . . . complications."

"I'm sorry."

Before she could question him further, the doctor yawned again, and nodded at the samples in front of them.

"We really should get back to work, Carrie," he said. "I'd

like to finish analyzing this before the end of the day. Can you check the video camera? We'll want to make sure it's still functioning correctly before we begin this next part."

"Sure," Carrie said, nodding.

She tried to remain upbeat and positive throughout the remainder of the day, but it quickly became clear to her that she had upset Dr. Barbet. They still spoke, but his tone and demeanor were perfunctory and professional, without his usual friendliness. Assuming she must have touched on a sore spot, Carrie let it go. His husband probably wasn't thrilled with the long hours the doctor was putting in here at the clinic, and obviously the adoption process had suffered some setbacks. It wasn't her place to pry. Instead, she focused on helping out, and learning what she could about the creatures.

She met Abhi for dinner in the cafeteria. That evening's offerings were chicken parmesan or seafood salad. Carrie chose to pass on both and went with the salad bar instead. Abhi, on the other hand, opted for a helping of both main courses, but somewhat surprisingly, he didn't eat much of either. Instead, he listlessly pushed the food around on his plate, like a child trying to convince their parents they'd eaten more than they had. Carrie noticed that he wasn't as talkative and outgoing as normal, either. More worrisome, he kept glancing around the cafeteria, as if looking for someone.

"Are you okay?" she asked, finally.

"Sure."

He nodded, but Carrie remained unconvinced.

"It's just that you haven't eaten much," she said. "Normally, you would have inhaled that plate by now and gone back for seconds."

"I had a late lunch," Abhi replied. "I guess I'm just not hungry now. My eyes were bigger than my stomach."

His tone was flat, and he didn't look at her while he
spoke. Instead, his gaze continued to flick around the room.
Carrie glanced around, trying to be inconspicuous, but saw
no cause for concern or alarm. The cafeteria was barely occupied. In addition to Abhi and herself, three nurses sat at one
table, chatting and laughing amongst themselves. The only
other people present were the cashier and the chef behind the
counter.

What the hell is with everybody today? Carrie thought.
Everyone must be just restless, she decided. Perhaps cabin
fever was setting in. Especially in Abhi's case, since he had nothing to do all day. Carrie resolved to mention it to Barbet and
Ochse. There was no reason Abhi should have to stay here any
longer, now that the media's interest in the crash had faded.

"You miss your paint thinner, don't you?" Carrie teased,
hoping to illicit a smile or maybe even a laugh.

Instead, Abhi uncharacteristically ignored the playful comment, and glanced down at her tray.

"Are you finished?" he asked.

"Yes."

"Good. Let's clear off our trays."

Without another word, he stood up abruptly, and carried
his still nearly full tray across the cafeteria, weaving around
the tables. Frowning, Carrie did the same, following along
behind him. She watched Abhi slow down as he passed beneath
a fire sprinkler in the ceiling. He glanced up at it, and then
quickly away. His posture stiffened. Her concern for him deepened. It occurred to Carrie that perhaps the older man was
suffering some form of post-traumatic stress disorder, brought
on by their multiple encounters with—and narrow escapes
from—the creatures haunting the trench. Abhi had lived an
adventurous life, but he'd also been through a lot these last few
weeks. Maybe the strain had finally gotten to him.

"Abhi, are you sure you're feeling okay?"

He didn't respond, and instead of turning around, he quickened his pace. Carrie followed him to an alcove where diners were supposed to leave their trays, plates, cups, and utensils for the staff to carry to the dishwasher. A small window offered a view of the kitchen. Next to the window was a door marked EMPLOYEES ONLY. Abhi sat his tray down and nodded at a woman in the kitchen. As Carrie placed her tray in front of the window, the woman walked out of sight. A second later, the door opened.

"Ah," Abhi exclaimed, suddenly sounding like his normal, exuberant self. "Rosalina! How nice to see you again. Carrie, come here. I want to introduce you to a new friend of mine."

Rosalina was middle-aged and rotund, and although she smiled at Abhi, she didn't respond to him. She simply held the door open and impatiently motioned at them to step through. Abhi did. After a moment's hesitation, Carrie followed.

"Carrie, this is Rosalina. Rosalina, this is my friend Carrie I was telling you about."

"Hello," Carrie said to the woman as the door shut behind them. "It's nice to meet you."

Rosalina didn't respond. Indeed, she didn't seem to acknowledge Carrie at all.

"She doesn't speak much English," Abhi said, "so don't be offended."

Without giving them another glance, Rosalina wandered back over to the window and retrieved their trays. Then she hustled them off to the dishwasher.

The kitchen was hot, humid, and noisy. A large exhaust fan in the ceiling seemed to do little in the way of clearing the atmosphere, and instead, thrummed like a jet engine. The dishwasher rattled and boomed. Carrie's sense of smell was assaulted from all sides with a bewildering array of aromas,

simultaneously mouth-watering and repulsive. Chicken parmesan and marinara sauce lingered strongly in the air, but so
did the stench of garbage and chemical cleaners. Steam seemed
to cling to everything, and already her hair felt damp and limp.

"Abhi." She had to raise her voice to be heard over the clat-
ter. "What are we doing back here?"

"I wanted to introduce the two of you to each other."

"Isn't that what you just did? She didn't seem particularly
excited to meet me."

"Aye. Well . . . come on. This way."

Abhi led her past a massive industrial oven, and a long
counter littered with the aftermath of an afternoon of food
preparation. Carrie turned back to look at Rosalina, but the
woman had already disappeared, apparently having work to
do elsewhere in the labyrinthine kitchen. Abhi stopped in front
of a pantry door, and glanced around. Then, apparently satisfied, he opened the door and motioned for Carrie to walk inside. She did, but the pantry was dark.

"Abhi, I can't see shit. And to be honest, I'm not in the mood
for jokes anymore. What's this all about?"

"Hold on."

He shut the door, plunging them both into total blackness.
Carrie heard him fumbling against the wall. A second later,
he found a light switch and flicked it. Carrie squinted against
the sudden glare. Then she gasped in surprise. The pantry was
a huge, walk-in affair, with floor to ceiling shelving on both
sides, packed with an assortment of bulk-sized canned and dry
goods. Standing in the center of it was Dr. Barbet.

"Are we having a party?" she quipped, recovering from her
initial surprise and annoyance.

"Did you tell her anything?" Barbet asked Abhi.

"Nothing yet," he replied, coming around to stand at Carrie's
side. "I figured it best to wait until we were all together."

"Good."

"Okay, what the hell is going on?" Carrie demanded. "Both of you have been acting weird all day, and no offense, but I think we're all a little bit too old to be hiding from the adults."

"Please," Barbet said. "Keep your voice down. This is one of the few places I'm absolutely sure isn't under surveillance, but we should still use an abundance of caution while we talk."

"Under surveillance?"

He nodded. "This entire facility is monitored. Alpinus has cameras and microphones in every room—hidden in the sprinkler systems, the ventilation shafts, the waiting rooms and lounges, even the televisions. All incoming and outgoing calls are monitored, as well as all Internet traffic. They even have aerial drones monitoring the outside grounds. The only place I know for sure isn't monitored is this pantry and the food-prep freezer."

She pointed to the grille of a ventilation shaft above them. "What about that?"

"I removed the covering earlier and checked," Barbet insisted.

"Maybe I should start at the beginning?" Abhi said.

"Yes," Carrie replied. "Maybe you'd better."

"This morning," Abhi said, "I noticed that all of the mercenaries from Takenaka's ship were gone."

"I noticed that two of them were missing this morning, too," Carrie said.

Barbet held up a finger, interrupting her. "Please. It is dangerous to stay in here for too long."

"I thought you said it was safe?"

"They can't hear us, but if we're gone too long, and not showing up on any of the cameras, they'll notice we're missing."

"At first," Abhi continued, "I thought perhaps a few of the

crew had recuperated and were discharged. But I'd gotten to know some of them over the past week. We'd been playing checkers and such. I mean, we're not friends, but they were polite enough. Social. You'd think at least some of them would have said goodbye. And then there were the ones who I know couldn't have recovered already. One of them, Etienne, this ex-French Legionnaire, had two broken legs, several broken ribs, and a broken collar bone. The man was in traction yesterday, but when I went to his room this morning, he was gone. When I asked the nurses about it, they didn't have any answers. When I pressed them, they were vague. I didn't get the idea they were lying to me, necessarily. It was more like they were just as confused as I was. That made me curious. So, I started checking around, and when I found out that all of the mercenaries were gone, I went to Dr. Barbet."

"Why didn't you tell me?" Carrie asked.

"You were with Paolo," Abhi replied. "I didn't want to trouble you. At least, not until I'd found out what was going on. There's no reason to hit the panic button if there's not really a panic. But I'm coming to you now, right?"

"So, where did they all disappear to?"

"They took them out last night," Barbet confirmed.

"Who did?"

"Ochse and his men. Alpinus security. And they weren't transferred to another hospital. If they had been, there would have been some record of it. I would have had to sign off on all discharge and transfer papers. Also, if they had been moved to other medical facilities, private or otherwise, they would have been transported in ambulances. For the number of patients we're talking about, that would have involved a caravan. Nobody saw anything like that. They were secretly removed from this facility overnight. One of my nurses saw it, but was too afraid to say anything about it to anyone, at first. She's a single mother with three children and she doesn't want to lose her job."

"What did she see?" Carrie asked.

"She said Ochse and his people took them all down to the loading docks and put them all into black vans. She didn't see where they went after that. She said the patients didn't seem concerned, and seemed to be going along voluntarily. We have to assume that either Ochse made a deal with them, or lied to them about their destination. I'm guessing it is the latter."

"So, where are they now?"

"I don't know," Barbet replied.

"See, I think you do know," Carrie pressed. "I think you know a lot more than you're telling us, Doctor. You seem like a good guy. Whatever it is that's really happening here, I don't think you like it. I don't know—maybe your conscience is bothering you after our talk in the lab, but there's a reason you're here with us now."

"Of course there is. After our discussion this afternoon, I had one of the nurses whom I trust slip Abhi a note, advising him of the surveillance procedures, and giving him instructions on when and how to meet."

"Then why lie to us about where Takenaka's crew are?"

"I'm not lying about that. I don't know where they are."

"You're not lying about that?" Carrie stepped closer to him, backing the doctor into the corner. "Then what are you lying about?"

Barbet seemed to deflate. His shoulders slumped and his face fell.

"Quite a bit," he admitted, "I've been lying all week, to you both, and to Paolo, as well."

Carrie stared him in the eyes. "About what?"

"About many things. Especially Paolo, and about his condition."

"He's not improving, is he? Even with the antivenom?"

Barbet averted his gaze and stared at the floor. "No, I'm afraid he's not."

"You son of a bitch . . . why would you lie to us about that?"

"Because Alpinus threatened me. Ochse said if I didn't do what they wanted, they'd make sure Paul got deported, and make sure our adoption process was unsuccessful. And they could. They could easily follow through on that."

"Who's Paul?" Abhi asked.

"His husband," Carrie replied. "What do they have on him, Doctor? I'm assuming it's some kind of blackmail?"

"Yes, although it feels more like bullying to me. Paul . . . he got into some trouble when he was younger, years before we met. It involved kickbacks and graft for a building he was designing. As I said, this happened years ago, and there was never a conviction. There's no record of it. But Alpinus knows about it, and they have access to certain documents and e-mails that the authorities never obtained."

"So they're a bunch of blackmailing bastards," Carrie said. "Okay. And I'm betting they lied about never receiving the egg, too."

Still staring at the floor, Barbet nodded in resignation.

"Those fuckers." Carrie spat. "I knew it. I knew I was right! Ochse was so condescending, insisting that I must have misheard them—that I was mistaken. And you went along with that, Doctor."

"I'm sorry."

"It's okay. I understand why now. But that still doesn't explain why they lied about the egg in the first place, and it especially doesn't explain why they wanted you to conceal the truth about Paolo's prognosis. Why would they want us to think he was getting better if he wasn't?"

"I don't know why they lied about the egg," Barbet said,

"but I can confirm it was indeed brought in with you, and I did perform an ultrasound on it. When that was finished, I stored it in the lab. At some point, it was gone. I have to assume Ochse had his men confiscate it. As for Paolo, Ochse ordered me to only administer small doses of the antivenom— enough to make your friend stabilize, but not enough to cure him."

"But why?"

Barbet took a deep breath. "Paolo is undergoing some changes, and Alpinus is very interested in studying them."

"What kind of changes?"

"These changes are taking place at a cellular level. To put it bluntly, Paolo's brain is mutating. It's a slow process, but it's definitely occurring. I don't know what is making it happen, but I suspect someone in Alpinus Biofutures does. In all my years, I've never seen anything like it. All I know is they want to allow his brain to continue mutating and they want me to record the results. If he dies, they'll take his body."

"And if by some miraculous chance he lives?" Carrie asked.

"Then the mercenaries won't be the only ones who have disappeared."

Shocked and stunned, Carrie clenched her fists. "Those motherfuckers."

"Aye," Abhi said.

"Again," Barbet apologized, "I am so sorry. But if I don't go along with them, then they'll ruin Paul, and destroy our chances at having a family."

"Well," Abhi said, "at least now we know why we haven't been allowed to leave this place. Media scrutiny, they said. We know that's not true. The question now is, what do we do about all of this?"

"I can try to double the dose I've been giving Paolo tonight," Barbet offered. "One of the security personnel is always with me when I administer it, but they don't pay attention to the dosage amount."

"Will that cure him?" Carrie asked.

"Hopefully it will begin the process. If I am correct, it should at least begin to halt the mutations. I don't know if the process can be reversed, but I'm fairly confident I can stop it from going further. Maybe that'll buy you time."

Carrie considered this carefully. If they could halt or slow the process, it might give them time to figure out a way to escape and get Paolo to a specialist.

"I'm putting a lot on the line here," Barbet continued. "If I start upping his doses and someone notices, I could lose everything. So could Paul."

"We've all got something riding on this," Carrie replied. "Certainly our reputations. Maybe even our safety. Isn't that reason enough to do the right thing and get out of here?"

"That's easy for you to say. You can go back to America. But this is my home. If my safety is threatened, there's nowhere for me to run."

"If it comes to that," Abhi said, "we'll keep you and your husband safe."

Barbet scoffed. "I need more than that."

"I met a reporter," Carrie said. "If they start to out Paul, or if they threaten you in any other way, we'll go to her. Reveal everything that's happened here."

"How do you know she'll believe you?"

"I'm a public figure," Carrie replied. "No, I may not be a movie star or a pop singer, but people know who I am, especially after all the recent news coverage of the collapse. She'll believe me, and she'll run with the story because it will get ratings—someone like myself bringing these allegations against a company like Alpinus? The media will be drooling for an exclusive with us."

"Well . . . ," Barbet paused, frowning. "Do I have your word you'll help me and Paul?"

"You have my word," Carrie promised.

"And mine, as well," Abhi said.

Barbet smiled slightly. "Thank you both."

"Could you manufacture more doses beyond the initial week," Carrie asked, "so we could smuggle them out with us once we get Paolo out of here?"

"Provided I have enough specimens, and I don't anticipate that being a problem."

"And you're sure you can fool Ochse and his men for that long?"

Barbet nodded confidently. "They aren't doctors or scientists. They're just thugs—bullies in nice suits. But once Paolo begins to get better, they will surely suspect something is amiss. What then?"

"I don't know," Carrie admitted. "But you said it will take a full week of regular doses, right?"

"Correct. That is my best guess."

"Then we've got a full week to figure out what our next move is."

As it turned out, they didn't have a full week.

They barely had any time at all.

THIRTEEN

Dr. Barbet administered the first full dose that night. By the next morning, Paolo already showed marked signs of improvement as the antivenom went to work on his system, counteracting the mutation's progress. Since they had to assume they were under constant surveillance, Barbet couldn't communicate the specifics to the other conspirators, but Carrie and Abhi could see the remarkable changes in Paolo's condition for themselves. His complexion changed, and his fatigue abated.

A second full dose was administered the following night, after which Paolo's appetite returned. More important, the hallucinations ceased and the constant pain in his head seemed to ease. He was able to get out of bed on his own and use the restroom by himself.

The next morning, Barbet slipped a note to Carrie and Abhi, informing them that, given the antivenom's success, a full week of doses might not be needed after all before Paolo was well enough to be transported. Carrie stepped up her planning, but was stymied by the cautionary ways she had to use in communicating her plan to Abhi and the doctor. They'd decided against using the pantry a second time, so as not to arouse suspicion. They had also agreed not to mention anything to Paolo, until they had no choice.

Their waking hours were filled with tension and nervousness, trying to keep up the appearance of normality, exchanging pleasantries with Alpinus officials whom they no longer trusted, and worrying about the ramifications if it was discovered that they knew about the blackmail attempts and the company's real agenda.

All the while, Carrie desperately planned.

On the third night, after administering another full dose of antivenom and checking Paolo's vitals, Dr. Barbet stepped out into the hall, thinking about how much he missed Paul, and about how tired he was. He was looking forward to sleep—the one place where this current bout of anxiety and depression couldn't reach him.

Unfortunately, Ochse and Maberry were waiting for him outside of Paolo's room.

"Dr. Barbet." Ochse kept his voice low but cordial. "Working late, I see?"

Surprised, Barbet fought to keep his voice from quaking. "Actually, I was just about to retire, gentlemen. You're right. It's very late."

"Could you come with us, please?"

"Is there a problem?"

"No problem, Doctor. No problem at all. It's good news, in fact. We've been told that this operation can cease, effective tomorrow morning."

"Really?" Barbet did his best to feign excitement. "Well, that's wonderful! But there's still so much to do. More testing on the specimens. And what about Paolo?"

"The specimens will be transferred to another Alpinus Biofutures research center, where they can be studied and analyzed better. After all, you're just one man, and you lack the equipment needed to really do an in-depth analysis. The company feels it would be better to have an entire team devoted to this. That way, you can get back to saving lives, rather than examining dead things."

"I see. And my patient? What of Paolo?"

"He's being transferred, as well. The company is dedicated to seeing that he gets the best care available. Don't get me wrong. That's not to say you haven't done a commendable job. You have, and my superiors are grateful. It's just that, again, there are specialists who might be better suited to accommodate him."

Barbet nodded dumbly, afraid that if he tried to ask any more questions he'd give himself away just as he was about to be allowed home.

Ochse's expression was quizzical. "I must say, Dr. Barbet, I thought you'd be glad to get rid of us and get things back to normal."

"Oh, yes. I am glad. I mean, not about getting rid of you, of course. No . . . I'm just . . . surprised?"

"That's perfectly understandable." Ochse smiled and nodded. "We just got the news ourselves."

"And it will really be over?"

Ochse smiled, patiently. "I give you my word. You and your husband can rest easy. I hate that we had to drag him into this in the first place, but I had my orders. Just know that it wasn't personal."

"And our adoption process? You'll leave us alone?"

"I wish you nothing but good luck with it. I have two kids of my own. It's a wonderful thing, to be a parent. Anyway, we'd like your assistance in preparing the specimens for transport. If you would, please?"

"Now?"

"Yes, unfortunately so. I'm afraid the company would like this entire process expedited. If it were up to me, I'd say wait till morning, but you know how these corporate bigwigs are."

"Of course."

"Then, please," Ochse said again. "If you would, come with us."

Maberry motioned down the corridor with his hand. Swallowing, Barbet walked in the direction indicated. He glanced around, hoping to catch sight of another staff member, or perhaps Carrie and Abhi, but he was alone, except for the two agents. They fell in step behind him, and, under the dim fluorescent lights, their shadows seemed to stretch over his own, engulfing it whole. Their shoes, echoing on the tiles, sounded very loud in the silence.

Barbet wondered if they could hear his heart pounding, as well.

When she heard the elevator door close, Carrie tiptoed out of her room. She glanced both ways, but the hallway was deserted. Mindful of the facility's surveillance system, she wondered what to do next. Although she'd only overheard pieces of the discussion between Barbet and the Alpinus agents, she'd heard enough to be concerned. As she stood in the doorframe, chewing her bottom lip and weighing her options, Abhi's door creaked open. He emerged, yawning and glancing around cautiously.

"You heard?" she whispered.

"Not all of it. I was asleep. But I heard enough to know it was bullshit."

"Yeah," Carrie replied, "that's what I'm thinking, too."

"What do we do?" He lifted a finger toward the ceiling, reminding her about the cameras and microphones.

"Hey, Abhi." Carrie spoke louder now, playing to whomever might be watching or listening. "What are you doing awake? Couldn't sleep, huh?"

He stared at her, blinking, his face aghast. Then, realizing what she was doing, he grinned.

"No, I was asleep, but then that conversation woke me up."

"Yes." Carrie nodded emphatically. "I heard that, too. Great news, huh?"

"Aye. Great news indeed. Sounds like we're going home soon."

"I know! Isn't it exciting? I thought I might go down to the lab and see if I can help them prep the specimens for transport. I have experience handling these remains, after all."

"Ah . . . um . . ."

Abhi shifted from one foot to the other, obviously unsure of what she wanted him to say or do.

"Why don't you check on Paolo?" Carrie suggested. "The noise probably woke him up, too. You can tell him the good news."

Understanding slowly crept across his features. "Ah, yes. That's a good idea, Carrie. I'll go check on Paolo. I just need to go to the bathroom first. The older I get, the worse my prostate is at night."

Carrie cringed inwardly, all-too-aware that the two of them sounded like they were reading from a script. She was suddenly gripped with indecision. Maybe this wasn't the right approach. After all, if they were being monitored, whomever was watching them could now inform Ochse that she was on her way down to the lab. Still, it was too late now. Things were already in motion.

Abhi opened the door to his room and slipped inside. Carrie started down the hall, pulse racing, expecting to be stopped or challenged at any moment. Instead, the corridor was silent.

She tried to step lightly, but her footfalls echoed in the stillness.

She was confident that Abhi had understood what she was implying—that he should watch over Paolo in case one of the agents arrived. She wondered about his bathroom comment, though. Obviously, he said it because there was something he wanted to retrieve from his room. But what? A weapon, maybe? Whatever the case, she felt confident of his abilities. Paolo would be fine. Dr. Barbet was her primary concern now.

She passed by an empty nurses' station. The computer was turned off. A cup of coffee sat next to it. She touched the mug with the tip of her index finger. It was cold. She frowned, trying to remember when she'd last seen one of the nurses or staff. This wasn't the first time she had encountered a deserted nurse's station, either. Had Alpinus been phasing the staff out, as well? Doing it slowly, so as not to arouse suspicion?

Just how far were they willing to go to keep things quiet?

After reaching the elevator undiscovered, Carrie pressed the button and waited. Watching the lights, she noticed that, instead of ascending from the sub-basement level where the lab was located, the elevator instead began its ascent from the garage level, where the loading docks were. Frowning, Carrie puzzled over that. They couldn't have already packed the lab specimens and the carcasses from the freezer.

The elevator arrived. The doors hissed open, and Carrie walked inside. She instinctually reached for the lab's sub-level but after a moment's hesitation, she pressed the button for the garage level. The doors slid shut. The elevator descended. Carrie noticed idly that someone had turned the music off. The silence was discomforting. Her muscles felt taut, like overstretched guitar strings. As the elevator stopped, she focused on her breathing, using her diving techniques to help steady her nerves, and rehearsed in her head what she'd say if caught sneaking around.

She was still thinking about that when the elevator doors slid open again, and she found herself staring down the barrel of a gun.

"Shit!" Carrie instinctively put her hands up to shield her face. "Whoa. It's just me. Don't shoot!"

The gunman, agent Legerski, stood with his feet shoulder-width apart, both hands controlling his weapon, arms outstretched, and elbows locked. One finger was on the trigger guard, a split second away from the trigger itself. Carrie recognized this as a professional shooter's stance. Heart racing, she tried out her best smile, the one she used during press interviews and to sway investors.

"Jesus, you really scared me. What's going on?"

Instead of answering her, Legerski spoke to his lapel. Carrie realized he had some sort of Bluetooth device in his ear.

"Ochse, I've got Carrie Anderson here."

There was a pause while, presumably, Ochse responded in his ear. Carrie glanced at the elevator's control panel, debating making a lunge for the button to close the doors.

"I don't know," Legerski said, not taking his eyes off her. "I thought he was on monitor duty, too. What do you want me to do?"

Carrie did her best to appear perplexed and surprised and frightened. For the latter, she didn't have to pretend.

Come on, you stupid doors, she thought. *Fucking close already!*

"Okay," Legerski said. "Affirmative."

Close, she silently pleaded. *Come on!*

"Ma'am, step out of the elevator please." Legerski motioned with the barrel of his handgun.

Sighing in resignation, Carrie slowly complied.

"What's going on, Legerski?" she asked. "Is there some kind of trouble?"

The agent lowered his weapon but did not holster it. Carrie took a cautious step forward. She estimated that he stood about five feet away from her. As she gauged the distance, she heard the doors slide shut behind her. The elevator dinged, cheerily.

I'm going to rip that thing's circuits out if I get a chance.

"We've had a security breach, Miss Anderson. If you'll just come with me, please?"

"Come with you where?"

"My orders are to get you to a secure location."

"Whose orders? Ochse? Maybe I should talk to him instead."

"He's right this way. Just come with me."

"I'm not going anywhere until you—"

Instead of responding, Legerski raised the weapon and pointed it at her face.

"Okay," Carrie shouted, putting her hands up again. "Okay, okay. Jesus fucking Christ!"

"Now that I have your attention . . ." Legerski waggled the gun barrel. "To your left, please. Walk slowly, and keep your hands up where I can see them."

Carrie stared Legerski down.

"I don't want to hurt you, Miss Anderson. Seriously."

"I don't believe you."

He motioned with the gun again. "Just walk."

Carrie did as ordered, and each step sent her further into despair. Her feet felt like blocks of lead and her leg muscles wobbled and tingled. In a strange way, the sensation was quite similar to what she had felt under the effects of the creature's neurotoxin. And the parking garage was just as dark and foreboding as the trench had been. Fluorescent lights ineffectually flickered here and there, seeming to add to the gloom rather than dispel it, much like their phosphorescent torches had done during the dive. But here, she didn't have to hold her breath. And here, she also knew exactly who the predators were.

She just didn't know why. At least, not all of the reasons why. Not yet.

Carrie wondered if she'd get a chance to find out.

An echo rumbled through the structure—a muffled bang, like somebody dropping a book onto a hardwood floor.

Carrie stopped. "What was that? Was that what I think it was?"

Legerski responded by pressing the barrel of his gun into the small of her back.

"Keep going," he said. His tone was flat, inflectionless. "That was nothing to concern you."

The parking garage echoed with their footsteps. There were only half a dozen vehicles in sight, three of which were black sport utility vehicles like the one Maberry and Mariotte had used to transport her and Abhi to the port. To Carrie, that now seemed like it had all taken place in the distant past. Another was a black Jeep. The other two were black four-door sedans.

"You guys like black, huh?"

"You're doing fine," Legerski said, ignoring her comment. "Just a little farther now. Nice and easy, and no one will get hurt. That's the way. I'm just as sick of this place as you are. Soon, we can all go home."

Carrie watched her shadow lengthen as they passed under another set of lights. She passed beneath them and back into the darkness, and considered making a run for it. If she was quick enough, and stayed out of the light, she might be able to lose him. She hadn't noticed a silencer or suppressor on his pistol. Would he risk the possible unwanted attention the sound of gunshots might raise? But then it occurred to her that it was possible no one else would hear them. She still didn't know where the clinic was located, or how close they were to a population center. And for all she knew, the only people in the facility, other than her, Abhi, Paolo, and Barbet, might all be Alpinus agents. And that was the other problem with fleeing. She didn't know where the other agents he was leading her toward were. If she managed to escape, she might run right into them.

She felt a cool breeze on her face and saw the darkness dissipate up ahead, and realized Legerski was leading her to the loading dock. The heavy garage door was open, letting in the night air and a sliver of moonlight. A huge box truck had been pulled up to the dock, and its rear door had been rolled up. She smelled a whiff of gun-smoke, and something else—something she couldn't quite place. A figure stood inside the back of the truck, watching her passively. As she got closer, she recognized the man as Ochse. He was also armed with a handgun, currently clenched in one fist and dangling at his side. His expression spoke of a resigned sadness, but she paid little attention. There was something odd about the box truck's windowless interior. The walls and floor seemed reflective.

What is that. It's not wood or metal.

"Go on," Legerski ordered. "Step into the truck."

Instead, Carrie stopped so suddenly that he nearly bumped into her.

Plastic. They covered the inside of the truck with plastic sheeting.

Then she realized why.

Dr. Barbet lay in the center of the truck. The smell she'd been unable to identify was his blood, which was jetting from the back of his head in a steady, ever-widening pool. Indeed, as she watched, Ochse took a step forward as the flow stretched toward his shoes. More blood was splattered across the plastic lining the truck's walls. Steam rose from Barbet's still-warm body, curling lazily in the cooler night air.

Carrie tried to speak, but could only retch instead. Her knees buckled, and she sank to the concrete floor, oblivious to Legerski's sudden alarmed shouts behind her.

"Get the fuck up!"

Her voice trembled when she spoke, not from grief, but fury. "Why?"

"Orders," Ochse said. His tone was sympathetic. "It's nothing personal, Miss Anderson. But with Dr. Barbet having administered the curing dosages, Alpinus has determined there's no more to be learned from the live experiment. We've been told to liquidate the witnesses and take Paolo's and the monsters' remains in for further study, along with the data we've collected."

Carrie shook her head in denial.

"It wasn't supposed to happen like this," Ochse continued. "Unfortunately, Mariotte decided to sneak off for a cigarette when he should have been monitoring you. And so, you were able to unintentionally stumble upon this situation."

"You still haven't told me why."

Ochse frowned in confusion. "I thought I just did."

"No," Carrie croaked. "I meant why? Why do all of this?"

"Well, there were simply too many existing witnesses to pay off. It wouldn't have been cost-effective. The mercenaries alone would have been financially prohibitive. And, of course, there's no guarantee that everyone would stay silent. They wouldn't. They never do. If it's any consolation, your sister and her family won't know the ugly truth. As far as they're concerned, you succumbed to complications from the bends, suffered after your dive with Peter Scofield."

"I posted on Facebook after that. They'll know better. They know I got out of the hospital."

"Well, it's funny. We all thought you were doing just fine. We had your discharge papers in the works and everything, but unfortunately a nurse—a nurse who I assure you will be dealt with quite severely—gave you a dose of the wrong medicine. You had a severe allergic reaction to it, I'm afraid. Given all the trauma you've recently been through, you were just too weak to recover from it."

Carrie stared at him, speechless. Her hands curled into fists. She began to tremble, not from fear, but from rage.

Shrugging, Ochse nodded at Legerski. "Bring her here. Let's make this quick."

"Fuck you," Carrie said. "Fuck you both."

Neither man responded. Legerski bent down and roughly seized Carrie's arm. He grunted, trying to pull her to her feet. Instead, Carrie flung herself forward, breaking his grip. As Legerski flailed, Carrie rolled herself into a ball, trying desperately to present a smaller target, however, the momentum carried her to the edge of the dock, only inches from the truck. She sprang into a crouch, but before she could flee, Ochse grabbed her hair in one fist and yanked her toward the truck.

"It doesn't have to be like this," he yelled.

Instead of answering him, Carrie kicked out with her foot, trying to trip him. Avoiding the blow, the agent leaped backward, taking a fistful of her hair with him. Carrie shrieked in agony. Her scalp burned. Out of the corner of her eye, she saw Legerski aiming his weapon.

"Don't shoot her," Ochse shouted. "Evidence, goddamn it! Get her on the plastic, unless you want to be scrubbing this dock all ni—"

Carrie launched herself from the floor and punched Ochse in his groin, grinning as she felt her knuckles smash into his testicles. Ochse made a breathless, whining sound, and tried to raise his gun, but he seemed paralyzed, and his arm merely trembled. He slowly sank to his knees. He attempted to speak, but only wheezed again. He knelt there on the plastic sheeting, seemingly oblivious as Dr. Barbet's still-steaming blood seeped into his pants.

"Bitch!" Legerski lunged.

And then a gunshot thundered through the parking garage, stopping all three of them where they stood.

"Don't move," Abhi yelled. "Let her go or we'll kill him! I swear to God I'll cut his goddamned throat!"

Carrie gasped in disbelief. Halfway between the elevator and the loading dock, illuminated under a row of fluorescent lights, were Abhi, Paolo, and Mariotte. Abhi stood behind Mariotte, peeking out from behind the taller man's shoulder. The visual would have been almost comical if not for the fact that Abhi had a surgical scalpel held to the agent's throat. Mariotte's expression was simultaneously angry and embarrassed. Paolo, meanwhile, occupied a wheelchair, and was parked slightly behind and to the left of Abhi and their hostage. He pointed a handgun at Legerski and Ochse, and Carrie thought that he looked more alert and lively than he had since their arrival at the clinic. His other hand was pressed to his chest.

"Come here, Carrie," Abhi said.

"Don't you fucking move," Legerski muttered.

"Drop your guns," Abhi shouted. His voice echoed throughout the garage, bouncing off concrete pillars.

Mariotte seemed frozen. Only his eyes moved, darting to each of his fellow agents, silently pleading with them to do something.

"Fuck you, Tubby," Legerski replied. "You drop the scalpel."

Carrie glanced at Ochse out of the corner of her eye, and saw that, while still incapacitated, he was slowly beginning to recover. Her gaze flicked back to Legerski, whose attention was completely focused on Abhi, Paolo, and their hostage.

"I'm going to count to three," Legerski warned.

"I mean it," Abhi replied. "I'll cut his throat."

"Go ahead. It would serve the dumb fuck right. One."

"Two," Paolo countered, his voice clear and strong.

Surprised, Legerski paused. Seeing her opportunity, Carrie sprang at him from behind. Ochse tried to call out a warning, but only managed to grimace and moan. He waved his hands, trying to get Legerski's attention. With both hands, Carrie grabbed Legerski's gun arm by the wrist and twisted savagely. Shouting, Legerski squeezed the trigger three times in rapid succession. The gunshots were deafening, and Carrie's ears immediately began to ring. One of the ejected brass casings glanced off her arm, burning it. The unexpected pain brought another surge of adrenaline. Keeping a firm grip on his wrist, Carrie used her momentum to swing the off-balance agent around, and then pushed him toward the truck. He stumbled, off balance and flailing. She raised one leg and kicked Legerski in the chest, sending him crashing into Ochse. Both men toppled onto the plastic sheeting next to the doctor's body. She heard the air whoosh from Legerski's lungs. Stunned by her own success, Carrie lunged for the strap dangling from the bottom of the truck's raised door. She pulled hard, slamming the door shut before either man could recover. The handle slammed into place, effectively locking the door from the outside.

She stood there, breathless and panting, as the two men began pounding on the door from inside the windowless box truck.

"Carrie," Abhi called. "Are you okay?"

Her ears still rang from the gunshots, and it sounded to Carrie as if Abhi was calling to her from underwater. Nodding, she wiped her brow with the palm of her hand and hurried over to them.

Abhi shoved a shaken-looking Mariotte away from him. The agent eyed them nervously, and rubbed his neck, scratching the spot where the scalpel had been.

"Keep him covered," Abhi told Paolo.

Paolo pointed his weapon at Mariotte. "Oh, I intend to. Believe me."

"What happened?" Carrie asked. "I thought you were going to stay with Paolo?"

Abhi frowned. "Why are you shouting?"

"Gunshots." She pointed to her ears. "I can't hear."

"Ah." Abhi then raised his voice. "I was in Paolo's room, until that man and another agent came to kill us. Then we thought it might be better if we came to find you instead. Looks like I was right, yes?"

Carrie nodded. "And thanks for that. But where's the other agent?"

"Locked inside a custodian's closet on the first floor."

"We need to hurry," Carrie said. "I don't know if they can get a signal inside that truck or not. The walls might be too thick. But if they can, then we have to assume more are on the way. And that big guy, Maberry, is around here somewhere. He came down with Ochse and Barbet."

She glanced around in apprehension, half-expecting the laconic agent to jump out from behind a cement column and start shooting.

"They've been spread thin so far, dealing with the mercenaries and other staff. But our luck won't hold." She turned to Paolo. "Are you up for traveling?"

Paolo smiled. "I'm fine, Gatito. And I'm glad that you're okay, too."

"What's the plan?" Abhi asked. "Because we need one, fast."

Carrie shrugged. "Steal a car, and make for the American Embassy in Port Louis."

"Sounds good to me," Abhi said. "The sooner we're out of here, the better. I've had enough hospital food for one lifetime."

The ringing in Carrie's ears subsided even as the pounding inside the truck grew louder. Carrie wondered how long they had before Ochse or Legerski tried to shoot their way out of the vehicle. Both men had been momentarily disabled, but she guessed they'd be recovering any moment now. Even in the dark, they'd be able to find their weapons. She wondered if such an attempt would actually work. She turned to Mariotte.

"Do you have the keys to one of these vehicles?"

He eyed her warily. "If I say yes, you're just going to have him shoot me anyway."

"Well, maybe. We might shoot you. We just won't kill you. Not if you cooperate."

"Bullshit. I don't believe you. I help you, then you'll kill me."

"We could have killed your partners," Abhi pointed out, "but we didn't. Unlike you people, we're not murderers. Now, answer the lady's question."

Mariotte's gaze shifted warily to each of them, and then settled back on Carrie.

"I'm going to reach in my pocket—"

"No," she interjected. "I'm going to reach in your pocket. You're going to hold very still. Maybe we won't kill you, but if you try anything, Paolo can still shoot you in the balls or your kneecaps. Understand?"

He nodded, trembling noticeably. Carrie wondered if it was from fear or nicotine withdrawal. Or maybe both.

Slowly, without taking her eyes off his, Carrie reached into Mariotte's pocket and retrieved a set of car keys. Up close, he stank of cigarettes and coffee and sweat. She stepped back from him and turned to Abhi.

"Did you search him, before?"

"Yes. He has no weapons on him, other than his breath."

Mariotte flinched at the insult, but didn't say a word.

Carrie held up the key fob and pushed a button to unlock the doors. A black SUV chirped in response. Its headlights flashed just a few rows from where they stood.

"That must be the one," she said. "Okay, what do we do with him?"

"Go get the vehicle," Paolo suggested. "I'll keep him covered. You drive back over here and we'll take him with us."

Carrie glanced at Abhi, who shrugged.

"Works for me," he said. "As much as I hate to say it, having a hostage might come in handy. Just be careful, Paolo. Watch him closely."

"You be careful, too," Paolo replied. "More of them are probably on the way. Be quick about it."

Carrie and Abhi ran for the SUV. They were climbing inside when a gunshot reverberated throughout the parking garage. It was quickly followed by another. Alarmed, they jumped back out of the vehicle and turned to see Mariotte sprawled on the concrete, blood already running from his body. Paolo sat in the wheelchair. Smoke curled from the barrel of his pistol. Mariotte's left leg jittered and twitched. Then he stopped moving.

"Paolo," Carrie shouted. "What the fuck?"

"He tried to attack me, Gatito. I had no choice."

Abhi frowned. "You killed him. . . ."

Paolo lay the still-smoking pistol in his lap and wheeled toward them, grunting with the effort. His hospital robe strained at the seams.

"Yes," he said, his tone flat. "I killed him. He lunged at me just as you were getting in the car. So I shot him. And unless we want to end up the same way, I suggest we go. Now."

A chime dinged, and they heard the elevator's hydraulics begin to whine.

"Somebody is on their way down," Carrie said. "Let's move!"

She slid in behind the steering wheel and started the ignition. The pounding and shouts inside the truck had grown frenzied now. As Abhi helped Paolo into the backseat, and then folded up the wheelchair and stowed it in the cargo section, they heard a muffled boom, followed by another.

"What was that?" Abhi asked, jumping into the passenger seat and slamming the door.

"They're trying to shoot the door open," Carrie explained.

"Will that work?"

"I don't know. But we're not going to be here to find out."

Two more gunshots echoed throughout the garage. Carrie caught a glimpse of muzzle flashes from inside the truck, coming from behind the door. That meant they'd managed to at least shoot through it.

"I think it will work," she muttered. "Time to go."

Carrie dropped the SUV into reverse and hit the accelerator. Their taillights flashed in the gloom. As they passed by the elevator, she was alarmed to see three more Alpinus security agents emerging. All three were armed. Carrie sped up. They glanced toward the SUV, and then ran toward the loading docks.

"Why didn't they shoot at us?" Abhi sounded bewildered.

"Tinted windows," Carrie panted.

"This is getting worse by the minute," Abhi said.

"Yeah," Carrie agreed. "It is."

She scanned the garage, looking for the exit, and followed the arrows painted on the columns and walls. After a few nerve-wracking moments in which she was convinced they'd gone in circles, they found the exit. The gatehouse stood empty, but a mechanical arm blocked the way.

"Punch it," Abhi said.

"That only works in movies," Carrie replied. She turned around to Paolo and stuck out her hand. "Give me the gun."

"Why?"

"Because I asked nicely."

Shaking his head, he turned the weapon over to her. Carrie flung the door open and sprang from the vehicle. She opened the guardhouse door and scanned the control panel, until she found a button to raise the gate. Hydraulics whined softly as it lifted into the air. Then, after making sure the coast was still clear, she got back into the vehicle and handed the pistol back to Paolo.

"Thanks."

"I'm just glad you didn't have to use it."

"Me, too."

They sped out of the garage and up a ramp. Bright flood-lights snapped on, momentarily blinding them. Squinting against the glare, Carrie focused on driving. They followed the road, which brought them around to the front of the clinic, and then arrowed through the thick foliage before terminating at another guardhouse. Unlike the booth in the parking garage, this one was occupied. Two more security agents stood in front of the gate, weapons drawn.

"Punch it," Abhi said again. "And hope this actually works outside of the movies."

Seeing that they had no choice, Carrie stomped the accelerator and the SUV roared forward. She ducked down as low as she could. Abhi and Paolo did the same. The agents opened fire. Flashes burst from their pistols in the darkness, bullets pinged against the SUV, and then the sound of the gunshots followed. The vehicle shuddered and rocked as the bullets slammed into it. The steering wheel jerked in Carrie's hands, but she managed to hold it steady. Then, the hail stopped as she closed the distance. The two men leaped aside as the speeding vehicle bore down on them.

"Hang on," Abhi shouted.

They slammed into the gate with a crunch that shook the vehicle, but the mechanical gate snapped on impact and the SUV blew through the opening, shuddering and bouncing on its suspension. Paolo groaned from the backseat. Carrie's arms were stiff as she gripped the wheel, expecting the airbags to deploy at any second, and was surprised when they didn't. She glanced in the rearview mirror and saw the two agents scrambling to their feet. When she turned her attention back to the road, a tree loomed large in the headlights. Carrie yanked the steering wheel to the left, gritting her teeth as the tires scudded against a curb.

Another agent rushed out of the foliage, his expression panicked and breathless. Armed with some type of compact machine gun, he opened fire as they sped past. The first few rounds slammed into their vehicle, but then the weapon's recoil pulled him off target, and he sprayed the trees. She stared into the muzzle flash. When she looked away, spots danced before her eyes.

"Anyone hit?" Carrie yelled.

Neither Abhi nor Paolo responded, but she couldn't risk glancing at them.

Then, much to her surprise, she realized that they had exited the grounds. A main road stretched out in front of them. Headlights winked in the distance. She hit the on-ramp without slowing, and sped onto the road.

Abhi sat up and glanced around. "Is everyone okay?"

"I am." Carrie nodded. "Paolo?"

"I'm fine, all things considered. But it's cold back here in just this hospital gown. Can you turn on the heat, please?"

Carrie looked at the dashboard and saw that the check engine light was on. She turned the switch for the heat, and warm air blew across her feet. Despite having been shot at and used as a battering ram, the SUV seemed to be handling okay.

Despite the warning from the check engine light, which seemed to glow balefully in the darkness, the temperature gauge seemed normal, and there was no sign of steam leaking from beneath the hood.

"I think we made it," she said. "This thing seems to be running okay. Although I'm surprised the airbags didn't deploy. I, for one, will be writing the manufacturer a strongly worded letter . . ."

"They're not mandatory in Mauritius," Abhi explained. "Probably never installed, or if they were installed, then they were never activated."

"Who cares?" Paolo sighed with relief. "Carrie's right. We made it!"

"Not yet," Abhi replied. "You can bet your ass they'll be coming after us. We should get off this road as soon as possible. Maybe even change vehicles, if we can."

"We've got no money and no identification," Carrie reminded him. "And Paolo's wearing a hospital robe. He looks like an escaped mental patient. I'm not hijacking another car. Stealing from those assholes is one thing. Carjacking from some innocent civilian is another."

"Well, then we had best lead them on a merry chase."

"Don't worry," Carrie said. "All we have to do is reach the embassy in Port Louis. Then we'll be safe."

"Yes," Abhi countered. "But to do that, we need to first figure out where we are."

"Good point. Watch for road signs."

They drove into the night, and the darkness seemed as oppressive as it had along the bottom of the ocean.

FOURTEEN

They rode in stunned silence for a while. Carrie assumed that Abhi and Paolo were each coming to grips with the situation in their own way. She felt nauseous and edgy as leftover adrenaline coursed through her system. Her hands and feet jittered, and her left eye kept twitching uncontrollably. Trying her best to ignore it, she guided the SUV on a bewildering series of turns, choosing at random, hopping from highways to back roads to service roads and then back onto the highways again, all in a desperate effort to lose any pursuit while also putting as much distance between them and the Alpinus facility as possible. She kept glancing in the rearview mirror, alert for any signs that they were being followed, but—beside a few nerve-wracking false alarms—the coast remained clear.

She had hoped to find one of the roads that Maberry and Mariotte had used when the two had driven her and Abhi to Takenaka's ship. At least then, she'd be able to find the harbor, and possibly help. But nothing looked familiar in the dark.

"Check around," she suggested, finally. "See if there's anything in here we can use. Maybe there are more guns."

Paolo found nothing after checking around the vehicle's rear. Abhi meanwhile searched the glove compartment and the other storage nooks, but came up empty other than an atlas of Mauritius, a packet of tissues, and a crumpled, empty cigarette pack. He consulted the atlas, squinting in the dark, and then glanced up at their surroundings.

"Is that mountain over there Le Pouce?" Abhi pointed out the window.

"I think so." Carrie nodded.

"Then that puts us in the Moka District."

"Not that far from Port Louis," Paolo said. "All we have to do is make it over the Moka Range."

"Easy as pie," Carrie muttered. "Nothing to it."

"You are much more optimistic than I am," Abhi said.

"Aren't I always?"

"The Moka Range is all winding mountain roads," Abhi said. "There's very little in the way of lighting or widely popu- lated areas. If they're going to hit us, those roads would be the best place for it. Great place for an ambush, too. How many bullets do you have left, Paolo?"

Fumbling, Paolo ejected the weapon's magazine and squinted in the dim light. "I think six? And maybe one in the chamber."

"We might need them," Abhi said. "We have to consider the very real possibility that they're following us right now."

"I haven't seen any cars tailing us," Carrie said.

"They don't need to tail us," Abhi explained. "Barbet said they had aerial drones as part of their security at the clinic. And we know they had high-tech listening devices. It stands to reason they've got a GPS or something else tracking this vehicle right now."

"Shit." Carrie's skin prickled. "You're right. In all the ex- citement, I never even considered that."

"It's okay," Abhi said. "I don't think any of us were in our right minds."

He paused, and glanced back at Paolo. There was an uncomfortable silence, and then Paolo cleared his throat.

"I had no choice," Paolo said. "I thought he was going to kill me, or take the gun and kill one of you. What would you have had me do?"

"I don't know," Abhi admitted. "And yes, I know very well what their plans were for us. But still, I just . . . it's the first time I've ever been involved in killing someone, Paolo. You'll have to excuse me if I'm a little . . . what do the kids say? Freaked out?"

"How do you think I feel, Gordo?"

Abhi swiveled around so fast that it startled Carrie. The SUV swerved into the other lane.

"I told you before," Abhi warned, "don't call me fat. And as for how you feel about killing a man, I don't know. Maybe you don't feel anything at all. You're always so goddamned smug. I don't know what Carrie sees in you."

Carrie's eyes went wide. "Hey!"

"I still don't understand your motivations for joining us in this," Abhi continued. "I know you said you were worried about Carrie and worried about your reputation, but—"

"Enough," Paolo interrupted, holding up his hand. "Enough, Abhi. Please. You're right. I haven't told either of you everything. And I will, right now. I swear it. But first, we must figure out what to do about this car. I think you are right. They are probably tracking us. Not counting Ochse, there are twelve agents assigned to the facility. We can account for the two in the truck, the one in the custodian closet, the three at the gate, and the two that got off the elevator as we were leaving."

"And the one that you shot," Abhi replied.

"Yes, him, too. That means the others are unaccounted for.

And have probably freed the others by now. Probably called the cops, too."

"I'll find a populated area," Carrie suggested. "The village of Moka is just up the road. We'll find somewhere with lots of lights and people. Somewhere they can't confront us in the open without witnesses. Then we'll abandon the SUV and get a taxi to take us to the embassy."

"How are we going to pay for it?" Abhi asked. "What little money we had left is back at the clinic."

"We'll figure that out when we get to the embassy. What we need to do first is ditch this thing and find us a cab."

After both men agreed with the plan, Carrie and Abhi stayed silent, waiting for Paolo to continue with whatever he had been about to tell them. When he didn't speak, Carrie prodded him gently.

"Now, what were you saying, Paolo? Something about not telling us everything?"

"I know what the creatures were," he said softly. "And I know why Alpinus is trying to kill us."

Carrie and Abhi glanced at each other. Then Carrie's eyes darted to the rearview mirror. Paolo stared out at the passing countryside, his expression one of grim resignation.

"And how did you come by all this information?" Carrie asked, afraid that she already knew the answer.

Paolo sighed. "Because I work for Alpinus. When the United Nations awarded Alpinus the expedition contract, it led to certain risks. There were things they didn't want uncovered. I was assigned to spy on the expedition, and keep anyone, including you—especially you—from discovering the wrong things."

"Which is?"

"The research and development arm of Alpinus Biofutures has been working on nanotechnology for the last decade. The progress they've made is absolutely stunning, but there is only so much you can do in a laboratory setting. Two years ago, they began testing nanobots in the wild."

"What the hell are nanobots?" Abhi asked.

"Tiny robots," Carrie explained. "Built on the scale of a nanometer. Microscopic in size. In theory, you could inject them into a human being and repair damaged tissue or attack cancer cells, or utilize them in molecular research."

Abhi shook his head. "And I have trouble sending an e-mail. Do these things actually work?"

"They were supposedly theoretical, for the most part," Carrie said. "A few primitive versions have been tested, but it sounds like Alpinus got much further along."

"You have no idea," Paolo said. "And that's the way it always is. Over the last five years, drones have dominated the news. You see them discussed everywhere as the latest in cutting-edge technology. They're used in everything from warfare to home deliveries. But your Central Intelligence Agency had developed drones and were using them in the field as far back as the Vietnam War. Not big, bulky drones, but sophisticated, advanced units, built to scale and designed to look like dragonflies, catfish, and other creatures."

"Why would anyone make a catfish drone?" Abhi asked.

"It's easy," Paolo replied. "Suppose there is an enemy dam you wish to destroy. You pilot the drone up the river and monitor the dam. You take pictures, via the drone, of the best place to plant explosives. If anyone sees it, there's no chance of discovery, because they assume it's just another catfish. But getting back to my point, drones aren't some brand new thing. They've been in development for decades. They're only new to the public. It's the same with nanotechnology. Carrie said that only a few primitive machines have been tested, but it goes way beyond that. Those primitive machines were being secretly tested back in the early seventies. They're much more advanced now."

"Hang on," Carrie said, noticing a pair of headlights closing fast on their rear. She held her breath and gripped the steering wheel tighter as the other vehicle approached. Then, it sped past them. She caught a glimpse of four young faces—kids, out having fun in a fast car. She exhaled, and her grip loosened.

"About a year and a half ago," Paolo continued, "Alpinus released nanomachines into the ocean here. As you know, with the exception of the northern fringe, the water temperatures in this area keep the production of phytoplankton low. As a result, life in the ocean is more limited than it is in other regions. That and the warmer temperatures made it an ideal location for their experiment, the intent of which was to ultimately create a temporary hypoxia that they could dial up or down at will."

"Hypoxia?" Carrie frowned. "Why would they want to do that?"

Paolo shrugged. "Control the oceans, and you control an array of natural resources. Some of the world's biggest oil and natural gas reserves are beneath the ocean floors. Consider how the oceans feed us. If you controlled the oceans, you could create famines, which do wonders for the prices of various commodities. If successful, Alpinus would have unprecedented control of not just their competitors, but entire populaces— entire nations. Billions of people would be dependent on them."

"Jesus," Carrie muttered.

"Well," Abhi said, "that settles it. Once we get to Port Louis, I'm calling Alpinus and quitting."

The joke elicited only a wisp of a smile from Carrie, who was struggling to control her anger at these revelations. And what bothered her more than Alpinus's unscrupulous experimentation and sheer arrogance, was the fact that Paolo had known about all this, and said nothing. Indeed, by his own admission, he'd been paid to keep her—and anybody else—from discovering the truth. Her emotions regarding Paolo had just started to warm. This betrayal was like plunging into the Arctic Sea.

"So, what went wrong?" Carrie fought to keep her tone neutral.

"There were unexpected . . . complications. The experiment led to a rapid mutation of the sea life near the trench. The nanobots began building, using various bits of the sea life around them. Tentacles, gills, claws—it was like they borrowed something from everything they encountered and used it to make their very own Frankenstein's monster. I don't begin to understand the science involved. In truth, I don't think there are many at Alpinus who understand what happened, either. Somehow, these mutations ultimately yielded the two massive nanomachine-enhanced apex predators we contended with."

"Wait a minute," Abhi said. "Those monsters were really just tiny robots?"

"No, they were biological," Paolo corrected. "They were flesh and blood. We don't know what their original stock was, but they were enhanced by nanobots. The machines took the best from a variety of sea life near the trench, and mutated it, the same way they were starting to mutate my brain. But while the process was halted in me, it went unchecked in the trench. Those two predators were the result. And somehow, their presence and the hypoxia effect have led to the rapid deterioration of the sea floor."

"That's a lot to swallow," Abhi mused.

"Perhaps so, but that doesn't make it any less true. There is also the very real danger of this spreading farther out into the ocean. Not only will they wreak havoc on other ecosystems, but they'll gain access to a greater variety of life from which to feed and build. And sooner or later, humans will be part of those raw materials. But unlike what happened with me, the process won't be halted."

Carrie's head throbbed. "So, why tell us now, Paolo? I mean, you strung us along. You goddamn knew what was down there when we dived—"

"I didn't know the full extent—"

"Shut up." Carrie spat. "I don't want to hear your excuses. Peter died because of this. You knew what was down there and you didn't warn us. Peter would still be alive now!"

"But I honestly didn't know," Paolo insisted. "I don't think anyone from Alpinus knew the true extent. The mutations— the impact on the trench—none of that was supposed to happen. The nanobots were just supposed to engineer a controllable version of hypoxia. Alpinus knew they would copy some lesser forms of sea life, but it wasn't supposed to be anything like this. Certainly not predators like the ones we encountered. Their size, their aggressiveness, the fact that they are breeding—it was unexpected. Nobody at Alpinus knew the true extent of it until after you and I dived."

Carrie gripped the steering wheel so tightly that her knuckles popped.

"They must have suspected," she reasoned.

"I know there was another research vessel—a private craft—one of theirs, that disappeared just after the collapse sped up. They sent it out here to investigate things discreetly. Do you remember Asselin and Edidin from when we worked at the Scripps Institute?"

"Janelle and Rachel?" Carrie nodded. "Of course I remember them. They were brilliant."

"They were both part of the original expedition."

Carrie sighed in dismay. "They were a part of this? They knew?"

"I don't think they knew, at all," Paolo said. "But Alpinus hired them to accompany a team out here."

"Where are they now?"

"Their boat disappeared. It was never found, nor were any of the crew's bodies recovered."

"The predators?"

"That's what I assumed," Paolo said. "Now, I'm not so sure. Perhaps it was Ochse and his men. There have also been some instances of other people disappearing—a few fishermen, but mostly tourists, and all of those back before the authorities banned people from diving in the waters around the trench. But these disappearances happened over a length of time, so nobody suspected anything like Alpinus could be behind it."

"The body count just keeps rising," Carrie muttered. "You must be very proud of yourself, Paolo. You talk about growing up in the shadow of Pinochet, but that old man had nothing on Alpinus. How could you work with people like that?"

"I swear, Carrie. I never meant to put you in danger. Need I remind you one of those things nearly killed me, as well?"

Abhi crumpled the atlas in his fists. "It nearly killed all of us, you little asshole."

"So," Carrie asked, "when you warned me about the Novak being under surveillance—was that just another lie?"

"No," Paolo said. "It wasn't a lie. The ship really was under surveillance. At the time, I just didn't know it was Ochse and his men. I wasn't told of their involvement. I thought perhaps it was a competitor—Globe or someone like that. Or maybe one of the journalists, trying to go rogue, and get a deeper story."

"You didn't know about Ochse," Abhi said, "but were he and his men aware of your involvement?"

Paolo shrugged. "I'm sure they were."

"Why are you telling us now?" Carrie asked.

She saw him smile in the rearview mirror, his perfect teeth flashing white in the dark.

"I'm hedging my bets, Carrie. Plain and simple. I think you would agree that my situation has drastically changed?"

She shrugged.

"And they lied to me. One of the reasons I was hired was because of our past relationship. I was promised that neither of you would be hurt. That changes things. Even after the United Nations shut everything down, I stayed on because I wanted to keep you safe. I had to answer to them, yes, but you were my number one priority. I couldn't let you discover the truth, but I couldn't let anything happen to you, either."

"Is that supposed to make me feel better?"

"No," Paolo said. "But it is the truth."

"I don't know what the truth is anymore, Paolo. And you know what's even worse? I don't think you do, either."

"Carrie . . . I am truly sorry for everything that has happened."

Carrie didn't respond. As they drove on, Abhi cleared his throat and shifted around in the seat, clearly uncomfortable with the tension in the vehicle. Carrie remained motionless, except for the almost imperceptible turns of the steering wheel. Her thoughts were swirling, chaotic turmoil. She was furious with Paolo, but even more enraged with herself—because, despite everything he'd done, and everything he'd revealed—she was already on her way to forgiving him. And that felt like the worst betrayal of all, because it didn't come from someone else. It came from inside herself. She stared straight ahead, into the darkness, afraid that if she tried to reply, she'd begin screaming instead.

When they reached Moka, Carrie's plan of finding a brightly lit area with lots of witnesses fell apart. Apparently, the entire village went to bed after sundown. Her temples still throbbed. Instead of abating, her headache had only grown worse, which just increased her overall tension. She cruised the dark and empty streets, looking for a place to abandon the SUV. Eventually, in a more run-down section of the village, they found a street lined with bars, where people were still awake. A group of young men loitered on the corner outside one particularly seedy-looking establishment. They eyed the black SUV warily as Carrie slowly cruised past them.

"They don't look like they're up to anything good," Abhi mused.

"No," Carrie agreed. "They don't. Which makes them absolutely perfect."

"What? Are we going to hire our own mercenaries?"

Instead of answering him, Carrie turned into a narrow, trash-strewn alley on the other side of the bar. The headlights glanced off a garbage dumpster, atop of which several fat, sleek rats scurried, fleeing in fright at the intrusion. Carrie turned off the headlights and killed the engine. Then they got out of the vehicle. Abhi went around to the back and began to wrestle with Paolo's wheelchair, but the younger man stopped him.

"Leave it," Paolo said. "I think I can walk on my own now."

"Are you sure?" Abhi seemed unconvinced. "You're still recovering from . . . well, whatever it was that was happening to you."

"I'll be fine. The wheelchair will only slow us down and make us more conspicuous."

"Conspicuous?" Abhi scoffed. "Look at how you're dressed."

"It's better than being naked. Leave the wheelchair."

Shrugging, Abhi closed the hatch. Then he turned to Carrie.

"He says we don't need the wheelchair. Go ahead and lock it."

"I'm not," she replied. "And I'm leaving the keys in the ignition."

"What? Why?"

Carrie smiled. "Trust me."

"You I trust."

Abhi made a point of glancing at Paolo as he said it, but if Paolo picked up on Abhi's implication, he didn't react. Instead, he pulled his hospital robe tight, and handed Carrie the pistol.

"Here," he said. "I don't really have anywhere to hide this right now."

Carrie tucked the handgun beneath her waistband and pulled her shirttail down over it. The metal felt cool against the small of her back. The sensation had a strange, calming effect on her.

"Let's go," she said. "I feel exposed, standing out here."

"You feel exposed?" Paolo indicated his hospital gown. "How do you think I feel?"

They walked down the dark alley and exited onto the sidewalk. When they did, Carrie made a point of not glancing in the direction of the young men who were still hanging out in front of the bar. Their conversation, which was being spoken in a mix of Mauritian Creole and Bhojpuri, abruptly ceased as the three of them emerged. Their surly glares turned to gaping surprise when they saw Paolo limping along, still dressed in his hospital gown. He kept one hand pressed to his chest, and the other clutched the string ties on the back of the robe. Trying to appear casual and relaxed, Carrie guided Abhi and Paolo in the opposite direction, and headed down the street.

"Oh shit," she exclaimed, raising her voice until it echoed down the street. "I left the keys in the car. Do you think it will be okay?"

Understanding flickered in Abhi's expression. Grinning, he played along.

"It should be fine," he said, slurring his voice. "As much as we've had to drink, we shouldn't be driving anymore tonight anyway. We'll come back for it in the morning."

They continued up the street, stumbling a bit now, and laughing a little too loudly. Abhi stumbled off the curb and walked into a light pole, then hopped back up on the sidewalk.

"Don't overdo it," Carrie whispered.

"Nonsense," he replied. "This is an Oscar-worthy performance. And you are a genius."

When they'd gone a full block, Carrie pretended to drop something so that she could risk a glance behind them. She almost cheered when she saw the gang of youths slinking into the alley. She straightened up quick and kept walking.

"They took the bait," she said.

A few minutes later, the SUV roared out of the alley and sped off into the night, tires screeching. The brake lights barely flickered as it rounded a curve and disappeared. The roar of the engine faded.

"Well done," Abhi said. "That was genius, Carrie!"

"It should buy us some time. If you're right about the GPS, then Alpinus will track the SUV. I'd hate to be those kids when Ochse and the others catch up with them." She paused, and a deep look of concern crossed her face. "Paolo, you don't think Ochse would kill them, do you? I mean, they're not involved. They don't know anything. All they did was steal a car."

"I don't know," Paolo admitted.

"Maybe," Abhi said, "and maybe not. But he definitely wants to kill us. I suggest we find a taxi."

The streets remained mostly deserted. A few cars drove by, but none of them were taxicabs. They found a bus stop, but according to the sign mounted on a pole, public transportation had stopped running several hours before and wouldn't resume until morning. Eventually, after growing increasingly frustrated, Carrie led them into a bar.

"What are we doing?" Abhi had to shout over the cheers of rowdy patrons and a live band who were playing French covers of heavy metal songs from the eighties. "And do I have time to get a drink?"

Carrie leaned over and put her mouth against his ear. Tiny hairs tickled her upper lip.

"You two wait by the door," she said. "I'm going to ask the bartender to call us a cab. Keep an eye on Paolo."

Abhi nodded his understanding. Then he tugged on Paolo's arm and positioned them in a dark corner near the door, where they hopefully wouldn't attract attention.

Carrie elbowed her way through the throng of drunken, rowdy people as the band segued from Guns n' Roses "Reckless Life" to a song by The Bullet Boys, the title of which she couldn't remember. The crowd sounded marginally better— and louder—than the band, and the clamor did nothing to ease her headache. Each throb of the bass guitar and every cymbal clash was like a spike being driven through her temples. Finally, she made it up to the bar and got the bartender's attention. She quickly pleaded her situation—telling him that her friends were too drunk to drive, and they had no cell phone with which to call a taxi service. She was relieved when the bartender agreed to help them. Carrie thanked him, wishing she had money to tip him.

Then they went back outside and waited, glancing around

nervously, expecting at any moment for a horde of Alpinus security agents to burst from the shadows and descend upon them. Paolo fidgeted with his hospital gown, repeatedly tugging on it and making sure it stayed tied, but also pulling it away from his chest, as if the fabric were too constricting. The behavior seemed odd, but Carrie chalked it up to tension and anxiety.

She glanced at Abhi, and was alarmed to see just how old and tired he suddenly looked, as if the events of the past few days had aged him. A deep sadness welled up inside of her. In a way, Carrie felt responsible for his plight. If she had never recruited him to help her, none of this would have happened to him.

As if sensing her thoughts, Abhi turned to her and smiled. "So, this is fun, isn't it?"

"You look like shit."

"It's the lighting out here. And you're not exactly catching me on my best day."

Despite everything, Carrie laughed.

"You sound just like her," Abhi said.

"Just like who?"

"Marissa. When you laugh like that, you sound just like Marissa used to sound. That's one of the reasons I've always liked you."

Carrie's voice softened. "You never did finish telling me about her."

"Aye, I didn't. Marissa was the one who got away. That may sound cliché, but there is often a lot of truth in those old clichés, no? If there is such a thing as a soul mate then she was mine."

"What happened?"

"I happened." He stared down at the pavement. "She was completely unlike any other woman I've ever known. She understood me—I mean really understood me, the good and the bad. And she didn't judge. I never understood the concept of unconditional love until Marissa. That makes what happened even worse."

Carrie smiled in sympathy.

"One night, I ran across an old girlfriend. Not one I loved in the same way I loved Marissa, but one for whom I cared very deeply still. You understand?"

Carrie had to restrain herself from glancing at Paolo.

"We were both drunk, and when the bar closed, she invited me back to her place. I genuinely had intended to sleep on the couch. It was nice, being with her. Sharing old laughs, but I had no plans to sleep with this woman."

"But you did?"

"Aye. We drank some more at her apartment, and caught up on things. Talked about old times. Old friends. We laughed a lot. It was . . . nice. But it was also nothing like what I had with Marissa. When it came time to go to sleep, she brought me a blanket and a pillow for the couch. I noticed that she was wincing, so I asked what was wrong. She said her back hurt. I offered to rub it. One thing led to another."

He paused, but Carrie didn't respond.

"The guilt was instantaneous," he continued. "It hit me even before we'd finished. I couldn't handle it. And it came back to me every time I was with Marissa—and I don't mean just intimately—it haunted me when we did anything together. Watching a movie or having dinner or just walking down the street holding hands. I couldn't take knowing that I'd cheated on her, and so I began to find reasons to break up with her. I nitpicked our perfect relationship apart, until finally, it didn't exist anymore."

"Oh, Abhi . . ."

"I know. I know. It was a cowardly, stupid act—the behavior

of a boy, not a man. A cruel and thoughtless boy. I tell myself that I was younger then. We all do things we are ashamed of when we are young. But that doesn't make it right. Rather than telling her the truth, rather than working through it, I chose the coward's way out. And Marissa never knew the real reason why. She still doesn't, to this day. I heard from friends later that it nearly destroyed her. She blamed herself, but the truth is, the blame was all on me."

"Why didn't you ever try again? Why not reach out to her?"

Abhi sighed. "I almost did. I guess it was about fifteen years ago, now. I tracked her down, and found out she was married to a man who worked as a welder in a shipyard in Naples. They had three children together. After learning that, how could I? She was happy."

"Is she still married?"

"I don't know."

"You should find out, Abhi. And you should still tell her."

"What good would that do?"

"Well, I'm not telling you to go break up her marriage, but at the very least, she still deserves to know the truth. You owe her that. And I think you owe yourself that, as well. You've been carrying this for a long time."

"It has been a long time," he agreed. "Perhaps I will try, if we make it out of this alive."

His words seemed to hang in the air, and they fell silent again.

The taxi arrived about ten minutes later. Carrie felt a surge of elation as it pulled up to the curb. The driver eyed them warily. His gaze lingered on Paolo's attire. The three of them climbed into the back, and asked the driver to take them to the American embassy in Port Louis. He refused at first, hesitant to make the drive over the mountains in the dark, but Carrie turned on the charm and finally convinced him.

Once the cab was on its way, she sank back into the seat and relaxed, breathing a deep sigh of relief. She couldn't completely relax, however. Her nerves were wound too tightly. It also didn't help that the handgun was pressing into her back. She shifted around, trying to find a more comfortable position.

Paolo and Abhi were both quiet, seemingly lost in their own thoughts. The driver apparently wasn't the chatty type, preferring instead to listen to an audiobook. He kept the volume low, for which Carrie—whose headache still hadn't abated—was grateful.

"You should rest, Gatito," Paolo murmured.

Nodding, Carrie decided to close her eyes for a minute and do just that, in the hopes that her headache would subside.

"Carrie. Paolo. Wake up. We're here."

Carrie blinked, unsure what was happening. When she opened her eyes and saw Abhi rousting Paolo, she realized that she had fallen asleep in the back of the cab.

"Come on," Abhi urged again. "We're pulling up now. Time to rise and shine."

The taxi slowed as the driver approached the guardhouse outside the American embassy. Carrie's hopes surged. An American flag fluttered above the building, illuminated by two bright spotlights. Two U.S. Marines stood outside the gate, checking the identification of a vehicle in front of them. A black Jeep was parked nearby.

"We made it," she said, ecstatic. "Oh my God, we made—"

The exclamation died in her throat as she caught sight of a familiar face. Maberry, the hulking and laconic Alpinus security agent, stood next to the guardhouse, conferring with a third Marine over a handful of paperwork. Carrie had no doubt that their names and photographs were on the papers. Then she realized that the black Jeep probably belonged to him.

She'd seen another like it in the parking garage at the Alpinus facility. Or perhaps this was the same one. If so, that meant Ochse and Legerski were surely free.

"Keep going," she shouted, slapping the back of the driver's seat with her hand. "Don't stop here!"

The driver checked the rearview mirror in confusion. "Lady, you said take you to the American embassy. This is the American embassy."

Abhi looked at her in concern. "Carrie, what's wrong?"

"I see it," Paolo said, pointing. "Over there. One of Ochse's men."

Abhi's shoulders slumped. "Well, shit. What do we do?"

"Please," Carrie said to the driver, "we can't stop here. We just can't. You have to keep going."

Sighing with exaggerated annoyance, the driver turned the taxi away from the guard shack. Carrie, Abhi, and Paolo ducked low in the backseat as one of the Marines noticed the taxi pulling away. Slowly, he started to approach the cab.

"Go," Carrie said. "Please, hurry."

"And where would you like me to take you now?" the driver asked, exasperated.

The Marine drew closer. Now Maberry and the others were also looking in their direction.

"I don't know," Carrie exclaimed. "Anywhere! Just fucking drive."

Shaking his head, the driver wheeled away.

"It's your meter," he said.

When they'd pulled away from the building, Abhi raised his head and risked a glance behind them.

"Anything?" Carrie asked.

"No," he replied. "Maybe they didn't see our faces. What do we do now?"

The cabbie glanced back at them. "Do you have a destination, or should I just keep driving around in circles?"

"Keep driving please," Paolo told him. Then he turned to Carrie. "What do we do now?"

Carrie sighed. "I don't know."

"But you always know," Abhi protested.

"Well, I'm all out of ideas. Who else would give us asylum? Better yet, who would help us stop Alpinus from killing the Indian Ocean's ecosystem with their nanomachines?"

"Australia," Paolo said, after a moment. "Australia would help. Eventually, this ecological disaster will impact them. They have a vested interest in what is happening here. And while Alpinus may be an international company, they have no branches in Australia, so that country's leaders are less likely to be compromised."

Carrie tapped the driver's shoulder.

"Yes? Did you decide where you're going? I'd like to get back home before dawn."

"The Australian embassy," she answered. "Do you know where that is?"

He nodded. "Of course."

"Take us there, please."

She glanced behind them, watching for Maberry's black Jeep, but there was no sign of pursuit.

"How did he know we'd try for the American embassy?" she wondered aloud.

"Well, you *are* an American," Paulo said. "It stands to reason they'd be waiting for you there."

Or, Carrie thought, *maybe you told them instead.*

Abhi shrugged. "It's possible they are still tracking us."

"But how?" Carrie asked.

He shrugged again. "They could have had the SUV bugged.

They could have been listening in the whole time. Or maybe they're tailing us with a drone, in the sky. Or maybe they inserted some sort of tracking device in Paolo or yourself. Both of you were stitched up in the clinic. They could have inserted something under your skin."

"No," Carrie said, "if they had done something like that, I'm sure Dr. Barbet would have told us. He warned us about all the other surveillance equipment."

"Maybe he didn't know. Or maybe he just didn't get the chance."

"Those are a lot of maybes," Paolo said.

Carrie was overwhelmed with the image of Barbet lying crumpled inside the truck, his blood running out in deep, widening pools around him while steam rose from his corpse. She wondered what would become of his husband. Who would tell him what happened? And what would they tell him? Would they *even* tell him? Or, would they kill him?

"His husband," she said. "Dr. Barbet's husband. We've got to warn him. And I need to get in touch with my sister."

"That would be a mistake," Paolo replied, lowering his voice. "We have to assume they're monitoring all of our family, friends, and co-workers. Reaching out to anyone else right now would only put them in danger."

"What's that about danger?" The driver sounded alarmed.

"Nothing you need to concern yourself with," Paolo assured him. "You didn't hear any of this, right?"

"Right," the driver agreed, clearly shaken. "And for the right price, I'll make sure that nobody else hears—"

"Just don't," Carrie interrupted. "Are you really going to try to blackmail us? Right here at the embassy? I'm pretty sure I could find an interested officer around here somewhere. Just get us to our destination, please."

Cowed, the taxi driver stared straight ahead, shoulders hunched, and didn't say another word.

Two traffic lights and five minutes later, the cab pulled up in front of the Australian embassy. Like its American counterpart, there was a guard booth outside the fence, manned with soldiers. Unlike the American embassy, there was no sign of anyone from Alpinus.

When the taxi pulled up to the gate, the driver rolled the windows down. A young, baby-faced soldier approached the car. The cab driver pointed his thumb at Carrie. The soldier then walked over to her window.

"Passports, please?"

"We don't have any passports," Carrie told him.

"I need to see everyone's identification, ma'am."

"We don't have anything," she repeated. "We're in trouble. All of our identification was taken—our passports, everything. We're seeking immediate asylum, please."

The soldier frowned. "Are you Australian citizens?"

"Yes," she lied.

"Funny," he said. "Where are you from? Because you sound American to me."

Abhi leaned forward. "I tell her the same thing all the time, mate. She's been abroad too long."

Carrie struggled to suppress her surprise. Although he sounded like Crocodile Dundee, Abhi spoke with a pretty convincing Australian accent.

Though apparently not convincing enough for the guard. He glanced back at the gate, and then at them.

"Where are you from?"

"I just told you," Abhi said. "Australia."

"No, I mean what town?"

Abhi paused. "Oh, it's a small village. You've probably never heard of it."

"You might be surprised. What's the name of the town?"

Abhi paused even longer this time, clearly flummoxed. "Um . . . Melbourne?"

"Melbourne's a small town, is it?" The guard spoke into his radio. "This is Addison. We may have a problem at the front gate. Requesting additional manpower."

"Please," Carrie begged. "We're in immediate danger. Even out here. We can prove everything to you once we're inside, but we need asylum."

"Pull ahead," Addison told the driver. "All of you will have to go through security screening."

The driver inched the cab toward the gate. Several more soldiers appeared, along with an officer. They scanned the car, swept beneath it with a mirror attached to a long pole, and had it inspected by a dog—Carrie wasn't sure if it was sniffing for drugs or explosives, or both. Satisfied, the officer then had them exit the vehicle. The cab driver was visibly pleased to see them go.

"Wait here," Carrie told him. "And we'll get your fare."

"Now just a minute," he protested. "You had me drive you here all the way from Moka. This isn't some quick trip around the way for a few dollars. Don't try to skip on me."

"We're not trying to duck you."

"Then pay me—now."

"I promise," Carrie assured him. "As soon as we get inside, I'll make sure you're taken care of."

"You'd better. I'll call the police."

"There won't be any need for that. I swear."

The driver scowled at her, and waved his hand in frustration. "Go on, then."

"Okay," Addison told them. "I need you to walk this way, single file."

Carrie stopped the soldier before they could go any farther.

"I need to inform you that I have a weapon on me," she said.

"What?" His hand moved to the holstered pistol on his hip.

"Please," Carrie said. "I'm declaring it. I'm not trying to sneak it in or anything. I'm not some terrorist. I just figured I'd be doing the right thing by informing you before you found it. I'm going to take it out, okay?"

"No, ma'am, that's not okay. I need you to get down on your knees, put your hands on top of your head, and interlock your fingers."

To punctuate the order, Addison unholstered his sidearm. Other soldiers gathered around them, weapons at the ready. Carrie felt their eyes boring into her. Moving slowly, she complied with his demands, trying very hard to demonstrate that she wasn't a threat. She stared straight ahead and kept her breathing steady as another soldier frisked her, removed the pistol, and handed it off to the officer.

"Are we okay?" Carrie asked Addison.

Nodding, he motioned at her to stand up. Carrie complied again, still moving with exaggerated slowness. The officer approached them.

"I'm Second Lieutenant Navarro, Australian Defense Force. You're Carrie Anderson."

"You know me?" Carrie was surprised.

"I watch the news, Miss Anderson. And while I can't speak for your friends here, I'm fairly certain you aren't Australian. Which means you lied in an attempt to gain access to the embassy. Also, unless I'm mistaken, that weapon we just confiscated from you smells like it has been fired recently."

"Like I said," Carrie explained, "we're in trouble. There are people trying to kill us. We're asking for immediate asylum."

"But you're not Australian."

"No, I'm not," she admitted, "but it concerns your country.

We have information about a conspiracy that will directly impact Australia. We just need to talk to someone. Look, you said it yourself. I'm not a terrorist or something. I'm a public figure. I'm not going to do anything. Handcuff us. Take us in at gunpoint if you need to. But please, we need your help!"

Navarro studied each of them for a minute. Then he nodded. "This way, please."

Carrie motioned at the taxi driver, assuring him to wait. The driver shook his head in agitation.

On the other side of the gate, Carrie, Abhi, and Paolo were lined up to be frisked. The soldiers looked quizzically at Paolo's hospital gown, but didn't question him about it as he limped forward. As the soldiers searched her, Carrie watched Paolo. He looked gaunt and exhausted. The toll this entire thing had taken on him was never clearer. Her emotions regarding it were conflicted, however. On the one hand, she felt a perverse sense of delight. After his betrayal, it served him right. But another part of her wanted to comfort him—to fix things and make them better.

She was still thinking this when Paolo collapsed. He hit the pavement almost face-first, and when he rolled over, she saw that he'd split his bottom lip open. More blood ran from a cut on his cheek. Shouting, she stepped toward him but the soldiers restrained her. Addison called for a stretcher, and Paolo was quickly loaded onto it. He seemed alert and awake, but clearly weakened. Two soldiers carried him inside.

"Where are they taking him?" she demanded, an edge of panic rising in her voice.

"To the infirmary," Navarro explained. "He's in good hands. Right now, it's in all of your interests to let us finish here, Miss Anderson."

Carrie nodded reluctantly. The screening process continued. After they had finished frisking Abhi, Navarro had them both walk through a metal detector. On the other side of the security cordon, he smiled in an obvious effort to reassure them.

"Okay," he said, "follow us please. Any deviation from the directed route, or any failure to follow my commands will, in fact, be cause to respond with deadly force. Do I make myself clear?"

"Crystal," Abhi responded for them both.

Addison, Navarro, and two other armed soldiers led them into the embassy. The officer led the way. Carrie and Abhi walked behind him, with a soldier on each of their sides. Addison brought up the rear.

"We made it," Carrie said in disbelief. "I don't know how, but we made it, Abhi. We're safe."

"Yes," Abhi whispered, low enough that the soldiers wouldn't hear him. "Until they decide they can't grant us asylum because we're not Australian citizens. Then we'll be right back out on the streets again, or in jail."

"We'll cross that bridge when we come to it. If we come to it. I think they'll want to hear what we have to say."

"But we can't prove any of it, Carrie."

"Sure we can. All they need to do is raid the Alpinus facility. All the proof is there. The remains of the creatures, for starters. And I'm sure they have documents and data. Barbet and I were recording things."

"I hope that you are right."

Inside the lobby, Second Lieutenant Navarro pointed them toward a group of ornate, beautiful chairs and couches, and asked them to have a seat. The man's tone made it clear that this wasn't a request that should be denied. He also promised to get an update on Paolo's condition. Addison and another

soldier departed, leaving the third soldier to guard over them
while Navarro conferred with a man in a suit who was seated
at a nearby desk.

Carrie glanced around the lobby. Classical music played
softly from a hidden sound system. In addition to the furniture,
there were several Persian rugs on the floor. Tapestries and oil
paintings decorated the walls, depicting scenes of both Australian and Mauritian flavor. Despite the early hour, there were
a few people about. One of them, seated nearby on a plush, red
velvet-covered love seat, seemed familiar to Carrie. The woman
was tapping on her phone with a bored expression. On the
end table next to her sat a silver tray with a small ceramic
tea kettle, an assortment of creamers and sweeteners, and a
steaming cup of tea.

Oh God, Carrie thought. *What I wouldn't give for a cup of
tea right now. And a hot shower and three days of sleep in a
real bed. But tea first.*

The woman, perhaps feeling eyes upon her, glanced up.
When she did, Carrie gasped. The woman's surprised expression mirrored her own.

"Carrie Anderson?"

"Jessamine Wheatley!"

The reporter got up and crossed the room, beaming with
evident curiosity.

"This is unexpected," she exclaimed. "What are you doing
in the Australian embassy?"

"It's a long story," Carrie said. "What are you doing here?
I thought you were on your way to Australia when we last
spoke?"

"Oh, it's been a long week." Jessamine rolled her eyes. "You
just wouldn't believe the headaches we've had. First, the network wanted us to cover preparations for the evacuation, and
the economic impact it might have. So we stayed a few extra

days to file that story. And then Khem caught a stomach bug, and the network wanted us to travel together because of some cost-cutting bullshit, so we had to wait another day for him to get better. He thinks it was some shrimp he bought from a roadside stand. Then, yesterday, we were finally ready to leave and we got to the airport only to learn that our flight was delayed and we were stuck here in Mauritius. So, Hank, Khem, Julio, and I came here. The embassy promised the network they'd pull some strings, and get us on a plane."

"Why are all the flights delayed?"

"The impending evacuation," Jessamine explained. "It's taken a while, but I think people are starting to get worried. Anyone who can afford it is trying to get off the island, just in case the evacuation is ordered. I guess they want to beat the rush. It's causing chaos at the airports, so we're stuck here until later today. Khem and Hank are in the lounge, playing cards with one of the diplomat's assistants and a few civilians."

"Do you think it will be ordered?"

Jessamine shrugged. "Eventually. What do you think?"

Carrie sighed. "I don't know anything anymore."

"There's a lot of that going around."

Carrie quickly introduced Jessamine to Abhi. While the two shook hands and exchanged pleasantries, Carrie glanced over at the desk, where the man and Navarro were still conferring. Then, the man rose, and the two officials began to walk toward them.

"Jessamine, listen to me." Carrie took a deep breath. "That man is about to come over here. He may decide we're here under false pretenses. It's very possible he won't believe what we tell him, and it's vitally important that he does believe."

"Why? What's going on?"

"I don't have time to get into it right now, but it's something that impacts us all. We're in trouble. What I need from you is to help me smooth things over."

"Sounds juicy." Jessamine smiled. "I'm intrigued."

Carrie smiled in return. "You wanted a big news story that would get people interested? Let's just say I've got something of a lead for you."

Navarro and the official reached them. The man cleared his throat.

"Miss Carrie Anderson?"

"Yes. I'm Carrie Anderson."

"My name is James. I'm an assistant to Ambassador Mc-Bean. I understand you have a story to tell?"

FIFTEEN

It was well past dawn before they convinced the Australian government of their sincerity, but eventually, it was decided that the three of them could have temporary asylum within the embassy grounds while the diplomats conferred with their government about what to do next, and tried to verify some of their claims. After being checked out by the embassy's medical staff, Paolo was allowed to rejoin them. His bottom lip had two stitches in it, to go along with the ones in his leg. Looking at it made the stitches in Carrie's arm itch.

"Are you okay?" she asked. "You took one hell of a fall."

Paolo smiled sadly, seeming to notice the genuine concern in her voice.

"They say I am just dehydrated and exhausted. They had me on a saline drip. Then they gave me some painkillers and told me to get plenty of rest. But I assure you that I am fine, Gatito."

Carrie flinched at his use of the old term of endearment.

"Don't call me that, okay? Not now."

"Oh, I'm sorry . . . I—"

"No, don't apologize. It's just . . . never mind. We'll talk about it later. But I'm glad you're okay."

"Are you, really?"

"Of course," she admitted. "Paolo, I still care about you. I don't think I could ever stop caring about you. I just wish you weren't such a goddamn asshole."

"I . . . I wish I wasn't, as well."

They were each given a private room, as well as clothing and toiletries. In some ways, it felt like they were vacationers checking into a hotel, rather than fugitives on the run from a criminal corporation. Mostly this was due to the allegations they'd brought forth, but Carrie's minor celebrity status certainly didn't hurt. It turned out that many amongst the embassy staff were admirers of hers. One even claimed to have met her years ago at a book signing in Melbourne, when she'd been on a publicity tour for her memoir.

After they were settled, the three of them met up again in Carrie's room.

"I'm going to shower and change," she said, "and then, while we wait for the embassy to confirm our story, I have to meet up with Jessamine to go over the details of Alpinus's malfeasance. I want to make sure she has everything, just in case. Did you guys want to join us?"

"I'm going to head down to the lounge," Abhi replied. "I'm too wound up to sleep. Those guys from the network, Hank and Khem, invited me to play cards with them. Hopefully, there are some free drinks in it, as well. My stomach feels like I drank battery acid. I need something to set it right again."

"Just be careful you don't get drunk," Carrie warned.

"Where's the fun in that?"

Carrie smiled. "I just mean, be mindful that they work for the media. Loose lips sink ships."

"No," Abhi said, "weird, pissed-off sea monsters sink ships.

But don't worry. I won't reveal anything more than what you've already told Jessamine."

"Perfect." Carrie turned to Paolo. "What about you?"

He shook his head. "I'm still exhausted, and my face really hurts. So does my ankle, for that matter. I think I'm just going to go back to my room and sleep."

"Okay," Carrie replied, "but . . . we need to talk at some point . . ."

"Agreed. But I need to sleep first. Fair enough?"

Carrie nodded. "Fair enough."

"Okay," Paolo said, "then I will see both of you later. I'm off to bed."

Paolo shut the door to his suite and locked it. He sighed, staring at the queen-sized bed with overstuffed pillows and crisp, clean sheets. More than anything, he wanted to collapse upon it, press himself into the mattress, and just sleep. Blissful, peaceful, comforting sleep. Never had something looked more inviting than the bed did right now.

Unfortunately, it would have to wait.

His lip throbbed in time with his pulse, and his leg ached from all the walking he'd done over the last few hours. The flesh around the stitches felt hot and tight. He dry swallowed a few pills to help manage the pain, grimacing at the chemical taste as they slid down his throat. That just made his lip hurt more. He paused, waiting for the pain to subside. When it did, he took a deep breath.

"Okay," he muttered. "Let's have a look."

Paolo walked around the room, meticulously checking every corner and cranny. He peered under and behind furniture and inside drawers. He pulled back the curtains and studied the windows. Standing on a chair, he examined the smoke detector and fire sprinklers. He investigated the electrical outlets and appliances, and rapped on the walls at certain intervals. He even stripped the linens from the bed and looked over the mattress and pillows. Then he did the same in the suite's adjoining bathroom, checking every inch of the space, including the vent in the ceiling and inside the toilet tank.

When he was finished, although he couldn't be one hundred percent certain the room wasn't under surveillance, Paolo felt secure enough to open the top dresser drawer and remove his hospital gown, which had been balled up and placed inside the dresser when he'd changed clothes earlier. Then he carried the gown into the bathroom and shut the door. He turned on the exhaust fan for noise. Finally, as an afterthought, he turned the spigot on the sink, confident that the running water would provide some additional shielding.

Paolo sat the soiled robe down on the counter and slowly unfolded it. Inside was a sealed plastic freezer bag, covered with tattered duct tape. Stuck on the tape's adhesive was a tangle of black hairs. The hairs were his, ripped from his chest when he'd pulled it off while changing. His skin was still red and irritated from where the bag had been taped to his chest all night. Paolo had affixed it just moments before Abhi, during his delusional rescue attempt, had burst into his hospital room at the Alpinus facility. Thank God he had also heard the commotion in the hallway between Dr. Barbet and Ochse, and Carrie and Abhi's subsequent conversation.

He'd panicked when they reached the embassy, unsure of how he'd get the bag and its precious cargo past security. He was beyond relieved when his gambit of faking a fainting spell had worked. Paolo had been certain that it wouldn't work but he couldn't think of another option. When they'd gotten him to the infirmary, the soldiers had left him unattended for a few minutes, lying on the gurney behind some closed curtains. He'd ripped the bag free, biting down on his burst-and-bleeding lip as the duct tape tore his chest hair from his pores. He'd been looking around for a place to hide it when a nurse walked in. Paolo had frozen, terrified that he'd been caught, but the nurse, obviously assuming the bag had already made it through the security screening, had simply offered him a drawer to put his belongings in.

Paolo chuckled to himself now, remembering. His first instinct had been to snap the woman's neck and make a run for it. It had taken him a moment to realize that she suspected nothing out of the ordinary.

He winced in pain. Laughing made his lip hurt. Focusing again, he turned his attention to the task at hand.

Inside the bag were two portable hard drives and a small phone. Paolo unzipped the bag, and removed the latter. Then he turned it on, and was relieved to see that it still had plenty of battery life left. That might be a problem later, given that the charger was still back at the Alpinus facility. The phone, according to his employer, was surveillance-proof—scrambled, encrypted, invisible from traffic analysis and network monitoring, unable to be tracked or listened in on by any third party.

Paolo caught a glimpse of himself in the bathroom mirror. He didn't like what he saw. Split lip and the abrasions on his forehead aside, he still looked like shit. His complexion was still pale and dark circles remained under his eyes. He looked as tired and haggard as he felt. Some of that was due to the after-effects of the toxin. But the rest . . .

Well, if it wasn't something money couldn't cure, he didn't know what could. And soon he would have all the money he'd ever need.

The mirror began to fog over with steam from the hot water flowing out of the tap. That was good. It added yet another layer of protection, in case there were any hidden cameras in the bathroom that he'd been unable to detect.

Paolo dialed a phone number from memory. He didn't pause to calculate the time difference. Regardless of the hour, the person he was calling—William Bevill, the head of Alpinus Biofutures Research and Development—would answer. He was always available to receive calls from this particular phone.

Paolo was all too aware of what a dangerous position he was in now. He'd been secretly spying on Carrie and the entire operation for Alpinus to make sure they didn't discover the man-made nature of the catastrophe. Getting attacked by the creature hadn't been part of the plan, but then again, discovering the egg hadn't been either. The fact that the creatures were breeding had been unanticipated. He'd gambled that his employer would want all of the data related to that unexpected development, and it was a gamble that had paid off. His only mistake had been in assuming he wasn't expendable. After learning that, he'd decided to let Carrie and Abhi see a few of his cards. But he hadn't been foolish enough to tell them everything, nor had he revealed everything to Alpinus. Recognizing what a peculiarly profitable position he'd now found himself in, Paolo saw little benefit in solely aligning himself with either side of this marine arms race. Now, like a good mole, he intended to report in as though his past days at death's door hadn't changed his relationship with his employer.

The phone was answered on the third ring.

"Yes?"

Bevill sounded breathless. Paolo wondered what activity he had interrupted.

"It's me," Paolo said.

"So it is. Where are you right now?"

"I'd rather not say. I'm sure you understand."

"Of course, of course. Though, I have to admit, I'm surprised to hear from you. We still don't have a complete handle on what exactly has happened in the last few hours. Perhaps you can fill in some of the blanks for me?"

"Your men were sloppy. Two of the loose ends found out, and escaped. They're with me now."

"Escaped?"

"That's correct. But as I said, they are currently with me."

"I don't understand. Could you elaborate a bit more? How did this happen? Do you have any idea what tipped them off?"

"Yes," Paolo replied. "As I said, it was a breakdown of operational discipline. Your men lacked the necessary discretion at a time when it mattered most."

"I see."

"Oh, you see? Well, I'm glad that you see. But I'm even gladder that I saw. Otherwise, I think we both know that I wouldn't be talking to you right now. I wouldn't be talking to anyone. I'd be another scientific curiosity—an experiment gone wrong."

"Listen, about that . . ." Bevill sighed. His tone turned conciliatory. "You need to understand, your situation, while precarious, was unprecedented. We didn't know what would happen to you, but given your dire medical prognosis at the time, we had a scientific obligation to follow through and learn whatever we could about your condition."

Paolo laughed. "So, it wasn't personal?"

"Absolutely. I assure you it was not. It was purely scientific. We had to make the most of things, given the situation. Remember, we didn't expect you to recover."

"But I did recover." Paolo was careful not to sound too forgiving, lest he show his hand.

"Indeed, you did. And I am very grateful for that."

"As am I. And let me be clear—I expect to be well compensated for the medical limbo your people left me in."

Bevill paused. "I think something can be arranged. What figure did you have in mind?"

"You tell me. I'll decide if it's fair enough."

"I'm sure we can reach an agreement. However, before we do that, there are still other matters to attend to. I still don't have a clear picture as to what happened at the facility. I gave orders to bring everything to a conclusion. The lead agent was to transmit all of the current data, prepare the remains for shipment, and handle any outstanding . . . obligations."

"Yes, I know," Paolo reminded him. "I was one of those obligations."

Bevill ignored this. "Several hours ago, the lead agent communicated that there had been a major security breach, and they were taking steps to contain everything. We've heard nothing since, and he never transmitted the final, conclusive report. We still need that data. It's absolutely essential. So, perhaps you understand why I'd be very grateful if you could fill in the blanks. What happened?"

"The lead agent didn't transmit the report because he was locked in the back of a delivery truck. Given that you have since spoken to him, I have to assume he got out, and took countermeasures to make sure your company wasn't implicated in anything. As far as I know, he still has the biological specimens, but as for the data? I have that now."

"Say again?"

"The data is in my possession. I extracted all of it earlier yesterday, when I first noticed your operational procedures going into effect. When the private contractors began disappearing, it wasn't hard to figure out just what was going on. So I acted."

"I see. And just how were you able to obtain all of that data without being caught?"

Paolo laughed, ignoring the pain it caused. "You really

should have assigned more personnel to that facility, overall. They were so distracted and spread thin dealing with the free-lancers and the staff, that they never noticed me slipping out of my room. As I said, they were sloppy."

"So, you have all the data? Everything?"

"That's correct. I stored it on two hard drives. I have them in my hands right now."

"I see."

"Do you now? Then I can assume you also see just how valuable I am to you."

"I think we can agree to double your compensation to account for the, uh, unanticipated biological data you are able to provide for us."

"That is fair," Paolo replied, "but there is still the matter of the past few days. You agreed earlier that I should be compensated for that, as well."

Bevill paused longer this time. When he spoke again, he sounded tired.

"Yes, of course. I'm sure I can get approval for another fifty thousand to cover your . . . medical costs."

"Fifty thousand? That's not at all satisfactory."

"Well, what would be satisfactory?"

"I was thinking more along the lines of triple my original compensation."

"Triple? Now, see here!"

"Given the sensitive nature of things, it's a small price to pay to ensure this data doesn't fall into the wrong hands—especially, the hands of one of your competitors . . . well, I think we both know what that might lead to."

"Fine. Enough. Agreed."

"Excellent." Paolo smiled. "I was hoping you'd see things my way."

"So, when can you deliver?"

"I'll be in touch to set a time and place for the hand off."

"Understand something," Bevill said. "While we still have the specimens under our control, that hand off has to include *everything* else . . ."

"The hard drives are yours."

"And the other two factors, as well. Those two loose ends that are with you? They'll still have to be neutralized."

Steam rose from the sink. Paolo stared at the condensation on the bathroom mirror, and thought of Carrie and Abhi. In the fog, it was almost easy to pretend that his reflection belonged to someone other than himself. He reached out and touched the glass, leaving his handprint behind. The moisture felt cool on his hand. The running water and the thrum of the exhaust fan both suddenly seemed very loud. With his index finger, Paolo slowly traced a smiley face in the condensation.

"Are you still there?" Bevill asked. "I need you to understand—there's no deal unless we have all three. That is non-negotiable."

"Relax," Paolo replied, finishing his drawing. "They'll be delivered with the hard drives. I guarantee it."

Later that day, a representative from the embassy staff called for a meeting with Carrie, Abhi, Paolo, Jessamine, Hank, and Khem. They were led into a dark, secluded conference room deep inside the building. Two men were already seated at the large table. They stood up when the others entered. One introduced himself as Brett McBean, the Australian ambassador, and shook each of their hands, in turn. The other introduced himself as Mr. Brown, a member of Australia's Secret Intelligence Service.

Carrie thought it was strange that the ambassador had

introduced himself by his full name, but the intelligence agent had only given his last name.

Brown verified that two soldiers were positioned outside the door before he closed it. McBean, meanwhile, directed them to a small buffet, which had been set up in the corner, with crystal pitchers of water and juice, a pot of coffee, hot water and tea bags, and a row of silver platters heaped with a variety of fruits, vegetables, finger sandwiches, and hors d'oeuvres. Abhi and Hank helped themselves to the food, but nobody else partook. Before the meeting started, the two men looked up from their plates, noticed that no one else was eating, and then shrugged sheepishly at each other.

"Miss Wheatley," McBean began, after they were all settled, "I have to insist that this conversation be strictly off the record. Is that acceptable to you and your crew?"

"Everything, or just what you and Mr. Brown say?"

"Mr. Brown and I can only speak on behalf of the Australian government. What is said in this room during this meeting is off the record. If anyone would like to repeat it to you elsewhere, well, that would be up to them."

"Then yes," Jessamine replied. "Of course."

"Very good. Well then, it is our position that the Australian government owes each of you safety, and I'm happy to report that we are approving your request for asylum."

"Even though not all of us are Australian citizens?" Carrie asked.

"Of course, Miss Anderson. At this point, your nationality is no longer important. You are, after all, whistleblowers to a major crime being perpetrated on the Indian Ocean. Granted, it is occurring in Mauritian waters, rather than our own, but given the current social uncertainty and upheaval here, we feel that our government is better positioned to respond to this.

Mauritius has its hands full, to say the least. They don't have the resources to tackle this. Not to mention that these allegations, if true, will potentially impact our country, as well. It has become an Australian problem."

"However," Brown added, "you have to understand that this is a short-term arrangement. While our initial intelligence lends some credibility to your story—satellite imaging of the trench, for example, which confirms the widespread hypoxia— we still need proof of these allegations regarding Alpinus Biofutures' involvement in the collapse. Without that, the asylum grant will be reversed."

"Did you check out the facility here on the island?" Carrie asked. "All the proof you need should be there."

"We did investigate it," Brown confirmed, "but first responders got there before us."

"First responders?" Jessamine asked.

Brown nodded. "The clinic burned to the ground early this morning. It is estimated that the fire started around the time you got here. We found no one inside, and recovered nothing of any intelligence value so far. The ruins are still too hot to comb through, but our chances of salvaging anything useful appear to be slim indeed. Apparently, the blaze was aggressive. There is very little left standing. It was almost certainly arson, and expertly conducted, but that's all we know."

"Son of a bitch," Carrie exclaimed, slapping her palm on the tabletop. "They're covering their tracks! I should have taken a sample when we left."

"It's not your fault, Carrie." Abhi sipped his water. "It's not like we had the time. Let's just be glad we made it out of there alive. A lot of other people didn't."

"But we've got no proof," she argued. "I mean, what do we have, Abhi? We've got Paolo's word of the conspiracy, our own experiences, the wreckage of Takenaka's ship, and yes, maybe—maybe—we can prove the collapse was engineered, but there's nothing to link it to Alpinus. They've got the egg, the remains of the creatures, and all of the data. This would never make it to court, let alone the nightly news."

"Unfortunately, you're right," Hank said. "We'd need concrete proof before we could ever air these allegations. I'm not saying I don't believe you folks. I do. But the network is going to want this extensively corroborated and vetted. Otherwise, they're just going to laugh at me and suggest you take the story to Infowars or one of the other conspiracy sites."

Carrie sighed in exasperation. "Maybe we'll have to. Maybe we'll take it to Alex Jones."

"You *could*," Hank replied. "But you might find your story discredited just by appearing there."

"Then we'll take it to Ben Swann, Jesse Ventura, Gardner Goldsmith—anybody who will listen."

"But, Carrie," Jessamine cautioned. "Any legitimate news outlet, even amongst the alternative media, is going to need proof. And even if they didn't require it, without documentation to back it up, Alpinus will sic their lawyers on them when they ask for comment. The story would get killed long before anybody saw it.

Hank and Khem nodded in agreement.

"So we're screwed." Carrie sounded close to tears.

"Not yet," Jessamine replied. "Not by a long shot. We just need to think. Is there another way to get the proof we need?"

Carrie snapped her fingers. "The nest!"

McBean frowned. "Um, a nest?"

Carrie turned to Paolo. "When you stole the egg, were there others like it?"

He nodded. "Yes. They were strung up like octopus eggs. But Alpinus would have destroyed them by now."

"Maybe," Carrie agreed. "But maybe not. We've made them

act fast. Whatever their original timetable was, our actions made them speed things up. They could have gotten careless as a result. If there are still more eggs in the Mouth of Hell, and we can get them, then that's a good start at providing physical proof. And the remains of the creature Captain Takenaka killed might still be down there, as well. We could get samples from that."

"But it still wouldn't tie things back to Alpinus Biofutures," Jessamine insisted.

"It might," Brown said. "If you are correct about their use of nanotechnology, there might be certain identifiers that would indicate their involvement in the manufacturing of these robotic units. It would take time, and there is a possibility nothing could be determined, but it sounds to me as if your other options are slim."

There was a brief silence as all of them glanced around the room at each other. Eventually, all eyes settled on Carrie.

"Well," she sighed. "That settles it. I guess I'm diving back down there again."

"And here I thought we might finally get a few days off work," Abhi complained.

"No, you still get time off. You're not going with me this time."

"Try to stop me, Carrie. I've followed you out there how many times now?"

"We'd like to come along, too," Hank said. "I can't imagine the network vetoing that idea. We won't get in the way."

"I'm not going out there," Khem murmured. "Haven't you been listening? There are monsters in that trench. People died! You heard what happened to those mercenaries."

"They're dead," Hank reminded him.

"Then I'd better get paid double-time."

Hank rolled his eyes. "You're salaried, Khem. You don't get double-time."

"Well, then this would be an excellent time to discuss a raise."

"I hear GNN is hiring," Hank quipped.

Khem folded his arms across his chest and pouted.

"Are you sure this is wise?" McBean asked. "If your allegations are correct then you'll be marked targets the moment you step outside these walls. We can protect you here, in the embassy, or on Australian soil, but we can't safeguard you out on the open water."

"You won't need to safeguard them," Paolo said quietly. "I can offer proof."

"Your testimony carries some weight," Brown agreed, "but it's ultimately hearsay so we'll need solid proof to act on this. This is a criminal investigation. Right now, it's just your word against theirs. For all a court knows, you're simply a disgruntled employee with an axe to grind, making up incredible allegations that have no basis in truth."

"Oh, I'm certainly that." Paolo's laughter sounded cynical. He folded his hands on the table in front of him. "A disgruntled employee, that is. But as for proof, what if I told you there are two hard drives containing data that would verify our story?"

Carrie and Abhi glanced at each other in surprise.

"What sort of data?" Brown asked, intrigued.

"I'd like to know that, as well," Jessamine murmured.

"Everything," Paolo said. "Scientific data on myself, the fetal specimen we brought ashore, and the remains of the mutated creatures. Analysis of the hypoxia zone. Background on the mercenaries Alpinus hired. Log entries by Ochse and the other security goons. Phone records and e-mails. Videos. Those are what I know is on there. I assume there is much more to be found, once your people go over them."

Brown appeared intrigued. "And you have access to these hard drives?"

Paolo hesitated. "I do."

Carrie sat up straight. "You've got fucking hard drives and proof? How the hell did you get them? What did you do—sneak them into the embassy inside your hospital gown?"

"I didn't say that."

"No," Carrie retorted. "You didn't say much of anything, did you, Paolo?"

"I'm sorry, Carrie."

"How do we know you're not lying to us again now? If you had these hard drives all along, then why did you let us sit here and waste our breath thinking of another way to get proof?"

Before Paolo could respond to her, Brown cleared his throat.

"I would like to see them at once," he said.

"So would I," Jessamine said. "If they contain what you say they do, we can blow this story wide open!"

"I'm afraid that's out of the question, Miss Wheatley." Brown shook his head. "This is a matter of national security, and we'll need access to the data first. Before we started, you agreed that anything said during this meeting was off the record. That applies to the information contained on these hard drives."

"We can share," she replied. "How about that? I vote we share."

"This isn't a democracy, Miss Wheatley."

"Really?" Jessamine arched an eyebrow. "Are you, a high-ranking official from ASIS, telling me that Australia isn't a democracy?"

"You know very well what I mean. Don't try to twist my

words. I'm afraid I must insist that we have access to these hard drives first."

"Okay." Jessamine shrugged. "Then I'll just go on the news tonight and talk about what I know."

Brown flinched at the threat and cleared his throat.

"You won't do that," McBean challenged. "Do I really need to remind you again that when we started this conversation, I told you it was off the record? Without the data on the hard drives, all you'd be reporting on is allegations."

Jessamine didn't back down. "And need I remind you, Ambassador, that I clarified what was off the record and what wasn't? All I'm doing is reporting the outrageous and shocking claims made by a world-class free diver and her fellow co-workers against their former employer, who just happens to be one of the biggest companies in the world."

McBean sputtered in exasperation. "But if you do that, you simply give Alpinus more time to conceal the truth, and further hamper this investigation."

Jessamine nodded, smiling. "All the more reason, then, for you to share the information on the hard drives with us. You want to stop the bad guys, don't you?"

"I think you had better leave, Miss Wheatley. Immediately."

"On the contrary, I think I have every right to be here. I am an Australian citizen and this is a news story. I'm doing my job."

"I've had enough of this." McBean stood up. "I'm going to have you removed from the grounds at once."

Jessamine smiled. "You don't want to do that."

"Watch me."

"Jessamine," Hank whispered. "What are you doing?"

"Mr. Ambassador," Paolo said, his voice firm. "Please sit down."

McBean slowly complied. His ears and cheeks were red with anger. Jessamine sat quietly, demurely folding her hands on the table in front of her, and tried to suppress another smile. Hank and Khem shifted nervously in their seats. Carrie and Abhi stared at each other, still stunned by this latest turn of events.

"First of all," Paolo continued after he had everyone's attention, "I haven't turned over the hard drives to anyone yet. None of you even know their current location, so there is no sense arguing about it right now. I haven't said if they're on embassy grounds. For all you know, I hid them in the jungle."

Brown pointed at him. "If you're willfully concealing evidence of a crime—"

"I'm doing no such thing," Paolo interrupted. "I just told you that I'm willing to turn them over. But both of the hard drives are encrypted and partitioned. I know the ASIS is good, but so is Alpinus. It might take you weeks, or even months, to break the encryption. That's time that frankly, we don't have. Not unless we want to live like fugitives. And while your people are struggling to decrypt the data, Alpinus will be furthering the cover-up, and this crisis would continue to spread throughout the ocean. What I'm offering instead is a way to get Alpinus Biofutures to implicate themselves. A way for you to catch them in the act, so to speak. And a way to do it quickly."

"Go on," McBean urged.

"We all want to expose what has happened here. Jessamine wants her news story. You want to arrest these criminals. And we want to live, and not have to look over our shoulders, wondering if there's a sniper scope trained on our heads or a bomb beneath our car. What I'm proposing is a way to achieve all of these things. We set up a data handoff in Perth."

"Why Perth," Carrie asked. "Why not right here in Mauritius?"

Paolo turned to the intelligence head. "You can't act unless everything is in the hands of the Australian government, right?"

"That is correct," Brown replied. "But you'll never get Alpinus to come here to the embassy, and our authorities can't act beyond these walls."

"That's why I propose we fly to Perth. Would that work?"

Brown nodded. "Yes. You could make initial contact with the official at Alpinus and offer them the data in exchange for money."

"Great," Paolo agreed. "Then Carrie and Abhi will dead drop the hard drives at a pre-appointed location."

"Wait a minute," Abhi said. "Me and Carrie? How did we get drafted into this?"

"Because Alpinus wants both of you, as well as the data. The two of you are witnesses."

"So are you," Carrie said.

"Yes, but I can convince them that I'm still loyal. Still working for them. In their minds, I can be controlled. They can't say the same about the two of you."

"So you're sending us to our deaths?" Abhi sputtered.

"Not at all," Paolo said.

"We can have authorities waiting to arrest them at the second location," Brown said.

Paolo nodded. "You show up to make the dead drop. Before they can react, ASIS swoops in and arrests them. At that point, Mr. Brown has the guilty parties, the money, and the hard drives, and Jessamine has her news story, and no harm comes to you or Carrie. Everybody wins."

The room was silent for a moment.

McBean turned to Brown. "What do you think?"

"I think it might work." Brown rubbed his chin, thoughtfully. "Yes, I think it might work, provided he can convince the guilty parties to go for it."

"I'm in," Jessamine confirmed. "We can sit on the story if it leads to this. But I still want assurances that we'll get access to the data."

"Something can be arranged," McBean assured her.

"I'd like some assurances, as well," Carrie said. "I mean, the way I see it, Abhi and I are the ones taking the biggest risk here. How do we know they won't shoot us in the head as soon as we make the drop?"

"We'll have people watching you the entire time," Brown said. "If they even twitch, we'll be on them. I give you my word that no harm will come to either of you."

"And what if Alpinus gets a whiff of it? What if they spot your people before we spot them?"

"Miss Anderson, we're the Australian Secret Intelligence Service. Unlike our American counterparts, we don't make mistakes. And if they do spot us, we'll make the arrests early. At that point, even without the exchange, we have them for conspiracy, weapons charges, and a host of other things we can use for leverage."

"Well, then," McBean said, "if there are no more objections, I'll arrange for your travel to Perth. Miss Wheatley, I trust you won't inform your superiors at the network about this yet?"

"We were supposed to be going to Australia anyway," she replied. "I'll let them know we're working on something, but I can't say what it is yet. Fair enough?"

"I suppose so, as long as they don't start asking questions."

"I can convince them not to," Hank said. "They trust us when it comes to things like this. They may nickle and dime us on the budget, but at the end of the day, they give us enough room to do our jobs."

"Very well." McBean turned to Carrie and Abhi. "Do either of you have anything to add?"

Abhi shrugged and shook his head.

"Okay," Carrie said. "The sooner we get this over with, the sooner we can get on with our lives."

McBean nodded. "Very good. I have some calls to make. I'm sure Mr. Brown has some to make, as well."

"I don't know about this," Carrie said later. "I think maybe I agreed to it too quick."

She and Paolo were seated in the embassy lounge, having dinner. A candle flickered on their table, casting dancing shadows in the dim light. Soft music played in the background. Abhi, Hank, and Khem were at the bar, watching a soccer match on television and working their way through the embassy's stock of tequila. Jessamine had retired to her room.

"You are worrying too much, Gatito," Paolo said. "You heard what the man said. There will be agents everywhere. You and Abhi will be safe."

"Yes, but something could still go wrong. There are a lot of variables in play here, Paolo."

He stifled a yawn.

"I'm sorry," she said. "Are my concerns boring you?"

"No," he protested. "It's not that at all. I am just very tired."

"We both are. And that's why I'm having second thoughts. I think we rushed into this plan without thinking it through."

Paolo shrugged. "If it will make you feel more at ease, when I make the arrangements, I'll tell them they don't get my encryption key until after you and Abhi are safe. That assures nothing will happen to you."

Carrie paused, her wine glass half-raised. "Your encryption key?"

"Yes. Remember, the hard drives are encrypted and partitioned. They are useless to Alpinus without my key."

"I'm sure they could crack them in time. You said so yourself during the meeting."

"Yes, perhaps, but they may not have enough time. I am betting they will not want to take that chance. Not after everything else that has happened. Time will be of the essence to them."

"I hope you're right." She sipped her wine slowly.

"Are you okay, Carrie? You seem . . . troubled. I know this is all very upsetting, but is there something else on your mind?"

"No . . ." She hesitated. "Like I said, I'm just tired, Paolo. I feel like we've been on the run for weeks. I've been in and out of hospitals, seen people die, suffered from the bends, been in a boat wreck. I'm exhausted. I just want to sleep for a week."

"I sympathize," Paolo replied. "I am tired, as well. I will be glad when this is all over."

"What will you do? When this is over? What are your plans?"

"Well, I guess that depends on you. We still need to finish our discussion, yes?"

The candlelight twinkled in his eyes, warm and inviting. Carrie smiled, and took another sip of wine.

"Yes, we do, at some point. But not tonight. I don't want to think about that tonight."

"Okay, then. What do you want for tonight?"

"You know what I want? More than anything right now?" She drained the rest of her wine in one gulp and set the empty glass on the table. "I want you to come back to my room."

"Oh?" Paolo's eyes widened in surprise. "I would be delighted."

"Don't get the wrong idea," she cautioned. "Nothing is going to happen. At least, not yet. I'm not ready for that, Paolo. You'll need to give me time. But we're both exhausted, and I thought it might be nice if we just slept together. You know, like actual sleep? I'd like somebody to hold me, and I'd like that somebody to be you."

Paolo's voice was thick with emotion. "I would like that very much, Gatito."

"Alright, then. We don't have to pay the waiter. McBean said this was on the house. I'm going to go say goodnight to Abhi. He's still pretty mad at you, so maybe it would be better if we didn't leave together. Meet you upstairs?"

"Yes." Paolo nodded. "Just let me stop off at my room first. I'll meet you at your suite."

"Sounds good."

They got up from the table and crossed the lounge, then veered in different directions. Carrie watched him head for the elevators. Paolo's step seemed renewed and there was a big smile on his face. She half expected him to start whistling or skipping.

After Paolo had gotten on the elevator and the doors had closed, she walked over to Abhi and whispered in his ear.

In his room, Paolo freshened up and changed his clothes. He grinned into the bathroom mirror. Doing so caused the stitches in his lip to pull tight, but he barely felt the pain. He was pleased by how well things were going. All he had to do now was make an early handoff of the first hard drive to Alpinus, with the insistence upon receiving his money in cash at that point, and then tell them the location of the dead drop so they could recover the second hard drive and kill Carrie and Abhi—after which he would give them his encryption key. He would, of course, neglect to mention to Alpinus that the authorities would be on hand for that second drop, just as he would neglect to mention to Carrie and the others that he was getting paid upon making the first exchange.

Whether Carrie and Abhi lived or died, he expected to be far gone into the Outback by the time the second drop took place.

He also couldn't deny that there was something delightful about sharing her bed one last time. He still remembered all the ways of convincing her when she was "tired" that had worked so well in the past—kissing the back of her neck, stroking her shoulder, gently nibbling her earlobe. Those old methods had always been reliable. He was certain they still would be.

What was it his father used to say? The old ways were the best?

Even if this evening didn't involve sex, it would be nice to hold Carrie one more time. He'd missed the smell of her hair, and the feel of her. He would be sure to commit those to memory one last time.

Paolo fixed his hair in the mirror. His smile vanished.

He hoped, if the Alpinus team did get the drop on Carrie and Abhi before the intelligence services could react, that the kill would be quick. He didn't care about Abhi, obviously. Indeed, he would have preferred to see the old fool tortured. But Carrie?

Carrie had suffered enough. She deserved a quick, merciful end.

SIXTEEN

Later that night, as they lay in bed together, Carrie held her breath, and felt like she was drowning.

She was tired. In truth, she couldn't remember a time in her life when she'd been more exhausted than she was now. And yet, despite her deep fatigue, sleep was the furthest thing from her mind. She could no more sleep right now than she could transport herself to the surface of Mars.

Maybe that's what I should have done, she thought. *All those years ago. Maybe I should have become an astronaut instead.*

She exhaled slowly and soundlessly, barely moving. Then, she took another breath and held it again.

Paolo snored softly next to her. She'd forgotten about that—forgotten that he'd snored. Forgotten what it sounded like, too—a quiet sort of snuffling noise, like a baby piglet searching for its mother's teat. She'd forgotten his scent, as well, but was reminded of it now, as he lay pressed against her, spooning, with one arm lying limp upon her bare waist. At one time, his scent had awoken something in her every time she smelled it—longing, arousal, and a desperate, hungry need. Now, it repulsed her, as did everything else about him.

She hated him. She realized that now. Any glimmer of romantic love, or even friendship, was forever destroyed. They lay buried at the bottom of the trench, frozen, unable to be thawed, covered in silt and darkness.

Yes, she absolutely hated him. She made her peace with that.

But what she hated more was the fact that, despite her loathing for Paolo, she still cared about him, deep down inside.

Carrie didn't know how to make peace with that second revelation. She wasn't sure that she ever would.

At the clinic, when Barbet had revealed the truth about the conspiracy, he'd told Carrie and Abhi that the creature's venom was causing Paolo's brain to mutate. They knew now that the mutations had been caused by nanotechnology. But the bad thing inside of Paolo—that had no cause, and no cure. That was something that had existed inside of him all along.

She'd just never let herself see it until now.

Paolo shifted slightly, and his arm slid farther down her hip. His fingertips brushed against the hem of her panties. Once, those fingertips had aroused her with just a touch. Now, they made her stomach churn. They felt like cold, greasy sausage links. Paolo murmured in his sleep—soft, unintelligible words.

She held her breath until spots danced before her eyes. Then, she slowly exhaled and repeated the process once again. She wanted to raise her head and check the time, but she was afraid that if she moved, Paolo would awaken.

Carrie had been dissatisfied with Paolo's high-drama plan of capturing the criminals. She was an empiricist, and thought that if they had the evidence, they should turn it over to the Australian authorities, rather than take risks for the sake of showmanship. She had agreed to the Australian involvement after their efforts at the American embassy were stymied, because it had made sense to gain asylum, but now, she thought it was time to do the reasonable thing. Unfortunately, when she'd seen how Jessamine and the others had gone for Paolo's plan, she'd stayed quiet.

After the meeting, she had still felt unsettled. She didn't know why. She thought that perhaps it was just exhaustion, or maybe the fact that she was still reeling from—and struggling to reconcile—Paolo's admission. She had ultimately chalked up her uneasiness to those very things, until her dinner with Paolo.

His mention of the encryption key had been what tipped her off. He'd mentioned it quickly, in passing, as a way of assuring her nothing would go wrong. But why would Paolo have an encryption key to the hard drives? He had specifically told Brown and McBean that the drives were encrypted by Alpinus. Then, he'd intimated the opposite to her, implying that Alpinus would need his key to access the data.

He was starting to mix up his own lies.

Tonight, when they'd met here in the room, it had been all she could do not to shrink away. When they lay down together, he'd stroked her shoulder with his fingertips and kissed the back of her neck and nibbled on her earlobe—all the things that turned her on. But instead of being aroused by his attentions, Carrie had been repulsed. Luckily, she hadn't had to fend him off for long. Paolo had fallen asleep after only a few minutes of muted conversation.

She breathed in. Held it. Released.

She breathed in again. Held it. And curled her hands into fists.

She wanted to scream. You couldn't scream underwater, but she could damn sure scream now. She wanted to elbow him in the throat. She wanted to roll over and dig her nails into his face, bloody her knuckles on his already split lip and feel his blood squirt between her fingers. She wanted to choke him and feel her hands sink into the flesh of his throat. She wanted to drive her knee into his balls until he sank into the mattress.

She wanted to shake.

She wanted to cry.

Instead, she lay there, listening to him breathe, ignoring the feel of his body against hers, ignoring his smell, ignoring his touch, and then—just as if she were going on a dive—she focused on her breathing.

She exhaled.

Inhaled.

Held it.

Exhaled.

Inhaled.

And held it again.

And tried to wait.

And tried not to drown.

When she heard the footsteps outside her door, she exhaled again. Sighing with relief, Carrie slid out from beneath Paolo's arm. Paolo stirred, moaning softly, and then rolled over. Carrie paused, waiting. His snoring stopped for a moment, and then started again.

Carrie padded across the room. Her hands felt like balloons, and her ears rang. She focused on the feel of the plush carpet between her bare toes, afraid that if she didn't, she might pass out.

She unlocked the door and opened it before they could knock.

Outside were Abhi, Brown, and four armed soldiers.

"Did you find them?" she asked.

"Aye," Abhi said. "They were in his room, along with a cell phone."

Paolo stirred again, fumbling toward wakefulness. He mumbled something unintelligible, and then groaned.

"The phone alone is probably incriminating enough," Brown told her, "although we won't know for sure until we can access it. It's locked. Password protected. And we'll still need the encryption key for the hard drives. But I'm sure he'll want to cooperate."

"Oh, I'm sure he will," Carrie agreed. "He's very good at caring for himself."

Carrie flipped on the light switch and stood back from the doorway as the men entered the room. The soldiers hurried in, weapons drawn and readied. Brown and Abhi entered behind them. Carrie noticed that Abhi was grinning, but there was no humor in the expression. Instead, it was malevolent.

It matched her own emotions.

Groaning, Paolo rolled over and propped himself up on his elbows, squinting against the sudden glare.

"What's going on?" he muttered. "Carrie?"

"You're under arrest for conspiracy," Brown informed him. "Please come with us."

"Conspiracy? What? What is this? Carrie, what are they—"

Abhi stepped toward him. "Leave her alone, you piece of shit. You've done enough."

Paolo sat up the rest of the way and glanced around the room. His eyes were wide with panic, and his hair was in disarray. Carrie had never seen him look so small and afraid and unsure of himself as he did in that moment.

The soldiers surrounded the bed and, at gunpoint, ordered Paolo to his feet. Then they handcuffed him roughly and led him toward the door.

"Wait a minute," he shouted. "Can't I at least get dressed first? I'm in my underwear for God's sake!"

The soldiers didn't respond. They simply shoved him forward.

Stumbling, Paolo turned to Carrie.

"I don't understand," he exclaimed. "What is happening? Carrie, help me!"

"I can't help you, Paolo. I thought I could, at one time. But not anymore."

Slowly, the confusion drained from his expression, and was replaced with a cold, emotionless glare. Carrie felt the urge to look away, but instead, she stared him in the eye, silently challenging him to speak.

Paolo said nothing.

The soldiers pushed him out the door and down the hall.

"The password," Carrie told Brown. "The encryption key for the hard drives? Try Gatito."

He frowned. "Gatito? Does that mean something to you?"

"It used to," she replied. "But not anymore."

SEVENTEEN

". . . but a source close to the investigation revealed to me, on condition of anonymity, that there is no truth to the rumor, and the prosecutors have not agreed to any sort of plea deal at this time. And with the trial scheduled to start later this month, the defense is running out of time. For GNN News, I'm Jessamine Wheatley, in Melbourne, Australia."

Carrie shook her head in admiration. She had to admit, Jessamine had gotten her news story and then some. For the last year, the Alpinus Biofutures conspiracy had remained in the headlines. Sure, it was occasionally bumped to second place by wars, terrorist attacks, political arguments and controversies, or the latest celebrity meltdown, but it always quickly supplanted those stories again, and remained in the public eye, capturing much of the world's attention. Much of that was due to Jessamine's reporting. The savvy newswoman had already parlayed her exposé into a position at GNN (and had even managed to get her producer and cameraman included as part of a package deal). Carrie could only wonder what Jessamine would do next. The trade blogs and magazines were speculating that she might have a primetime anchor desk when this was all over. Carrie figured that was already a given. Something told her that Jessamine wouldn't be satisfied with just that position. Given time, she'd probably be running the network.

The thought almost made Carrie smile, but all she could muster was a slight grin.

Smiling was something she rarely did these days.

Carrie turned away from the television and glanced around the prison's waiting room. It was filled with wives, girlfriends, and children, as well as a few lawyers, all of whom were waiting to visit inmates. In addition to the television, which was permanently tuned to just one channel, there was a magazine rack and a few tables with children's books strewn across them. In one corner was a toy box filled with dilapidated old toys that had seen better days.

This is where toys go to die, Carrie thought. *From the factory to the toy store to some kid's home to a yard sale to the children's ward at a hospital and then to here—a prison waiting room. The circle of life . . .*

Across the room was a small window, behind which sat a bored-looking prison guard who kept snapping her chewing gum loudly as she flipped aimlessly through a magazine. Occasionally, she would call out a visitor's name, with a begrudging, impatient tone.

None of them—the visitors or the guard—had recognized Carrie yet, which was a relief. In the past year, her face had been on television almost as much as Jessamine's had, especially in the first few months of the story. It had brought Carrie an uncomfortable, unfortunate level of fame far beyond what she had experienced as a world-class free diver. There was nothing flattering or comfortable about it at all. Feeling self-conscious, she reached up and adjusted her sunglasses. Then she patted the red silk scarf covering her hair.

"Carrie Anderson?"

She looked up as the guard called her name. Then she got to her feet and approached the window. People were staring at her now, but whether out of recognition or simple mindless curiosity, she couldn't be certain.

"Yes. I'm Carrie Anderson."

The guard shoved a clipboard through a slot in the window. "Sign and print there, please, next to your name. And I need to see your I.D."

The pen felt greasy between Carrie's fingertips. She scrawled her name where indicated, and slid the clipboard back through the slot, along with her passport. The guard gave it a perfunctory glance and slid it back to Carrie. Then, without looking up, the guard pressed a button, and a buzzer rang loudly.

"Step over to the door, please."

Carrie did as instructed, and was met by another prison guard, who had her stick her arms out to her sides. His face had the same bored expression as that of his co-worker. Wordlessly, he then ran a wand from Carrie's head to her feet, front and back. When that was finished, he quickly and perfunctorily frisked her, checking for weapons and contraband. His hands felt rough. Carrie was reminded of their initial entrance at the embassy, the night they had escaped Ochse and his men. Something sour rose in her throat, and she grimaced. Satisfied with his search, the guard stepped back.

"Is this your first visit to this facility, Miss Anderson?"

She nodded. "Yes."

"Okay. You are required to be in the company of a prison guard at all times. Don't stray off anywhere by yourself. If you need to use the restroom during your visit, one of us will accompany you. The inmate will sit across from you. You may communicate by phone. Please be aware that these conversations are monitored and recorded. Is that clear?"

Carrie nodded again. "Absolutely."

"This way, please." The guard indicated another doorway.

"Okay."

She followed him through the door, and down a short corridor lined with drab, gray tiles, and then a third door. On the other side of that door were a series of cubicles with seats in front of them and a large partition of glass. Some of the cubicles were occupied by other visitors, talking to inmates on the other side of the glass through phones wired into the wall.

"Wait here," the guard told her.

After what felt like an hour, but was in reality only a few minutes, Paolo was brought out on the other side of the glass, and directed to a seat. He wore an orange jumpsuit. Either it was too big for him or he had lost weight. She couldn't be sure of which. Then she got a good look at his face and decided it was the latter. His hair was much shorter than it had been when she'd last seen him. She also noticed that he no longer limped.

Time does heal some wounds, she supposed.

But while time could heal injuries, it could never take away the scars.

Scars were timeless.

"Okay, go ahead." The guard nodded toward the cubicles.

Carrie crossed the floor slowly. Her feet felt like lead. She focused on her breathing. In and out. Paolo smiled when he saw her. She did not return the gesture. She sat down in the chair and took off her sunglasses and her scarf. She shook her hair out. Then, after a moment's hesitation, she picked up the phone.

"You came." Paolo sounded genuinely pleased and surprised. "I wasn't sure you would."

"I wasn't sure I would either," Carrie admitted. "But your lawyer convinced me."

"It is good to see you, Carrie."

At least he didn't call me Gatito, she thought. *At least there's enough decency left in him for that.*

"You look good," he said. "God, you look amazing!"

Carrie nodded. "Thank you."

"You are well, I hope?"

Carrie shrugged in a noncommittal way. "I'm doing great, Paolo. How's prison treating you?"

Paolo chuckled. "It is not like the movies. There are no gangs or riots, and no one has molested me in the shower."

"You almost sound disappointed."

Paolo's smile didn't falter. He shrugged.

"I read a lot," he said. "And play chess."

"Chess? That's good. You really needed to work on improving your game anyway. I'm glad you've got the time to do it now."

"Ah, very good. I have missed your sense of humor." Paolo's smile slowly faded, but he kept his tone cordial and warm. "And Abhi? How is he these days?"

"He's married."

"Married? You don't say!"

"Yep. Happily married now. They tied the knot a few months ago. They're living together in Italy."

Paolo shook his head in apparent wonder, and was then quiet for a moment.

"So . . ." Carrie stared at him, waiting.

"Yes, I'm sorry. The thought of marriage . . . I had hoped that one day . . ."

"How about we get down to business, Paolo?"

"Very well." He sounded sad. "My lawyer explained why I asked you to come?"

"Yes." Carrie nodded. "Your conspiracy trial starts later this month. He wants me to testify that I knew about the hard drives and your secret cell phone all along, and that my turning you over to the authorities was part of the setup plan, because we suspected that various individuals on the embassy staff might be compromised by Alpinus Biofutures."

"Exactly," Paolo said. "And did he mention anything else?"

Paolo's eyes darted to the guards and back to her. He tapped the phone receiver with his index finger, reminding her that the conversation was most likely being recorded.

Now, for the first time, Carrie smiled. It felt good, after not having smiled for so long.

"Yes, he did, in fact. He mentioned you have a bank account that the authorities don't yet know about. He also mentioned that Alpinus Biofutures was making untraceable direct deposits into that bank account. And he told me that you would split the money with me if I agreed to lie under oath with that bullshit story you concocted."

Paolo gaped at her through the glass, almost dropping the phone. Sweat stood out on his forehead as he fumbled with the receiver. When he'd recovered, he shook his head.

"Carrie! Always such a joker! Though, I have to say, this one is not very funny."

"No, Paolo. It's not a joke. But you are."

"Carrie, please. I . . . I know what I did was wrong . . ."

"Oh, really? Well, that's a big step for you, isn't it, Paolo? Knowing what you did was wrong? That's a first. Did you find Jesus while you were in here, too?"

"Please," he begged. "Please now, just hear me out. These things you are saying—they aren't true. My lawyer would have never said those things. I know that you are angry, and you have every right to be. I know that I can't begin to make things up to you. I'll never be able to do that. And I know you probably won't understand, but I was . . . what is the expression? Between a rock and a hard place? I was trapped, Carrie. Trapped between Alpinus and my loyalty to you. I didn't know what they would do if I betrayed them. All along, I thought the best way to keep you safe—to keep you from harm—was to do as they asked."

"I see? So you did all this for me, Paolo? Is that what you're saying?"

"I won't deny there was a financial gain, at first. But when I learned what they were truly capable of—when I saw that you were in danger—yes, I did it for you, Carrie. I still care about you. I always have. The truth is . . . I love you. I've changed. I know how much I hurt you. I know I don't deserve your trust, but all I have in here is time, and all I do with it is think about you. I want to make things right. I know I can make things right. I just need the time to do it. If you are willing to testify on my behalf, my lawyer is confident I can get a reduced sentence. Perhaps even an acquittal. I know I have a lot to make up for, but this gives me the opportunity to do just that."

Carrie stared at him, long and hard, until finally, Paolo looked away.

"You need time?" she asked. "You're asking me to give you time?"

"Yes. That's what it will take between us. Time."

"I need time, too, Paolo."

His expression brightened again. "Does that mean you'll do it?"

"No. That means I think we should both get all the time we deserve. You, especially. I think a conviction on three charges of conspiracy, and the nice, lengthy jail term that follows should give you all the time you need."

"Carrie . . . please don't do this."

"I already have."

"Goddamn it, Carrie . . ."

"You know, after we recovered that poison gland, Dr. Barbet told us your brain was mutating. After we found out about your betrayal—and the despicable fucking lengths you went through—I told myself maybe it was because of that. Maybe it was what the venom had done to your brain. But it wasn't, because you were doing those things long before you got attacked. This is who you are, Paolo. This is who you've always been."

"Not anymore," he insisted. "Carrie, I've changed. I can prove it."

"No, Paolo. You really can't."

"I love you, goddamn it. Don't you see? Did you hear me? I love you, Carrie. And I know that you still love me, too. Maybe you can't admit it right now, but I know that deep down inside, you still love me."

"I . . ."

"Please," he begged again. "I know you want to help me. I know you'll do it."

"Don't hold your breath."

"Carrie . . ."

She stood up, still clutching the phone.

"No, seriously, Paolo. Don't hold your breath. We both know I could always hold my breath longer than you."

He stared up at her from behind the glass, tears running down his cheeks. His eyes were wide, wounded circles of pain.

"Goodbye, Paolo."

Carrie hung up the phone and turned her back on him. She nodded at the guard, indicating that she was finished with her visit. Then she took a deep breath and held it.

She didn't breathe again until she was outside the prison walls, and the sun shone down upon her.

EPILOGUE

Off the coast of Mauritius, life on the seafloor had finally come to an end. The once warm waters were now frigid and dark, even in the places where the feeble sunlight was able to penetrate. Still, even in death, there was movement amidst the gloom.

But that didn't mean the ocean was alive.

Shrimp and crabs were dragged along the bottom by the undertow, their carcasses saved from decomposition only by the cold temperatures. Armies of deflated jellyfish floated on the currents, lifeless and drifting. A school of dead tuna bobbed in their way, tossed and spun like driftwood by the undercurrents. Below them, the corpses of sea anemones still perched precariously to the seafloor with their adhesive feet—sticky even in death—but their once vibrant, multi-colored tentacles were now gray and brittle, and no longer waved. A female octopus lay frozen in her nest, her arms contorted in a reflection of the agony of her final moments. A string of frozen eggs hung above her lair, swaying in the current. Their once soft outer shells were now hardened, as were the embryos inside of them. A deceased green sea turtle lay wedged in between two large rocks. The turtle was the last of its kind in these waters, and had died alone, without ever finding a mate. Two dugongs floated slowly to the surface, their bodies swollen with gas and putrescence. Orange-and-white striped clownfish lay scattered amidst the banks of now colorless, broken coral, and massive schools of sapphire devils littered holes and crevices, their color now a permanent black. The bottlenose dolphins were gone, having moved on when they sensed the change around them. So, too, had the Great White shark, when it was faced with the knowledge that it was no longer a predator, but mere prey.

In the silence, a blue whale sang out from somewhere farther out to sea, beyond the dark depths. The tune was a haunting, phantom melody that still echoed of the past—but its mournful song would never be answered again. Not in these waters.

There was no life here, off the coast of Mauritius. It was a cold, silent, darkened wasteland. Nothing lived. Nothing moved, except for dead things, caught in the currents.

Then, something squirmed amid the devastation, something small and new, and very much alive. Something that, even in birth, was already dark and predatory.

One by one, the eggs began to hatch. Dozens of spindly, pointed arms pierced the hardened shells, and waving tentacles pushed their way through, flexing and stretching.

Slowly, the already frigid waters began to grow colder.

The darkness deepened, spreading in concentric circles.

And the newly hatched creatures began to hunt, searching for new areas still full of life. Soon they would feed.

Then, when the feast was over, they would breed and make more of their kind.